JANE HILL
GRIEVOUS ANGEL

arrow books

Published in the United Kingdom by Arrow Books in 2006

3 5 7 9 10 8 6 4

Copyright © Jane Hill, 2005

First published in the United Kingdom in 2005 by William Heinemann

Arrow Books
The Random House Group Limited
20 Vauxhall Bridge Road, London, SW1V 2SA

Random House Australia (Pty) Limited
20 Alfred Street, Milsons Point, Sydney, New South Wales 2061, Australia

Random House New Zealand Limited
18 Poland Road, Glenfield, Auckland 10, New Zealand

Random House (Pty) Limited
Isle of Houghton, Corner of Boundary Road & Carse O'Gowrie,
Houghton 2198, South Africa

The Random House Group Limited Reg. No. 954009
www.randomhouse.co.uk

A CIP catalogue record for this book is available from the British Library

Papers used by Random House are natural, recyclable products
made from wood grown in sustainable forests. The manufacturing processes
conform to the environmental regulations of the country of origin

ISBN 9780099476573 (from Jan 2007)
ISBN 0 09 9476576

Typeset by SX Composing DTP, Rayleigh, Essex
Printed and bound in the United Kingdom by
Cox & Wyman Ltd, Reading, Berkshire

GRIEVOUS ANGEL

Jane Hill was born and brought up in Portsmouth. She has worked in radio for twenty years, first as a journalist and then as head of programming for an award-winning group of commercial radio stations. She is now a freelance writer and broadcaster and is also pursuing a career as a stand-up comedian. She has a passion for live music and also for travelling, particularly in the USA.

Praise for Jane Hill's *Grievous Angel*

'A new voice in psychological suspense fiction'
Daily Mail

'A sensational new addition to the psychological thriller shelves'
Daily Record

'By turns playful and poignant, sexy and sinister, Hill's darkly comedic portrait of a woman scorned packs a captivating surprise'
Booklist

Also available by Jane Hill

The Murder Ballad

For Cheryl, who called the plumber

Acknowledgements

Thank you to my agent Luigi Bonomi: this wouldn't have happened without you. Thank you also to Susan Sandon, Nikola Scott, Justine Taylor and Claire Wachtel.

I'd like to thank the friends and family members who read early versions of this book and offered encouragement, praise and criticism. You know who you are.

In particular, thank you to Michael for helping me lead a double life, Melissa for nagging me to finish this book, Rachell for nagging me to get an agent, and Chris for being Chris.

Finally, I'd like to thank Wilco for being there.

1

'Nicky Bennet Disappears', it says, the newspaper story that Anna has helpfully ringed in fluorescent-yellow marker pen and handed to me. It's tucked away in the middle of yesterday's *Guardian*: just a small paragraph, a minor but entertaining diversion from the day's real news. I'm sitting on top of the washing machine in Anna's kitchen, watching her cook. I'm enjoying the motion of the spin cycle and a bottle of very good Rioja, so for a moment I don't fully understand the words that I'm reading. *Nicky Bennet Disappears*. The headline dances and swims in front of me; I have to close one eye to keep the words still. What can it mean?

And then, suddenly, I can see it in my mind's eye. He's standing tall, smiling his inscrutable half-smile, his hands pressed together in a gesture of prayer, his long elegant fingers touching. He clicks his heels (in tooled, spurred, expensive cowboy boots), bows his head and disappears in a giant puff of smoke, vanishing by sheer will-power. 'Nicky Bennet disappears?' I read out loud, doing a theatrical double take. 'God, probably up his own backside.'

Note my inability to moderate my language when it comes to Nicky Bennet. We have unfinished business, Nicky and I. Your classic love-hate relationship. Talking about him seems to make me blaspheme or use childishly rude words like 'prat', 'arsehole' and 'bastard'. I read on: 'Hollywood film star Nicky Bennet has disappeared from the set of his latest project, a romantic thriller being shot in Canada, according to newspaper reports in the United States. The 36-year-old actor was last seen on set a week ago, and was presumed to have gone to visit his fiancée, model Clio Callahan, in Los Angeles. However, Ms Callahan (22) is reported as saying that she has not seen Bennet for at least a month. Sources described as close to the maverick star claim he had been "depressed and unsettled" recently.'

I get goose pimples on the backs of my hands and I shiver. Anna looks at me, worried, and asks, 'Where do you think he's gone?'

I stare into space for a moment, then laugh: a hollow, humourless 'huh'. 'Fuck knows,' I say (thinking, what's the matter with me? I haven't said 'fuck' out loud since I was a teenager). 'Nicky's very good at disappearing. He's had a lot of practice. Trust me, I know.'

I look at the story again. 'Maverick star?' I spit out the words. 'Pretentious git, more like. And if he's thirty-six then I'm, I'm . . .' and I search limply for a comparison. 'Then, well, so am I.'

As we eat our regular Friday-evening meal we talk about what might have happened to Nicky. I suggest alien abduction, preferably the kind that entails a painful anal probe. Anna, who has never met him, speculates that maybe he's gone to find himself in the Canadian wilderness, worn out by the demands of the twenty-two-year-old model, and is now living in a log cabin with only a tame grizzly bear for company. I catch her eye and we both laugh: this is what we love about our evenings together, the ebb and flow of our conversation as we try to outdo each other with ridiculous suggestions.

We're still discussing the domestic arrangements in the log cabin when Anna's husband Gray wanders in from his studio in the back yard in search of dinner, looking as always like a cuddly garden gnome. His hands are covered in clay and he absent-mindedly tousles my hair, then leans into the fridge to get a beer. Anna places her arm round his waist and pulls him towards her. 'We're talking about Nicky Bennet – you know, the actor Justine used to know? He's gone missing.'

Gray looks at Anna, then at me, deeply puzzled. He's famously bad on actors. He's heard of Clint Eastwood, I think, but hasn't yet realised that there's a difference between Tom Hanks and Tom Cruise. 'Nicky Bennet,' he says, turning the name over in his mind. After a few seconds his face lights up. 'Oh, is that the fellow who used to play the policeman in Yorkshire in that series that was on Sunday nights? I didn't know you knew him, Justine.'

Anna stares at him with her characteristic mix of love, exasperation and wonder. I snort loudly and nearly choke on my wine. It occurs to me that my life might have been a great deal simpler if only I'd fallen in love with Nick Berry out of *Heartbeat* instead of an enigmatic American with a penchant for letting me down.

Nicky Bennet comes from Savannah, Georgia and has the world's most seductive accent. His voice is soft and husky, with slow twisted vowels like those of a courteous elderly Southern gentleman. When I first met him he was twenty, like me, and so obsessed with the country-rock singer Gram Parsons that he regularly wore what he described as a genuine Nudie jacket that he'd bought in Nashville. At the time I wasn't at all sure who Gram Parsons was, only that he'd died in a motel room somewhere in the desert back in the drug-addled 1960s or 1970s. I didn't know what Nicky meant by 'Nudie'. I recognised it as one of those jackets that old-fashioned country-and-western singers wear, covered with appliquéd embroidered shapes of cowboy boots and flowers. But as for the word 'Nudie', I could only guess that to Nicky it meant that it felt like a second skin, like being in the nude. He told me about his home town, how Sherman presented Savannah to Abraham Lincoln as a Christmas present at the end of the American Civil War, and how it was full of shady squares, beautiful ante-bellum houses and trees covered in Spanish moss. To be honest, I barely understood a word. I didn't know who Sherman was and I certainly didn't know what 'ante-bellum' meant. It sounded like Latin for 'against beauty' but I wasn't sure. I had played truant during so many Latin lessons that I'd failed my A-level and had had to rely on my headmistress phoning London University pleading traumatic family circumstances before they'd let me in. Somehow, though, because Nicky's voice was so mesmerising and beautiful I didn't care that I didn't understand the phrase. I remembered every word he told me.

I met Nicky during the summer I spent at college in America. Later he stood me up in spectacular style, leaving me alone and scared and sitting on a brick wall in Brooklyn. The following year he walked out of my life for ever.

Anna once asked me whether I would have made more effort to stick with Nicky if I'd known how famous he was going to be. It's a question I have often asked myself, and I simply don't know the answer. You see, when I knew Nicky he showed absolutely no signs of future Hollywood stardom. He never even mentioned acting. He wanted to be an artist. He took moody black-and-white photos and mounted them on canvas with weird random daubs of oil paint all over and around the photos, in shades of lilac and turquoise and pale orange. I thought the results were quite nice to look at but I wasn't sure if they were art.

He even took some photos of me. He persuaded me to pose nude, against my better judgement. You probably wouldn't be able to tell it's me because the photos are quite dark and arty and splodged all over with paint, but I used to worry about their existence. Suppose I became famous myself, or married into the royal family or something like that? Suppose a newspaper got hold of them? As things have turned out, I don't think I need to worry any more. I can't imagine any of the tabloids paying big bucks to run a story with the headline 'Assistant manager of South Coast bookshop in nude photo shock'.

According to all the articles I've read (and — yes — cut out and kept), Nicky Bennet became a film star completely by accident. A friend of his from film school asked Nicky to take some stills to generate press interest in the no-budget film that the friend was making. Then the lead actor dropped out so Nicky got the part. Naturally the film went on to become a big hit at all the independent film festivals that year, and Nicky predictably became the next big thing. That was nearly fifteen years ago, and what was less predictable was that somehow Nicky managed to segue from a role in an indie art movie to a career as a bona fide, Oscar-nominated, thinking woman's heart-throb kind of film star.

I must admit that for a while I enjoyed the kudos I got from boasting that I used to know Nicky Bennet. I would put a special emphasis on the word 'know' so that people were left in no doubt what I meant. I'm getting fed up with it now. At work Nicky is always described as 'you know, Justine's ex-boyfriend' with a smirk of incredulity behind the words. My mother, who for years had been asking me, 'Whatever happened to that lovely American boy you used to know?', phoned me one day to say, 'That film on television last night. Was that . . .?' and I said, 'Yes' before she could finish the question.

'Oh love,' she said, which meant something like, 'How could you let someone so gorgeous slip away?'

But I didn't realise he was gorgeous. Or,

rather, *I* thought he was gorgeous but I couldn't imagine anyone else agreeing with me. I thought his gorgeousness was my unique discovery. Nicky Bennet is tall, thin and fair, almost ginger, with skin so pale that it's nearly blue. His veins are extraordinarily prominent, so close to the surface that you think they're going to pop. His skin looks dry and you expect it to be powdery to the touch, but in fact it's smooth and cool; it's as if he never sweats.

What Nicky always had was presence. His amazing green eyes would draw you in and make you tremble, as if just by standing near him you had entered a magic place. I had seen him around campus in his ridiculous embroidered Nashville jacket and found myself mesmerised. When I was finally introduced to him, he bowed his head to me and said, 'I'm Nicky Bennet. One T,' with an air of surprise as if to say, 'Who else could I possibly be? And how could you possibly think of spelling it any other way?' I sat next to him in the bar, sneaking sideways glances at him, and my knickers got so wet that I thought my period had started early.

I last saw him eighteen years ago, so of course I'm over him. I've had the standard number of relationships since then, some of them quite satisfactory. They usually end in much the same way. Just at the point when the current boyfriend starts annoying me so much that I want to scream, they dump me. 'This isn't working,' they say, and I say, 'Yeah, I've been thinking the same thing myself,' and wish I had the courage to add, 'Oh, and by the way, I never liked your taste in music' (or leather blouson, or straggly ponytail, or tiny penis, or whatever). A couple of years ago I made the classic mistake of getting involved with a married man, and the end of that relationship was so disastrously awful that it's put me off dating to this day. Maybe that's why I still think about Nicky sometimes when I'm down. On those grim premenstrual evenings when I forget to eat and find myself knocking back whole bottles of cheap Bulgarian red wine, I've been known to cry and say out loud (though there's nobody there to hear me), 'Nicky Bennet, you're the only man I ever loved.'

Sometimes I actually mean it.

Please don't imagine that I'm a pathetic lonely spinster. It's only on bad days that I feel down. Just as my long-healed broken wrist twinges only on cold days, so my long-healed broken heart only gives me gyp at times when I'm hormonally predisposed to feel miserable. Most of the time I'm happy to dismiss Nicky Bennet as a pretentious poser I once knew who had a nifty way of making a girl feel special and who walked out on me in the most cowardly way possible. But on those desperate, depressed evenings when there's nothing on the telly, when a panicky kind of loneliness clutches at my stomach and I imagine my life slipping globbily, sluggishly away like lumpy cheese sauce being poured down the plughole of the kitchen sink, that's when I remember him as the love of my life and the great lost opportunity.

At Anna's kitchen table, as we run out of beer and wine and suggestions as to what's happened to Nicky, a phrase from the newspaper report bubbles up to the top of my mind. 'Depressed and unsettled'. I shudder. Anna flicks a quick, perceptive glance at me. 'You're worried, aren't you?'

I shrug. Gray says, 'You're afraid he might be dead, aren't you?'

I look at him, shocked, and half nod. I think,

of coffee and settle down to read what they're saying about Nicky. There are lots of photos of Clio Callahan wearing Raybans, climbing in and out of cars and looking bored (or 'distraught', as the *Mail on Sunday* puts it). Lots of photos of former girlfriends (only the famous and beautiful ones; not me, of course). Shots of Nicky looking variously moody, deep and sensitive. The *Observer* has that famous photo of him that Annie Leibovitz took, posing him bare-chested in jeans in a rodeo paddock, waving his T-shirt like a bullfighter's cloak. I remember buying *Vanity Fair* the month that picture was on the cover, and I tore it off and kept it in my sock drawer for years. I used to look at it for minutes at a time, to prove to myself that I was over him. The accompanying newspaper story is ominously full of words like 'misunderstood' and 'mercurial' – and, that phrase again, 'depressed and unsettled'.

Unexpectedly I find myself getting teary, so I do what I usually do in such cases. I get undressed, sit in the empty bath and turn the shower on full blast. I allow myself a good sob under the pounding water, and then I run the kind of bath my dad used to call a Choirboy's Collar, with way too much Radox and foam up to my neck. I'm still in the bath when Gavin rings. Covered in bubbles I answer the phone and Gav says simply, in his quiet, flat, ordinary voice, 'I called to see if you were okay.'

That starts me crying again, trying to talk but getting the words caught in the back of my throat, pouring out all sorts of incoherent snotty mush. Gavin says stuff like, 'Shh,' and 'I know,' and listens quietly for a while. Then he says, 'I'm coming round and I'm going to take you down the pub.'

Gavin is the kindest man I have ever met and I wish I fancied him more. He's my semi-ex-boyfriend. Semi-ex and semi-boyfriend. We never exactly split up because we never exactly went out. I suppose I keep him metaphorically on the back burner, just in case. He's the standby I take to events when I really need a partner. Anna describes him as 'the fall-back position'. She'll listen to me rant on about my disastrous love life, then smile shrewdly and say, 'Of course, if all else fails there's always Gavin, isn't there?'

She thinks I take him for granted. I do, but I think he likes being taken for granted. I think he'd miss it if I didn't.

I met Gavin about six years ago when I

crashed my car into the back of his at a set of traffic lights. I was on my way out for the evening so I had my hair up and earrings in and was looking my best. I thought he was good-looking in an obvious way (fair hair, crinkly eyes, nice teeth) but not my type – and besides, he was several inches shorter than me. He was in his mid-twenties then, a full seven years younger than me; I think he's always had a thing for older women. He told me once that the secret of my appeal was that I looked like a hippie art teacher but was really hot in bed. Gavin is the manager of one of the big DIY superstores out of town, so I suppose we have an interest in retail management in common. He owns a disturbingly tidy two-bedroom starter home on one of the new estates. He wears short-sleeved shirts and ties and claims to make a mean spaghetti Bolognese; these attributes are, incidentally, two of my strongest irrational pet hates in men.

On my last birthday, when I turned thirty-nine, Gav took me out for an expensive meal at a new French restaurant on the seafront. After-wards we went back to his spotless house for what I assumed would be a quick old-times'-sake fuck in his neatly made bed with its navy-blue chevron-patterned duvet cover and matching pillowcases. But afterwards I went to the fridge to get a beer and that's when I realised that he wanted me to stay the night. He'd bought loads of food for breakfast: honey-cured rashers from the deli counter, free-range eggs, proper coffee, croissants, unsalted French butter and freshly squeezed orange juice. It made me feel very uncomfortable. Making a limp apology and clutching the shreds of my self-respect around me like a skimpy bath-towel, I made my getaway in a taxi.

Gavin takes me to our favourite pub down by the docks and buys us each a pint and a bag of dry roasted peanuts. 'So,' he says, 'Nicky Bennet has disappeared. And you're worried about him. Your eyes are all puffy.'

'Yeah. Stupid, really, isn't it?' I sniff. 'I mean, I haven't seen him for years and years, and I don't even know him any more. I scarcely give him a moment's thought from one day to the next, and now suddenly I'm all upset because he's gone missing. I guess it just reminds me of all the times he disappeared on me . . .' And I proceed to tell Gavin selected stories from the short but colourful relationship of Nicky Bennet and Justine

Fraser. How we met; the time he stood me up in Brooklyn; the story of Live Aid Day. Gavin sits and listens and keeps handing me clean Kleenex Man-size that he must have stuffed in his pocket before coming out, knowing I'd need them. I suppose half my brain realises that the poor bastard has heard these stories many times before and is a saint to put up with it. I wonder why he doesn't just say, 'For God's sake, Justine, get over him.'

We agree over our second pint that the whole thing is a misunderstanding: that the most likely scenario is that Nicky probably told someone where he was going and they've forgotten. Maybe he's just gone back to LA to score some drugs, or perhaps he's secretly married to a girl in Alaska or Montana or somewhere, and he's simply gone to visit her. These conclusions reached, we go to the pier and play pinball for a while.

Nicky and I used to play pinball on the pier during the eleven glorious days in the summer of 1985 when he lived in my bedsit and we were going to get married. We'd come down to the beach most evenings after I got home from work and go for a swim, and then we'd spend an hour or so in the arcade. When we played pinball I would stand in front of him, leaning back against his chest, and he would reach his arms around me to play, resting his chin on the top of my head. Now, eighteen years later, I'm still playing pinball on the pier while Nicky's a big Hollywood star. How could we ever have thought that we were meant for each other?

Gavin walks me home. We stop for chips and eat them out of the paper as we walk. Gavin kisses me chastely on the lips when we get to my front door and saunters off towards his car, his hands in his pockets.

I close the door behind me, open a bottle of red wine, and go straight to my computer.

3

You see, I know exactly why I'm so upset. It's not because I think Nicky Bennet's dead, or that I'm particularly worried about him. It's because he's disappeared. I don't know where he is. Normally I can at least imagine where he is, imagine him on a film set or at home in the tatty yet glamorous house that I imagine he owns in the hills above Hollywood. But now I feel as if he's getting away from me, disappearing from my past as if he's going down the plughole, whirling around like a newspaper headline in a film and getting further away all the time.

I love the Internet. I upgraded my computer a few months ago to give myself Internet access from home for the first time and that was when I realised how much information is out there. You know what the Internet's like; it's a kind of deep-space wormhole that leads you (via a dark and twisted route) to places that you never meant to visit. You sit at your computer on a Sunday afternoon, meaning to order a book from Amazon or to investigate cheap flights to France, and three hours later it's dark outside and you're reading some sad anorak's strangely fascinating home page that you stumbled upon by accident. Gavin introduced me to Google and to the joys of vanity surfing, and I was delighted to find myself on the second page of the search results for Justine Fraser: two links, both to the on-line edition of our bookshop chain's newsletter. If you've ever vanity surfed you'll know how addictive it can be. Soon you're typing in names of family and friends and inevitably it wasn't long before I did a search on Nicky Bennet's name.

There are mad people out there: people who have weird, religious interpretations of Nicky Bennet's film oeuvre; people who've convinced themselves that they know Nicky Bennet; people of both sexes who have written long, pornographic stories in which they have extraordinary sex with Nicky Bennet. It struck me that I could write up my own true experiences, post them on a Nicky Bennet fan-site message board and sound like just another stalker. One site called itself 'The Cruel Nicky', presumably in reference to his first film and to the general nature of the pornographic fantasies in the section marked 'Fan Fiction'. Another site claimed that Nicky Bennet often visited their message board and sometimes responded. Fans told of receiving warm, friendly messages from their hero. I'm ashamed to say that one particularly bleak premenstrual night, after far too much cheap red wine, I found myself on-line and leaving what I thought was a fairly non-committal message. The next morning I read over what I'd written: 'If Nicky Bennet is reading this, I'll always remember our two summers together. It would be nice to hear from you again. All the best, Justine Fraser.'

Fuck. Of course he didn't reply.

Today it's the official Nicky Bennet Fan Club site I'm after. It's the best source of information about him that I've found. They update it regularly with news of the films he's about to make. When he changed agents they had the details, and the site was the first to confirm his engagement to Clio Callahan (his third fiancée, incidentally, so there seems little chance of them ever getting married). I want to find out that it's all a mistake, that Nicky Bennet is alive and well and has been spotted in his local supermarket.

Except he hasn't. Emblazoned across the home page of the site is this: *Nicky Bennet Missing From Film Set – Fears Grow*, and then some stuff about how everyone is baffled by his disappearance. There are the same quotes from friends and Clio Callahan, and then there's a message page where fans can post their messages of support for Nicky and Clio. I read through some of them, and then – I shouldn't, but I do. Just a short note. Brief, functional, to the point: 'Nicky, I hope you're okay. You know where I am if you need a friend. JF.'

As soon as I log off, my phone rings and I know it's my mum using ringback. 'Hello, love, it's only me. I saw the papers. Are you okay?'

'Fine,' I say briskly. 'Absolutely fine.'

'I just thought, you know, what with Marie and everything, I was worried about you.'

'Mum, I'm fine. I'll call you later in the week,' and I put down the phone. That's when I get scared. I can feel it, physically: a cold,

4

I suppose almost everyone's got a Nicky Bennet in their past. Not necessarily your first love, but your first overwhelming can't-live-without-him love. The person about whom you sometimes stop and think, 'I wonder. Suppose it had lasted? What might have happened?'

Then you lose yourself for a while in a kind of reverie that's close, but not too close, to regret: a dream of yourself leading another life in a parallel reality. The difference for me is that for eleven days of my life eighteen years ago I was going to marry Nicky Bennet and that's a lot of what-if to deal with. Most people who get their heart broken by a bastard at least get to recover in peace. I get reminded of Nicky almost every day. Even at work. Decorating the walls of the main staircase of the shop we have film posters pinned up, posters for films based on books mostly. Right at the top of the stairs there's a poster for the John Grisham film that Nicky starred in, with Nicky's face looming in the bottom right-hand corner. One of my colleagues has added a thought-bubble: 'I wonder what Justine Fraser's doing now,' it says.

Leading a perfectly respectable, moderately happy yet vaguely unsatisfying life in the town where I was born, is the answer.

I like working in a bookshop. I write those 'If you enjoyed this you'll like . . .' signs to hook over the best-seller shelves, and then I feel a glowing sense of pride when customers come back again and buy a book by one of the authors whom I've suggested. I like dealing with nervous spotty new students and guiding them through their booklists. I like helping worried middle-aged women trying to buy the Michael Palin travel book that they've seen advertised on the BBC only they don't know where to find it. I like organising evening events: meeting authors and the inevitable posh blonde girl from the publishers at the station, driving them to the shop, briefing them on the local area and the kind of customers we get. I like making the authors laugh with sly jokes that surprise them, coming as they do from a provincial bookshop woman.

Sometimes in the evening I go to the pub with friends. Sometimes I go straight home to my warm womblike house, cook a nice meal and watch telly. Occasionally I indulge myself with one of the cathartic little crying jags that Holly Hunter popularised in the film *Broadcast News*.

When you get to my advanced age and find that nothing you'd predicted (marriage, babies, maturity) has actually happened, you become casually fatalistic. 'Would you like to find someone? Would you like to have children?' people say, and I shrug and think, how should I know? If it happens it happens. I'm not exactly being eaten up from the inside by a nagging, all-consuming maternal instinct; I can't hear a metaphorical clock ticking. I'm not considering sperm banks or dating agencies, but I do occasionally read my horoscope just to see if I'm likely to bump into that special someone, maybe in the supermarket checkout queue or at a 'Meet the Author' evening. Most of my friends are married with children; some of them feel sorry for me. They shouldn't. I have freedom. I can go on great holidays, stay out all night, invite strange men back for sex. I could, but of course I don't, not often.

Like Nicky Bennet, I'm thirty-nine. Like

Nicky Bennet, I'm tall, pale and thin. But there the similarities end. While he's officially the seventh sexiest film star in the world (thanks to *Empire* magazine for that statistic), the most anyone could say about me is that I'm not unattractive. I have bluish eyes and fairish hair (at a pinch you could call it blonde) that's long, straight and flyaway. Often I wear it caught up at the back of my neck with a tortoiseshell clip; I let annoying little tendrils escape around my face in the hope that they may look sexy, but I end up pushing them untidily behind my ears before the day's half over. I have a fairly decent figure, for which I'm very grateful: long, slightly gangly legs, angular shoulders and a flat stomach. I don't have much to speak of in the way of breasts, but there again I'm one of those lucky people who can eat what they like and never exercise and yet remain 'enviably slim' (Anna's words). There's nothing about my face that anyone could particularly object to. I have two eyes, a nose and a mouth that are more or less the right size and sit in the right places on my face in relationship to each other. The only things I wish I could change about the way I look are my tendency to red blotches when I'm embarrassed and the way the corners of my mouth droop downwards even when I'm reasonably happy. From time to time, people I don't know come up to me and say, 'Don't worry, love, it may never happen.'

I don't wear much make-up because I've never mastered the art, which I blame on my older sister topping herself before she could pass on the arcane secrets of foundation and eyeliner. In fact, foundation seems to me to be something that only women who work in offices should wear, and I'm lucky that my skin is – mostly – good enough to go without. I wear a bit of mascara, which always flakes off, and a bit of lipstick, which always feathers away. When I was a child I asked my dad if he thought I'd be beautiful when I grew up. He said, 'Every woman becomes beautiful when she's loved,' and it's only in the last few years I've realised that meant 'No.'

Instead of beautiful I tend to settle for, 'You know, you can be really attractive when you make the effort,' which is the kind of thing boyfriends have said to me. Scrubs up well, that's how I like to describe it.

Clothes-wise, I like to be distinctive. 'Stubborn,' my mother says. I like to wear things no one else would wear. Amateur psychologists might describe it as the result of being a third child, a second daughter. Throughout my childhood I was consistently two years out of step with fashion because I always had to wear Marie's hand-me-downs, until the supply dried up when I was sixteen. I couldn't wait to wear exactly what I wanted to wear. A friend once described my look as 'very bohemian', and I thought: I like that. I can't resist charity shops and market stalls. I'm a sucker for velvet and silk and things with beads and embroidery all over them. I like to customise clothes: even my newest, unpatched jeans have little daisy-chain patterns sewn around the hems. Sometimes I worry. If I were undeniably beautiful I could wear almost anything and look fabulous in it, but sometimes I wonder if I'm attractive enough to be as unconventional as I am. Occasionally I get it absolutely right, and people stop and ask me where I get my clothes, and that is one of the best feelings in the world. There are other times, though, when people look at me, and then take a second look, and I think they're about to mention what I'm wearing, but instead they don't say anything and just look away. That's when I know I've got it badly wrong. On a good day, and with a bit of effort, I can be Carrie in *Sex and the City*. On a bad day, I look – as Gavin put it – like a hippie art teacher from the early 1970s. But then, he knows my little secret. Even though I sometimes look like a freak, I can give blow jobs that make men squeal with pleasure. Unexpected talents are so useful.

Apart from the eleven days with Nicky I have lived alone for all of my adult life so far. To start with I rented a bedsit in the attic of a tall Victorian house, with sloping ceilings that had Athena posters Blu-Tacked to them. Now I'm the proud owner of a mortgage on a turn-of-the-century two-bedroomed terraced house built of warm red brick in a yuppified street. Most of us in the street have now replaced the 1970s louvres with facsimiles of the original sash windows. Inside, my walls are painted in shades of yellow and terracotta that I occasionally regret. The walls are supposed to be hung with framed posters from famous art galleries: I always come back from holidays abroad clutching a cardboard tube from a gallery but never get around to buying the right-sized frames. I have window boxes and a tiny backyard where I grow herbs and weeds in an old Belfast sink. In my kitchen I have a cafetière, a mezzaluna (never used) and a set of French saucepans that are so heavy I'm developing really great muscle definition in my arms.

Since Nicky I have had sex with nine other men. Four of those sexual partners have been one- or two-night stands. There's Gavin, of course, my emergency date on standby for moral support at weddings or office Christmas dos or evenings when I really can't face being alone. But there's no one in the world who loves me more than they love anyone else.

My trouble is that I'm not very good at being a girlfriend. I always get it wrong, misjudge the situation, misjudge the bloke. I never know whether to do the girly thing (lie on my back while he sucks my tits, write soppy poems, wait for his phone calls) or play the part of a wisecracking ladette (drink pints, insult him, get on with his mates). Blokes generally agree that I'm funny. There's this thing I do, call it my shtick – I think that's the word. I get into my element, my groove, on a subject – you could almost call it a rant – and I end up doing a whole comedy routine. Maybe it's supermarket queues or how bad I am at cooking, or some imagined defect about one of the guys I'm talking to.

There's always a moment when I know I've connected, when I make someone's face suddenly crease up in laughter. The eyes go first and then the rest of their face always follows. I can get Gavin to laugh every time I try. I think I would do or say almost anything to achieve that perfect, satisfying moment; and that includes running myself down or insulting almost anyone. The trouble is, I'm not very good at drawing the line and knowing when to stop. It appears that there are plenty of men in the world who find it a real turn-off to be insulted by a moderately attractive woman wearing strange hippie clothes.

Fortunately Nicky Bennet found it a turn-on. With him I was hard as nails, so sharp I'd cut myself, up for almost anything. He called me the vinegar in his pitcher of water, the ginger in his lemonade: the sharp taste added to make a drink truly thirst-quenching, a Southern-boy image that enchanted me with its foreignness. 'Nothing touches you, does it?' he said admiringly as we said goodbye for the first time, under the clock tower of Lowell University. 'You just don't care about anything.'

And I felt a pang of half pride, half pain. How

5

I t was the summer of 1984. I had never been abroad before. My brand-new passport photo showed me with wild, unkempt hair held off my face with a tatty piece of cloth, except for a heavy bit of fringe that I'd allowed to dangle in my eyes. I was wearing way too much blusher, badly applied, and a pair of earrings in the shape of frogs that I'd bought from a market stall in Covent Garden. I hoped I looked like the missing fourth member of Bananarama. With the benefit of hindsight I realise that I actually looked more like Boy George's ugly sister.

Into my new lightweight suitcase I packed a selection of nail varnish in bizarre colours, some clothes I'd bought at jumble sales or made from bits of fabric I'd found lying around at home and the Sony Walkman that my father had bought me as a going-away present. On cassette I took *Blue* and *Hejira* by Joni Mitchell, a couple of albums by Echo and the Bunnymen and three compilation tapes recorded off Radio One.

I had been selected from all the English Literature undergraduates at my college to spend an exchange term at the Ivy League Lowell University in New England. I couldn't shake the feeling that my course tutors had made a mistake, or had otherwise taken pity on me. My parents were excited while I was just dazed. They bought my plane ticket and put five hundred pounds in my bank account for spending money. I felt a bit guilty about this because I wasn't sure my dad's business was doing well enough for them to afford it. But they said they'd done the same thing for Simon when he went Interrailing around Europe so it was only fair. I promised them I would pay them back at some unspecified date in the distant future. They also gave me a credit card and witnessed me placing it in a sealed manila envelope. 'For extreme emergencies only,' said my mother. 'I'm trusting you with this. Try to bring it back in the same envelope. Sealed.'

I saw Nicky Bennet for the first time at the Greyhound bus station in Boston when I was waiting for the bus that would take me to Lowell. It was crowded, noisy and dirty, and full of people who could only be heading for an Ivy League university. Everyone was dressed in chinos and polo shirts, with luggage and sports equipment strewn around their feet. They all seemed to know each other. Still jet-lagged (I'd arrived at Logan Airport the night before), scared and lonely, I curled up on my seat in the waiting room to watch and wait. That was when I saw him.

The tall, thin, sandy-haired boy was standing in a corner, leaning against a vending machine, with a small, old-fashioned leather suitcase between his legs, ignoring the bustle all around him. It was as if there was a space around him that no one was allowed to enter. He was wearing jeans faded to the palest possible blue and frayed around the bottom, a pair of black cowboy boots complete with spurs and the most wonderfully ridiculous jacket I had ever seen. If I had found it at a jumble sale I would have bought it for myself. It seemed to be made of white satin, with red, black and green appliquéd patterns all over it, in the shape of guns, boots, cacti, dice and leaves of a plant I was too naive back then to identify as cannabis. The only place I'd ever seen jackets like that was on the sleeves of old country-and-western albums in charity shops. All he needed to complete the outfit was a cowboy hat. The boy was reading Carson McCullers's *The Heart Is A Lonely Hunter*, holding the paperback open with one hand while his other hand played with a pencil, passing it repeatedly backwards and forwards across his knuckles.

I stared and stared at him. I'd never seen anyone so outlandishly dressed and yet so self-assured. I was still searching for my own style; he'd found his. I stared until he looked up and caught my eye. He raised one eyebrow slightly, twitched the right-hand corner of his mouth and went back to reading his book.

The first time I heard Nicky Bennet speak was half an hour later when he helped me put my bag up on the luggage rack in the Greyhound bus. 'Let me help you with that, ma'am,' he said.

The last word came out in two long syllables as something like, 'may-yam'. I felt two bright red ovals form high up on my cheekbones. For a split second I thought about sitting next to him and striking up a conversation about *The Heart Is A Lonely Hunter*. I hadn't read the book, but I'd seen the film late one Sunday night on BBC2, starring Sondra Locke as the girl and Alan Arkin as the deaf-mute. But my nerve went and I scurried silently into the window seat immediately behind his, busying myself with my Walkman to hide my embarrassment. I stared intently out at the passing New England countryside for most of the journey, although I found that if I angled my head just right I could see the ginger-haired boy's reflection in the window. He propped his feet in the cowboy boots up against the back of the seat in front of him, read his book and didn't look out of the window once.

When we arrived at our destination, a small New Hampshire town two miles from the campus, I joined the throng of students waiting by the sign that said *Bus for Lowell University*. Nicky Bennet didn't. He strode across to the nearest phone box with a walk like Clint Eastwood's, dialled a number, said something like, 'Hi. I'm here,' then stood against the wall and carried on reading his book. A few minutes later a huge 1950s car with an open roof and shiny sci-fi fins roared into the parking lot. At the wheel was a girl who looked like a little boy, with short spiky blonde hair and a scowl. 'Y'all want a ride?' shouted Nicky in the general direction of the queue but looking at me.

I turned away, pretending to read a notice on the station wall, and the car roared off again.

I turned to look at the students in the queue to see if the cowboy had had the same impact on them. They were all looking studiedly unimpressed. I caught one girl's eye. She shrugged her shoulders at me. 'Whatever,' she said.

'Just plain weird,' said another of the girls, and that was the final word on the subject.

Lowell University was red-brick and white-clapboard buildings around a large central green that was criss-crossed by paths and surrounded by trees. At one end of the green the ivy-clad college library was topped by a clock tower, complete with a white cupola that was floodlit at night. Leading away from the green and down towards the river half a mile away was a road known as Frat Row, full of fraternity houses: once-elegant but now dilapidated mansions with balconies, turrets and white pillars and tatty old sofas out on the porches. Each of them had three Greek letters on the pediment. You'd recognise the street if you've seen the film *Animal House*.

I got into a routine early on. I made friends with a group of slightly subversive students and let myself drift into their way of life. If I didn't have a lecture I'd get up around four in the afternoon and meet up with friends. After iced tea and tuna salad sandwiches in the canteen, we'd sit around on the green watching the evening sun set over the white painted cupola of the library. We'd talk about the meaning of life, as students do, and sometimes we'd go to the bar or back to someone's room to listen to music. Somebody would know where there was a party; or maybe someone somewhere was having a barbecue so we'd all just turn up. Things seemed to happen as if in a dream. We'd wander down Frat Row around midnight looking for evidence of parties. We'd walk boldly in, heading for the beer keg that we knew we'd find in the basement of every frat house. When the keg was dry we just moved on to the next party.

Sometimes I think we even started parties, walking in on an unsuspecting fraternity, putting a tape on the deck and dancing, drinking their keg dry. Once or twice we got threatened or thrown out: a couple of the guys I hung out with were gay, one of the girls was the campus feminist and they weren't welcome at some of the houses. Eventually, around four in the morning when I'd been sick once or twice and couldn't possibly drink any more alcohol, I'd wander back to my dorm to go to bed. It was in the summer of 1984 that I discovered the true meaning of the word 'hangover'.

Perhaps because I was thousands of miles from home I became a bolder person. I took my tapes to the parties and made people play them. I single-handedly introduced Lowell University to the music of Echo and the Bunnymen. I even persuaded the head of music on the campus radio station to playlist 'The Killing Moon'. I'd say, 'Listen, I'm English, trust me, I know what's big in London.'

I told them that I knew Boy George and Princess Di; or rather, they asked me if I did and I said yes. All the American students wore madras-checked shorts, polo shirts and loafers, and danced in boy-girl pairs. Almost by tacit agreement they would pull back and leave a space in the middle of the dance floor for this whirling English dervish, dressed in rags and pointy suede boots, with green fingernails and frog earrings. I thought I looked really cool.

It was on one of those nights that I saw Nicky Bennet again. I was wearing a ra-ra skirt made out of the floral print Etam dress that I'd worn for my confirmation, and I was dancing to 'The Message' by Grandmaster Flash and the Furious Five, from one of my Radio One compilations. I had all my steps worked out. When they sang that bit about being close to the edge I would teeter forward on my toes, hands out, as if I was about to lose my balance. I was midway through this move when I noticed the tall, thin ginger bloke with the weird jacket from the Greyhound bus leaning against the fireplace on his own. He was looking at me with a half-smile on his face. Literally a half-smile: the right-hand corner of his mouth was turned up, the other was completely straight. I wobbled and nearly fell over. He laughed at me. I felt my cheekbones burning so I turned away and started dancing with the first guy who asked. A few minutes later I turned back and Nicky had gone.

It was a few days later that we were properly

introduced. He was in the bar as I went in, sitting with my usual crowd as if he belonged there. He was draped languidly on the banquette seat, talking to my campus feminist friend Nancy as if he'd known her for years. There was space next to him on the seat so I sat down and, during a lull in the conversation, cleared my throat and said, 'I don't think we've been introduced.'

Yes, those stumbling, over-polite, oh-so-English words were the first thing I ever said to Nicky Bennet. He turned, looked at me and bowed his head. Then he lifted the right hand corner of his mouth into that superior half-smile of his and said, 'I'm Nicky Bennet. One T.'

The way he said it made me blush, as if I should have known the answer, as if it had been a very stupid question. But in fact his answer surprised me. I'd heard a name, Alexander Esterhazy, mentioned by one of my Lowell friends, and had thought the name so wildly beautiful that it could only refer to the ginger boy. Nicky Bennet. Nicky Bennet. I said it in my head a few times, slightly disappointed. It seemed tame, normal. Only the pride with which he said it, the insistence on Nicky, not Nick, and on the one T, gave it distinction. Nicky Bennet. I said it again to myself, and this time it began to have poetry. Nicky Bennet had turned away by now and was about to resume his conversation, so I took my courage in both hands and said, 'I'm Justine Fraser.'

He looked at me again, for longer this time, and finally he did a proper smile. 'Yes, I know,' he said, then turned away and ignored me for the rest of the evening.

I struck up a conversation with the guy sitting on the other side of me, whom I didn't know from Adam. I talked far too loudly all night, trying to talk away the little red circles I could feel burning on my cheekbones and the tingling wetness in my knickers. From time to time I sneaked a look at Nicky's profile. The tip of his nose moved up and down as he talked.

6

I got very homesick at Lowell. At home when I get sad or moody I like to go down to the seafront and watch the grey sea make shapes on the shingle beach while the breeze whips my hair into a frenzy. I say to friends that the eternal movement of the ocean puts everything into perspective, but what I really mean is that the beach, particularly out of season, is a good place for a bit of self-indulgent melancholy. At Lowell, miles from the sea, I had to make do with the river. I'd walk down Frat Row in the early evening, down to the river bank where there was a wooden swimming dock. I'd take my shoes off and let my feet dangle in the river. At that time of the evening I'd be all alone except for the gnats and midges and the voices of the rowers from the boathouse a couple of hundred yards upstream. I'd think about life and stuff, letting the seductive swish of the water put me in a thoroughly melancholy mood. I'd think about time passing and poems I wanted to write and all the normal things an introspective English Literature student thinks about when she's miles from home and a little bit depressed.

One evening, out of the blue, Nicky Bennet joined me. I heard the swimming dock creak and there he was behind me, barefoot and holding his cowboy boots in one hand. It was the first time I'd seen him without his jacket, and I could see that his arms were freckled and wirily muscular. 'Mind if I join y'all?' he called.

'No, I mean, I was just leaving,' I blurted, as I turned away to hide my reddening cheeks.

'Stay,' he said, with at least one redundant syllable in the word, so I did.

We sat in companionable silence for a while, our feet trailing in the water, slapping away the midges with our hands. Looking down into the river he said, 'You have feet like mine. Long prehensile toes.'

'I suppose.' I didn't know what he meant, but I could see that we both had long, thin, bony toes.

'I like the crazy way you dance.'

'Thanks,' I replied, kicking myself inwardly

for being unable to deal with his simple conversational gambits.

'Don't you get scared when you're dancing and everyone's looking at you?' he said, making another effort to get me to talk.

'Not really,' I said, and pretended to look at my watch. 'Look, I've really got to go.'

Shit, shit, shit, I said to myself as I walked back up the hill towards the campus. When did I start being shy? Nicky Bennet was starting to get to me, churning me up inside in a way that I wasn't used to. It wasn't as if I wanted to fall in love with him. I had a more than adequate boyfriend back in London. Daniel was clever and funny and wrote for the college magazine; he was everything I'd ever wanted in a boyfriend. Nicky, meanwhile, seemed to be involved with the girl with the great car, the scowl and the very short hair. I didn't know what was going on in my mind.

A couple of days later I went down to the river again and Nicky was there. 'Hey,' he called. 'Don't go! Talk to me.'

So I stayed.

He suggested that we talk about music. I told him, in an embarrassed, blotchy-faced, blurted-out way, that deep down the singer I really liked was Joni Mitchell. He didn't turn up his nose or say 'typical female English undergraduate' like most men say. He started telling me about Gram Parsons. He told me that he wore his Nudie jacket as a kind of tribute. He gazed into the middle distance as he talked, and his eyes started to get teary. I said, 'Didn't he die in a motel room or something?'

'Yeah. His friends stole his body and cremated it in the Joshua Tree desert. I hope someone does that for me if I die in dramatic and tragic circumstances.'

Nicky was silent for a while, stirring the water with one prehensile toe (I'd looked the word up in the dictionary since our last conversation and could use it – at least in my head – quite properly). Then he turned to me and said, 'Do you ever think about killing yourself?'

'No,' I said sharply. 'I'm not allowed to.'

'Why? Are you a Catholic?'

'No. It's just that my sister killed herself, and for my parents to lose two out of their three children to suicide would be more than just careless, it would be downright irresponsible.'

He coughed suddenly and I think he was choking back a laugh, so I turned to look at him and said, 'It's okay. You're allowed to laugh. It's no big deal. I didn't like her much anyway.'

'Why not?'

'She was a stupid cow with fat legs who wrote really bad poetry.'

That time he did laugh. He looked at me and I could see that his eyes were surprised and his whole mouth joined in the laugh. I laughed too, then turned away, embarrassed. I felt his hand on the back of my neck and he pulled my head back round towards him and kissed me on the lips. His mouth was cold and dry and the kiss was a chaste one; he pulled away just as I parted my lips. He flicked his knuckle against my cheek. 'Justine Fraser,' he said, 'I love the crazy way you dance.' He said it with several irresistible extra syllables.

Then he walked away with his Clint Eastwood swagger, leaving me confused and tingly.

I didn't speak to him for a while after that. I saw him around campus with the short-haired girl. Once I saw them together in the classic car, cruising round the green late at night. Another time I saw them dancing together at a fraternity party, doing an old-fashioned American country dance with all the intricate steps, do-si-do-ing like mad. They looked as if they were made for each other. I don't think he saw me watching. Either that, or he was deliberately ignoring me.

I didn't know what to think. I wanted Nicky Bennet to like me, but I didn't want to date him. I wrote to my boyfriend Daniel, who knew a lot about pop music, asking him to tell me all about Gram Parsons so I could at least hold a conversation with Nicky. Daniel never replied, and it was only later that I found out why.

7

It was with a certain sort of inevitability that I eventually had sex with Nicky Bennet. The night it happened, I was curled up in the corner of a tatty old sofa in the front room of the house that Nancy and her friends rented. It was around three in the morning, the tail end of a party, and I was sharing my second-ever joint. The house was on a quiet tree-lined back street that petered out into the woods. It was made of clapboard, weathered a dull brownish-grey, and it was untidy and fusty-smelling in the way you'd expect from a house that's been colonised by students.

The front door was open with just the screen door shut; out on the porch I could see Nicky and the short-haired girl. They were sitting on the porch swing and Nicky had his booted feet up on the low wall, gently pushing the swing back and forth.

One of my Echo and the Bunnymen tapes was on the stereo in the front room. Over the dirge-like music I could hear Nancy clattering glasses in the kitchen, a couple making out in the corner of the room, the creak of the porch swing and the murmur of the conversation outside. I was sharing the joint with a fat girl in velvet who'd provided the dope. Every so often she'd take a long drag, hold the joint out in front of her, squint at it and say, 'This is good shit.'

I wasn't experienced enough in the ways of drugs to be able to tell good shit from bad shit. I was just enjoying the warm, dreamy, comforting feeling it gave me.

I slowly became aware that the conversation out on the porch had become an argument. I couldn't make out many of the words, but the girl's voice was raised and shrill. She'd say something, then Nicky would murmur in reply and she'd shout back, her voice getting louder with each exchange. The swing stopped creaking and I could see her standing over Nicky, holding the lapels of his jacket and shaking him. I heard the words 'fucking' and 'bastard', and then she stomped off down the street.

I curled up in an even tighter ball on the sofa

and took another drag on the joint. I heard the creak and dull thwack of the screen door opening and closing, that evocative American sound I knew from hundreds of episodes of *The Waltons*. I looked up and there was Nicky Bennet, posed in the doorway like a hero in a western.

Maybe it was the effect of the drugs, but this is how I remember it: I watched myself participate in the scene. He walked across the room in two strides and grasped the wrist of the surprised, blotchy-faced English girl. His hand was cool, dry and strong. Without taking her eyes from his face, she held out the joint for the fat girl to take. She stood up on legs that felt like jelly, and fell forward into his voracious, searching kiss. 'Justine Fraser,' he said, as he eventually took his lips away.

'Nicky Bennet. One T,' was her witty retort.

We ran out of the house and up the street towards the centre of the campus, criss-crossing diagonally across the road and back again, waiting for each other to catch up. Suddenly we were in a cop movie or an episode of *Starsky and Hutch*: hiding in alleyways, shouting, 'Cover me!' and running from an imaginary gunman.

'Just twenty seconds to make it – can you do it?' he said, still in character, and I said, 'Sure.'

He grasped my wrist again and we ran hell-for-leather towards the green and into the centre of it, skirting the sprinklers that seemed to start up as we ran past them. We collapsed into the grass laughing and he began to tear my clothes off.

It wasn't difficult. I remember exactly what I was wearing: a badly finished hand-sewn wrap-around skirt fastened with a couple of press studs, and a 1950s cardigan from a jumble sale, held together with a diamanté hairgrip. As Nicky pulled out the hairgrip he laughed, pinned it in his hair and did a quick little girlish moue. Then he was kissing my eyes and my nose and my mouth, and his dry, flaky lips worked their way down until they fastened on my left breast. I could feel his hands between my legs, and I couldn't tell whether the dampness was me or the wet grass. I scrabbled to help him pull down his trousers, and then suddenly his long, elegant penis was lying on my stomach. 'May I?' he said, and I nodded.

I don't think I've ever screamed so loudly. It hurt like nothing had ever hurt before. I felt I was being impaled on a rod of cold steel. I screamed words like 'Jesus!' and 'Shit!' and bit into Nicky's shoulder so hard I could taste blood. As the pain ebbed and flowed I fastened my knees behind his

8

When I met Nicky Bennet I was both naive and unshockable. If that sounds an impossible combination, think about this: I knew I was an innocent; I knew that my experience of sex amounted to just a few childish fumblings. But I also knew that there were lots of things I didn't know and, being naive, I had no way of knowing how to judge them. How could I know whether one sexual act I knew very little about was worse than another? Which is a long-winded way of saying that with Nicky, I was up for anything.

Not that we did anything particularly outrageous: a bit of nude photography, the merest hint of bondage and sadomasochism, that was about it. And besides, I was thousands of miles from home so none of it really counted.

After that first time, on the green, I spent the

next day worrying I might be pregnant. Maybe I should have asked Nicky to use a condom, but I was new to all this and didn't know the etiquette. I got out my diary and counted the days since my last period and more or less convinced myself it would be okay. Clutching my courage in both hands, I went to the medical centre, got myself on the Pill, and then I felt cool and grown up and ready for anything Nicky Bennet might want me to do.

My room became a little nest for Nicky and me. He'd knock on my door at strange times: the early hours of the morning, mid-afternoon, whenever. I was always ready for him. It was a standard-issue dorm room with a single bed, built into a set of cupboards against the wall. There was a desk, a washbasin, bookshelves above the bed specially designed for hitting your head on during sex, and a built-in wardrobe that never closed properly. Soon some of Nicky's clothes were hanging in it.

I preferred having sex in my room. Nicky's was covered with his strange pictures. I'd expected him to have a Confederate flag on his wall. In fact my expectation was so strong that I think someone must have told me he had one; it was exactly the kind of maverick Southern-boy thing that he'd do. But in fact all he had on his walls were his artworks.

I didn't know they were his to start with. I didn't know he was an artist. I only knew that he was majoring in history of art, in itself unusual enough to cause comment around campus. After the second time we had sex I pulled on his jeans, wrapped my cardigan around myself and took a good look at the pictures. By now the dawn was breaking in the sky and I was stone-cold sober and starving hungry. 'Did you do these?' I asked.

'Yeah,' he said.

I took a long look at one of the pictures. It was a black and white photo of a white-pillared Southern house, and purple paint was smeared across the sky and over the roof. A good photo ruined, I thought but didn't say. What I did say was, 'Do you think you've obscured quite enough of the picture with paint?'

He was standing next to me, naked, and his half-smile in the right-hand corner of his mouth suddenly shot across to the other side and his eyes lit up in a laugh. My heart did a leap and I decided I wanted to dedicate my whole life to turning that half-smile into a laugh.

Nicky asked me if I would pose for his

photographs, and after about a day's hesitation I did. Over the next few weeks I posed many times. I posed naked except for his spurred cowboy boots, naked except for his Nudie jacket, naked doing a handstand against his bedroom wall. We snuck down to the college darkroom late at night to develop the photos. Then he painted them, with broad swathes of yellow or turquoise acrylic paint obscuring my breasts, my face, my pubic hair. Should this have worried me? Maybe, but I was in America. And besides, he was a Southern boy and I'd read enough Tennessee Williams to know that this type of behaviour was comparatively normal for someone from the Deep South.

Nicky and I became inseparable. We sat opposite each other in the library, my bare feet in his lap. I took to wearing a silver ring like the one he wore so they would clank together when we held hands. We played games with each other. We'd arrange to meet at parties and then ignore each other. He would leave messages on his door for me: 'Tri-Delt at 11 p.m.' or 'I'll be in the bar from 9.' I'd nonchalantly turn up and catch his eye; he'd wink at me, throw me his lopsided smile. Then we'd turn our backs on each other and spend the evening flirting and dancing with someone else. Much later — sometimes, not always: the not knowing was part of the fun — he'd knock on my door and we'd have the most exquisitely delayed dirty sex. People talked about us, pointed at us, made jokes about us on open-mike night at the campus comedy club. I had never imagined that one day I'd be part of a couple that everyone was talking about.

I glowed. Looking at myself in the mirror, I remembered my dad's words: 'Every woman becomes beautiful when she is loved.'

I proudly bore the marks of our passion. I'd emerge from my room after Nicky had left, my cheeks raw from the rub of his stubble and his dry lips. I had bite marks all over me, and little finger-shaped bruises around my wrists and neck. We punched and kicked and bit each other during sex, going a little further every time. Sometimes he'd blindfold me with an old red bandanna, or he'd dig out a pair of handcuffs he kept in my desk drawer and we'd take turns at being in charge.

When we had to be apart I'd wear his jeans with no knickers, feeling the seams rub against my swollen genitalia and the raised sore welts on my inner thighs where Nicky had bitten me.

Being in love with Nicky made me feel all turned inside out: dirty, sleazy, moist and constantly in pain. I could get aroused just thinking about his kisses, the way my mouth was always sore from his rough, dry lips rubbing hard against mine.

There was one night with Nicky that I will always remember. He'd discovered I'd never heard any Gram Parsons music so he brought a tape round to play for me. His green eyes lit up as he slotted it into my cassette player. 'This is cosmic American music,' he told me, and then he closed his eyes and put his hands together in a gesture of prayer as the music began. I was expecting something mystical and strange and passionate, and was disappointed at first when what came out of the speakers sounded just like country and western. I picked up the cassette box and read the inlay card. The song was called 'Return of the Grievous Angel'. I closed my eyes and tried to listen with Nicky's ears. The song finished and he rewound it and played it again, and then again, and eventually I got it. It was the voices working together, Gram Parsons and a woman with a voice like an angel, with harmonies that didn't go where you expected them to go, and the lyrics, about travelling miles across America but all the roads leading back home. I looked at Nicky's face. He still had his eyes shut, a curious expression on his beautiful face: a kind of rapturous melancholy. I knew then that we were made for each other, that we would always find each other, wherever we travelled. He was my own grievous angel, I thought then; I guess I still do.

9

I nevitably we came to the end of term and things had to be sorted. I had two weeks left to run on my visa before I left the States, and only a half-arranged visit to some friends of friends of friends of my parents in Washington DC to look forward to. I dropped heavy hints to Nicky. 'I really don't know what I'm going to do at the end of term,' I said one night, grimacing as he bit my nipples. 'I guess I should travel around a bit, see the country before I have to leave . . .'

I put three dots on the end of the sentence to give Nicky room to say, 'No, don't. Just stay with me.'

But instead he put his hand over my mouth, said, 'Shhh' and did something rather nice to my clitoris.

This scene repeated itself, more or less, every time I started to talk about what would come next.

I wanted to kneel on the floor, throw my arms around his knees and say, 'Let me go with you wherever you're going. Take me to Savannah. Show me your white-pillared ante-bellum home in a shady square covered with Spanish moss, whatever that is.'

But I didn't want to sound desperate so I skirted the issue instead. I started to plan my stay in Washington DC out loud, hoping that he'd pick up on my lack of enthusiasm for the project. 'I want to go to the National Gallery, of course, and maybe the Hirshhorn. That's always the first thing I like to do when I visit a new city, go to the art galleries.'

At that point Nicky snorted. He was lying in bed, wrapped up in the crumpled sheets, as I was getting dressed around three in the afternoon. 'What's so funny?' I said.

God, how I wanted him to say, 'What's funny is that you're not going to Washington. You're coming home to Savannah with me.'

Instead, he said, 'Your voice. It's so light, so toneless, like a little mouse. Pitter-patter, pitter-patter, no emphasis, no feeling. It's so cool, so English, so couldn't-give-a-shit. I love it.'

The night before the end of term I tried the

same tack again. 'Actually, maybe I won't stay in Washington. Perhaps I'll travel around and see a bit of the country,' I said casually.

It worked. 'The thing is,' he said, 'I have plans for next week. But maybe you want to meet up later in New York? I've got a friend who might lend me his apartment for a few days.'

'Yeah, that sounds all right,' I said, as I struggled to hold down my leaping heart.

'If you don't want to that's okay,' he said, looking away but holding my wrist tightly. 'New York for the first time. That's probably something you want to do on your own.'

'No, no, that'll be great,' I said, struggling to keep the relief out of my voice. I turned to kiss him, and at that moment I wanted him so much that I was sure it was written on my face. But if it was, Nicky had chosen that same moment to become illiterate in the language of love.

We said goodbye late at night under the floodlit clock tower, and then I caught a cab to the station. I sat on the platform, waiting for the midnight train to Washington DC. I had a Gladys Knight song playing in my head. I was leaving my man and catching the midnight train. Does life get more romantically melancholy?

It was hot and humid in Washington DC. The couple I was staying with were elderly, friendly and God-fearing, and lived in a clean, affluent suburb. They asked me all about Lowell, clearly impressed to have an Ivy League house-guest. I gave them the bowdlerised version in which I studied hard and went to only a few parties. They fed me on unfamiliar food like squash, clams and soft-shell crabs, and wanted to know about England. Every morning they drove me to the nearest metro station and I would travel into the centre of Washington DC on the clean, efficient subway, its cavernous graffiti-free grey and silver stations looking like sets from a sci-fi film.

Washington DC made me blink. It was white, glaring and unreal. I stuck firmly to the centre, scared by my hosts' tales of ghettoes and black gangs preying on tourists who got lost. I visited the National Gallery and looked at American landscapes from the last century. I admired the sculpture garden at the Hirshhorn. I went to every branch of the Smithsonian, up and down the length of the Mall. I queued for the lift to the top of the Washington Monument to see the long Paris-style symmetry of the city. I paid my respects to

Abraham Lincoln and Thomas Jefferson at their
memorials, and toured the White House, the
Capitol and the National Cathedral. I ate my lunch
each day in museum cafés. I wrote postcards to
family and friends. And I tried ringing the phone
number that Nicky had given me.

It was a week before he rang back. It was late at
night, after eleven, and my hosts and I were
already in bed. I was summoned to the phone by
the man of the house. 'Some fella, says his name's
Nicky Bennet. I told him it had better be important
to wake us all up like that.' His tone was distinctly
disapproving.

'Sorry,' said Nicky when I picked up the
phone. 'I didn't realise you were the kind of girl
who went to bed before midnight.'

We made plans to meet up in New York two
days later. I told him that I would take the Greyhound, and I wanted him to offer to meet me at the
station. Instead he gave me the name of a subway
stop, and detailed and complicated directions to an
apartment above a corner store in Brooklyn, full of
phrases like 'walk six blocks against the traffic and
cross at the next intersection.'

Brooklyn sounded scary. The Port Authority
Bus Terminal, where the Greyhound bus would

arrive, sounded even scarier. As my elderly hosts saw me off on the bus, I assured them that my friend was meeting me there, at the terminal, and that my parents knew all about my plans.

The bus station, when I arrived, was even noisier, dirtier and more full of homeless people than it had been in my wildest imaginings. It was Labor Day, America's nearest equivalent to August Bank Holiday Monday, the last day of the summer vacation when everyone returns home. The terminal was heaving, hot and smelly. I stood in a queue for ten minutes or more to check in my suitcase, which was growing heavier by the second. I'd transferred the few things that I'd need for the next week to a small rucksack. Then I went to the toilet to try to make myself look beautiful, or at least like someone Nicky Bennet might fancy. As I washed my face and put on some blue mascara, I took a frank look at myself in the cracked, pock-marked mirror. Nothing special. A lanky, blotchy-faced English girl in an old lacy camisole top from a vintage-clothes shop, a pair of flip-flops and a long Indian cotton skirt made out of a sundress I'd bought from a market stall. I was scared stiff that he'd take one look at me and realise he'd made a mistake.

I found the apartment more easily than I'd expected and rang the bell marked 'Andersen' as instructed. I was carrying my backpack over one shoulder, and swayed from side to side as I waited for the door to be answered. I knew there'd be several flights of stairs so I took off the pack, leaned it against the wall and waited, my face preparing the smile with which I'd greet Nicky. As the smile started to hurt I realised that not only had there been no answer, there was no noise at all, no sound of someone galloping downstairs to welcome his girlfriend. There were two other doorbells with other names on them. I tried both of them, thinking that maybe Nicky had popped out for supplies and had left the key with a neighbour. Again, no answer. It was, after all, three in the afternoon on a hot Labor Day in New York. Who'd stay in on a day like that unless they'd arranged to meet their girlfriend?

I reluctantly hoisted my backpack again and stood there for a while, trying to decide what to do. Across the street a group of Hispanic kids were playing in the water streaming from the kerbside hydrant. Their shouts and screams were benevolent, not threatening. One of them waved at me and I waved back. I looked around. It seemed like an okay neighbourhood, at least at this time of the day.

I went into the little store on the corner under the apartments. It was an Italian general store and deli, with smelly sausages hanging behind the counter and plastic tubs of olives and tomatoes in oil. A fat, elderly Italian man in a white apron looked up at me as I walked in and I asked him if any message had been left. He knew nothing. He didn't know Nicky's name, he didn't even seem to know anyone called Andersen. I thanked him and hurried out before I began to cry. Outside the shop was a low brick wall so I sat down and tried to think. And all I could think to do was wait.

I sat on that wall for nearly three hours. I sat there so long that it felt as though the pattern of the bricks was imprinting itself on the backs of my thighs. I read my guidebook to New York cover to cover – twice. Nicky had obviously been delayed. All I had to do was wait and he'd turn up. After about an hour the Italian man brought me out a cold can of Coke and refused to let me pay for it. He tapped me on the shoulder gently in a gesture of sympathy. Later a girl came by, wearing a shiny blouse and carrying a lily; she started talking to me about God. She offered to take me back to her hostel where she would presumably initiate me into a cult. I politely declined, but for a while I let her talk and keep me company.

It was only when the sun got low and shadows got longer, as the Hispanic boys finished their game and went back to their respective homes, that I let myself admit that I'd been stood up.

I settled my rucksack on my shoulders and walked slowly back to the subway station. Using my guidebook and my emergency credit card I booked myself a room for the rest of the week in a hotel described as 'dull but adequate; a safe mid-price choice in Manhattan'. I took off my clothes, sat in the tiny bathtub, turned the shower on full blast and howled my eyes out.

10

There's a painting by Marc Chagall called *The Birthday* that hangs in the Museum of Modern Art on West 53rd Street in New York. In it a woman's holding a bunch of flowers that her boyfriend has just given her. It looks as if she's going to put them in some water but her boyfriend can't bear her to turn away from him even for just one moment. So he flies through the air from behind her, twists his head round at an impossible angle and kisses her on the lips. You can see a bed in the background of the picture and you know they're about to have wonderful sex.

I stood and stared at the painting for many minutes and realised with a clammy shiver of freezing cold embarrassment why Nicky had stood me up. It was as simple as this: he didn't love me. What I had thought was the all-time great love affair had been merely a fling. How could it compare to the painting in front of me? That was passion, that was true love: a force that can make lovers fly through the air, their lips unable to stay apart. I'd been fooling myself. Now I realised that what had connected Nicky and me wasn't love at all, just a pale imitation: a piece of shoddy knicker elastic with all the give gone, not the all-powerful electromagnetic force that gave Chagall's lovers wings.

And to think that I'd spent most of that morning sitting hopefully in the museum foyer. I'd been giving him one last chance. I'd toyed with the idea of going back to the Brooklyn apartment, just to check. But I stopped myself just in time. I decided instead to make the most of my time in New York, to sightsee as if nothing was wrong. But when I arrived at the Museum of Modern Art I felt a faint stirring of hope. If Nicky knew me at all, he'd know that would be the first place I'd go. And so, alone and teetering desperately on the verge of a broken heart, I sat on a bench in the museum foyer and tried to convince myself that the next person through the door would be Nicky Bennet, tall and elegant in his Nudie jacket and his cowboy boots. He would materialise in a puff of smoke and suddenly everyone else would go into blurry slow motion. There'd even be a kind of halo of light around him, and I would run into his arms and kiss him. He would kiss me back and then, in his wonderful, twisted Southern voice, he would say – what?

It was as I tried to imagine what his first words would be that I realised it wouldn't happen. 'Justine Fraser', those were the only words I could think of him saying. He'd never called me anything else, never used any term of endearment; he just described me as the ginger in his lemonade, the vinegar in his water. That's not how a man describes the woman he loves. That's how he describes someone he quite likes having around. He laughed at the sound of my voice, said it was toneless, lightweight, pitter-patter, like a little mouse. And, oh God, he'd laughed at me when I said that the first thing I liked to do in a new city was to visit an art gallery.

I knew what had happened. Since he'd been apart from me, he'd realised my true nature. He'd found himself involved with a plain, naive English girl who went to bed before eleven and who loved him with a passion and intensity that was scarily off the scale. He felt nothing for me. I had been just an amusing diversion for a couple of months. No wonder he had stood me up.

I spent the rest of the week in New York as just another sightseer; a pale, forlorn figure drifting along the tourist trail. I drifted to the top of the Empire State Building and the World Trade Center, past the Statue of Liberty on the Staten Island ferry, down to the noisy Oyster Bar at Grand Central Station. I bought take-out sandwiches to eat in my hotel room while watching TV each evening, too scared to go out on my own at night. I bit my fingernails down to the quick for the first time since I had given up the habit at the age of twelve. And at the end of the week I flew back to Heathrow.

On the plane I thought about Daniel back in London, so nice and clever and funny, with his lovely ugly face full of interesting, knobbly bones, and the way we'd snuggle up on the settee together to watch television. That's the kind of love designed for someone like me. Not a grand passion, just something comfortable, sensible and English, like a super-soft machine-washable acrylic cardie from Marks and Sparks.

I'd met Daniel soon after the start of my second year at university. One of my two flatmates, Katie, came in one day and told us about the student who'd tried to chat her up in the library. 'He had a really clever face,' she said, blushing.

Katie was a stalwart of the university Christian Union and had strict rules on dating. So when the clever-faced student had asked her out, she had said, 'Are you a Christian?'

'No,' he'd said. 'Why?'

'Because if you're not I can't really go out with you.'

'Oh,' he'd said, crestfallen. 'I'm Jewish – halfway there. Is that any good? We could talk about God and the Old Testament; discuss the lives of the prophets. It's an unmissable opportunity to convert the Jews. This one, anyway.'

The way Katie told the story made me laugh. I liked the sound of Daniel Green. He sounded too good to waste. I told her to invite him round to tea with us one evening. He arrived carrying a packet of fondant fancies. 'I've not been invited to tea anywhere since I was about eight years old, but these are what we ate then so I hope they prove to be an acceptable gift.'

Daniel was interestingly ugly, with a mobile

mouth and light brown floppy hair that had a distinctive cow-lick. He had pale skin, with a spattering of neat little moles and freckles. I liked the look of him. My other flatmate, Caroline, was looking her usual glossy self, dressed in a crisp men's shirt and beautifully cut jeans, her hair hanging in an immaculate bob. I was wearing something bizarre, I forget what, and was acutely conscious of a massively disfiguring spot on my chin. So I had to employ my most dangerous weapon. I moved into clever, sharp-tongued mode, made Daniel laugh and won the day. We became an item.

He was perhaps half an inch shorter than me, and hugely funny, but he spoke in a muttered voice that I sometimes had to strain to hear. Subversively funny, that was the phrase that came to mind. He wrote surreal pieces on pop music for the college magazine: 'The Smiths: Why?' was the title of one of them. Daniel was thoughtful and understanding. He accepted with good grace the fact that I was incapable of leaving the house if *Hill Street Blues* was on the television and instead of forcing me to go out with him when it was on he would turn up on the doorstep with some cans of beer and a pizza and watch it with

Caroline and me. He even tried to learn the names of the characters. Daniel occasionally played drums rather well in a not very good student band. Caroline, Katie and I would go to see them play, feeling like groupies. Daniel couldn't go into a kitchen without rummaging in the cutlery drawer and then playing the spoons. He could also play recognisable tunes by cracking his knuckles. These were all things that I admired. I wouldn't say he made the earth move for me, but sitting on the settee with Daniel Green was always comfortable.

I thought hard about Daniel all the way home, holding the thoughts close to me as I hugged the lightweight airline blanket. By the time my plane landed I was relieved that Nicky had stood me up. I was sure Daniel was the man for me and that he would be at Heathrow to meet me.

He wasn't. Alone, I lugged my suitcase and my rucksack onto the Tube and travelled all the way to Finsbury Park, where I got off and dragged my luggage to the flat I shared with Caroline and Katie. It was about eight-thirty on a sunny September morning and I was dog-tired. I let myself in and, leaving my case in the hallway, climbed the stairs, calling, 'Hello! I'm home!'

I squealed with delight when Daniel appeared on the landing. So he'd decided to wait for me there. How thoughtful. I went to kiss him, my arms outstretched. He looked sheepish and turned his unshaven cheek to me, which surprised me: both the fact that he turned his cheek and the fact that it was unshaven. It took several seconds for my befuddled jet-lagged brain to work out that he had just come out of Caroline's bedroom dressed only in a T-shirt and a pair of underpants.

Two weeks later I dropped out of university and went back home, scared of what I might do to myself. I wondered if this was how my sister Marie had felt. Her suicide note had read, in part, 'I've discovered that we need the love of others. But love breeds hurt and I can't stand the pain.'

At the time she wrote it, when I'd been cynical and sixteen, I'd thought it a load of pretentious tosh, almost as bad as the poems she wrote. But suddenly I knew what she meant.

Daniel phoned, half apologetic, half defensive. He said he was sorry he'd upset me, sorry I was upset he was sleeping with Caroline, but after all there'd been nothing serious between us, we were just good friends. And anyway, I had a boyfriend, didn't I? I'd written to him saying that I'd met some bloke called Nicky Something. He'd completely misunderstood. Of course, you could argue that I had been unfaithful. But that had been in another country, another world, in some kind of parallel universe. I couldn't make Daniel understand what he'd done wrong.

I couldn't stop crying, although I couldn't have said if I was more upset about Nicky Bennet or Daniel Green. I spent a lot of time up in my room tearing things up: paper, old clothes, magazines. My parents were worried about me. They speculated that it might be delayed reaction to my sister's death; I knew it was just a simple case of double heartbreak. They hesitantly suggested that I should go to see a psychiatrist, which shows how worried they were: no one in our family goes to see psychiatrists. Psychiatrists are for seriously mad people. Instead, I snapped out of it and pulled myself together. I got myself a job I enjoyed in a safe, friendly bookshop; then I found a cosy little bedsit and embarked on my destiny as a reasonably contented spinster.

Until Nicky Bennet turned up again a year later out of the blue and proceeded – oh so

11

'Well, you see, I had no idea. I'd always assumed he was her brother.' The crisp Edinburgh voice of my boss Paul floats out of the staffroom on Monday morning as I climb the stairs, hungover and late for work. I drank most of a bottle of wine while I was on the Internet last night and that was on top of the two pints I'd had with Gavin. I slept badly, my dreams full of disturbing images that kept waking me up with a start. I'm still shaky when I arrive, feeling as if I'm just hanging together. I walk into the staff coffee room just before nine, looking and feeling like death warmed up. The room immediately falls silent but there's still an echo of whispering bouncing around the walls. Everyone seems to have heard the news about Nicky. Everyone seems to be itching to ask me how I feel about it.

'So, Paul,' I say. 'Are you going to sell your story, about the Nicky Bennet you knew?'

I want to break the taboo, to make it clear I don't mind if everyone wants to talk about the disappearance. Paul glances at me, guesses what I'm doing and plays along. 'Och yes, my agent's already instigated a bidding war. I hear the *News of the World* is up to half a million.'

Paul is the only person at work who has seen Nicky Bennet and me together with his own eyes, living proof that I'm not making up the whole thing. Ironically, though, he never even realised that Nicky was my boyfriend: he thought he was my weird, scary, over-protective older brother.

Whenever I have to describe Paul the word 'dapper' is the first that springs to mind, even though it's not in my usual vocabulary. He always wears immaculately cut suits, he has a slightly camp Miss Jean Brodie accent and his nails are so beautifully manicured that I originally assumed he was gay. We are the only two survivors of a huge upheaval a few years ago when the shop was taken over by a chain that introduced late opening hours, comfy sofas and an espresso bar. Paul did some superb sucking-up to the new management and ended up in charge. Fortunately, he sees me as his protégée.

In the summer of 1985, when I was still the new girl and Paul was second in command of the popular-reference department, we lived near each other and he would walk me part of the way home. He was in his late twenties then, and because I thought he was gay I enjoyed the gentlemanly attention he paid me. There was a low wall at the corner where my street turned off the main road, and most evenings Nicky would wait for me there. He would greet me wordlessly with a kiss on the cheek or a chuck under the chin. I'd say a perfunctory goodbye to Paul as Nicky took me by the wrist and led me to the pier or the beach or our favourite pub or sometimes straight home for sex.

One evening Paul asked if I wanted to go for a drink. I assumed he was asking us both, so I said, 'I don't know. I'll have to see what Nicky says.'

'Nicky?'

'You know, Nicky,' I said, gesturing with my head towards the corner where he was sitting, waiting impassively for me.

'Och, forget Nicky,' he said. 'You're a big girl now. Come out and have some fun on your own.'

I stared at him as if he was mad. 'Why? I don't want to. I want to be with Nicky.'

We stood staring at each other for a while, and then he gave me a really sympathetic smile and said, 'I'm sorry. I'll leave you alone. I didn't mean to upset you.'

Years later, at the pub with Paul, his new wife and my short-lived ponytailed boyfriend, the conversation turned to films and Paul revealed his mistake. 'Ellie's annoyed that I came so close to going for a drink with Nicky Bennet. If only I'd realised he was your boyfriend. But you seemed too young to be living with someone, and you looked so alike.'

'Alike?'

'Tall and pale and thin, with such odd clothes. I felt sorry for you. I thought you must have a terrible home life with your overprotective older brother who had obviously brought you up. You never dared to be late home. I thought you were scared of him. And I thought you must be very poor since you both had to wear second-hand clothes.' Paul adjusted his cuff link as he said this.

'Oh my God, is that what everyone thought?'

'Justine, I know we've always had a lax dress code at the shop, but I think most of us felt that wearing an old school science overall as a frock went some way beyond mere eccentricity and had to be a sign of direst poverty.'

I was shocked. I'd been so proud of that science overall. It was a beautiful bright emerald green and made of heavyweight cotton drill in a wrap-around style. I thought it was far too good to throw away so I'd made a feature of the acid holes by blanket-stitching around them and incorporating them into an embroidered floral pattern, based partly on the designs on Nicky's Nudie jacket. It was one of my favourites.

Paul's obviously about to finish his story but then catches sight of something in my face. He stops, and instead he reaches out a hand to me and gathers me to him in a kind of hug. He's a kind man, is Paul, a good friend and a good boss, on the whole. He looks closely at my eyes, which I know are bloodshot, and says, 'Are you sure you should be at work?'

I nod, and I mean it. Of course I should be at work. But I'm grateful it's a quiet Monday. I find something that needs doing up on the deserted second floor, where the academic reference books are kept. It's a good place to be on my own, to daydream. And the daydream I want to play repeatedly in my mind is this one: I'm standing over by the bookshelves with my back to the shop floor. I feel a presence behind me. I turn around and there is Nicky Bennet, just standing there, smiling his half-smile at me. 'Justine Fraser,' he says.

'Nicky Bennet. One T,' I reply, and I fall into his arms and we kiss.

Later, we sit in the espresso bar on the first floor sipping lattes while he tells me why he's come to find me again. 'All this time I couldn't get you out of my mind,' he says in his seductive Southern drawl. 'The time we spent together was so special. I hoped against hope that I'd be able to find you again. And here you are.'

Through the morning I work on several different versions of events, honing the daydream until I'm almost acting it out. In one version I'm angry with Nicky for walking out on me all those years ago, but I know in my heart of hearts that if he came back I would just sink into his arms and forgive even the flimsiest of excuses. It happened before, when he came back to me on Live Aid Day; it would happen again. And the thing is, it could happen. Nicky knows where I work. He's actually been to the shop. The one reason I'm pleased I haven't changed my job in nearly twenty years is that Nicky Bennet will always know where to find me.

12

'Sorry to let you all down. When you know why, you'll understand.'

My mum rang me at work a few minutes ago and said, 'Have you seen the *Daily Mail*?' She never rings me at work. I know it must be important.

'Why?' I can feel my heart start to race.

'Oh love, it may be nothing. It's just that there was something about a note and it reminded me of Marie.'

In a panic I ran across the road to the newsagent's and grabbed the paper and now I'm reading it in the staff coffee room.

'Sorry to let you all down. When you know why, you'll understand.' The *Daily Mail* has printed those words in a typeface that looks like handwriting, as if they'd been written on a lined sheet of paper torn off from a notepad, and superimposed them over a huge recent photo of Nicky Bennet emerging from a Hollywood night-club dishevelled, drunk and apparently drugged to the eyeballs. 'Are these the final words of a maverick talent doomed to self-destruct?' the headline blares. 'Or merely a cry for help?' The story compares Nicky to James Dean, River Phoenix and Kurt Cobain. There's a sidebar written by 'a psychologist' that analyses the note and concludes that it could be a suicide note, citing 'the apology impulse' and the inability to give a proper reason as 'classic indicators'. We didn't have a psychologist around all those years ago to explain that Marie's note was a classic suicide note, but her dead body and the empty pill-bottles kind of gave the game away.

It's Paul who finds me curled up in the corner of the staffroom, a cold cup of coffee and the *Mail* on the table in front of me. I think I say something about my sister, and how I know Nicky's dead because the note's almost the same, and then Diana and a couple of the other girls are there too, and someone mouths to someone else that my sister killed herself and I'm trying to explain the most important thing, which is that I know absolutely that Nicky Bennet is dead because he deliberately copied my sister's note.

And then I'm at my mum's house in my old bed, and it's still daytime, and yet she's tucking me up with a hot-water bottle. I'm trying to tell her something, and it becomes terribly important to me that she understands this one thing: 'He knew about Marie's note.'

'What do you mean?'

'I mean, he must have copied it because he knew what it said.'

'How would he know?'

'Because I told him. Years ago. In America. He must have remembered it.'

'Oh love,' my mother says, brushing my hair away from my face.

Nicky Bennet found my sister's suicide fascinating, and I was flattered that he was interested in the only interesting thing about me. He considered it an ideal subject for post-coital conversation. We'd lie there on his bed, sore and aching, and he'd aimlessly trace circles around my navel with his index finger and ask me things like, 'How did it happen?' and 'Did she leave a note?' and 'Do you ever blame yourself?'

'No, course I don't,' I'd say in reply to the last question. But the real answer was yes, I blamed myself, because everyone else seemed to think it was my fault.

The weekend before it happened my parents had gone away on a Trust House Forte mini-break to Oxford that my dad had won for being the top sales rep that quarter. Mum filled the freezer with Sainsbury's lasagnes and chicken pies, issued instructions on how to override the central heating and left the hotel's number on the scribble pad by the phone. I had the house to myself. When I got home from my Saturday job at around six o'clock I was surprised and annoyed to find Marie at home. She'd gone off to university six weeks before and was supposedly having a great time. I assumed she'd come home because she wanted to do some washing.

That evening we had a huge row. Before Marie had gone away we all used to watch *Dallas* on Saturday evenings as a family. Since she'd gone my parents and I had developed a taste for *The Professionals* on the other side. I had a massive crush on Martin Shaw who played Doyle. I'd been looking forward to this Saturday's episode of *The Professionals* all day at work in the shop because, according to the trailers and the *TV Times*, Doyle would get shot and hang between life and death. I couldn't wait. In my head I'd been acting out versions of what might happen, with me playing the part of his weeping yet courageous girlfriend. Okay, so he didn't have a regular girlfriend in the series, but that was only because the producers hadn't been into the shop on a Saturday, spotted me behind the counter and instantly signed me up.

Of course, Marie wanted to watch *Dallas*. The argument began quietly but inevitably escalated until it incorporated every single little grievance either of us had ever had. 'Mum and Dad let you have everything you want,' I shouted.

'That's not true. You're the favourite because you're the youngest,' said Marie. It really was that childish. Suddenly Marie, exhausted, gave in. 'Oh, watch the bloody programme. I don't care, anyway.'

But I turned the argument round. 'No, you watch *Dallas*. *The Professionals* will be spoilt anyway if you watch it. I'm going up to my room.'

To sulk, I might have added. I sat on my bed and sobbed and got angry and sobbed again, and thought about how horrible Marie's fat thighs looked in the short skirt she was wearing. Then I hated myself for hating Marie and for being so babyish. A couple of hours later Marie knocked on the door, came in and said, '*Dallas* was rubbish. You were right.'

We had an uneasy cuddle and I went to bed.

Marie caught the train back to university on Sunday, swallowed three bottles of painkillers, lay down on her bed in her hall of residence room and died. When Mum discovered she'd been home for the weekend she said, 'Oh love, you should have called us. Couldn't you see she was unhappy?' and I felt like saying, 'When was Marie ever happy?'

For weeks afterwards I felt physically sick, constantly on the verge of throwing up. I felt as if there was a hard ball of food slowly making its way down my throat to my stomach. I didn't cry; instead I misbehaved. I played truant and went for long moody walks along the seafront. When I did go to school I was late. I dyed my hair black (it went green after two washes). My teachers were mostly understanding, my parents less so.

They told me that I was being 'selfish and silly', and that I should 'grow up'.

The local paper ran a story on Marie's death. The headline said, 'Suicide Riddle of Brilliant Student' and I wanted to ring them up and tell them that her A and two Cs at A level didn't make her brilliant at all, just fairly intelligent and a bit of a swot. My mum said, 'How could she do this to us?' and smart-alec me said, 'She didn't do it to you, she did it to herself.'

My kind, loving father slapped me round the face for that remark, and that was the first time since Marie's death that I'd cried.

13

You can drive yourself crazy asking why. It makes grief even harder to bear. Believe me, I know. When Marie died, that was all my parents wanted to know. Why did she do this to us? She didn't; she did it to herself. But why? Part of her note said, 'Sorry it has to be this way out and no other. If you knew why, you'd understand.'

Which is, of course, bollocks. 'If you knew why, you'd understand.' Surely 'knowing why' is the definition of understanding something? That's probably why I told Nicky Bennet about Marie's note: because the way it was written was stupid and cruel and hurt my parents so much. She could at least have given a proper reason.

My parents looked hard enough for a reason and they couldn't find one: no obvious boyfriend or drug problems, no struggle with academic work, no unwanted pregnancy. I think they would have coped better if there had been. Instead, all they had was that bloody note. Our well-meaning family doctor recommended a counsellor who, he said, specialised in 'family issues'. We all trooped along one evening and sat in an awkward circle while the woman tried to get us to talk about 'how we felt'. There was a long embarrassed silence. I remember staring at the carpet and trying to work out how often the pattern repeated itself. In the car on the way home my dad cleared his throat, said, 'I don't think we'll go again,' and that was it.

Maybe one of the reasons I coped comparatively well with Marie's death was that I knew perfectly well why she'd killed herself. I knew it better than anyone. She killed herself because she was eighteen and wanted to be profound. She spent too much time by herself in a small hall of residence room, got melancholy and decided that no one loved her. Then she decided no one understood her, either, including her own sister, and then she killed herself. I knew all this because I'd often felt like that, even at sixteen, sitting in my bedroom listening to John Peel on Radio One. Maybe he understood me but no one else did.

What has always annoyed me about Marie's death is that she stole a march on me. 'Snap out of it' became our family motto. Marie got there first and took callow teenage depression to its logical conclusion. It left me no option but to cope, brave-faced, with all the shit that life and Nicky Bennet later threw at me. Killing myself just wasn't an available choice, much as I wanted it to be.

It was my brother Simon who made the most effort to find out the reason for Marie's suicide, but I didn't realise that at the time because he was so much older than me and on the verge of getting married when she died. Older brothers are mysteries. One assumes they have emotional lives but, if they do, those lives are invisible and submerged. We've never been particularly close, Simon and I. He's eight years older and that's like a whole generation when you're a child. You might think we would have grown closer after Marie died, but if anything it made us grow further apart. When you can't trust yourself to talk about emotions with your own family, that's what happens.

It was only a few years ago, when my niece Katie, Simon and Sue's middle child, was quite ill, that Simon opened his heart to me over a bottle of brandy while Sue did the hospital-vigil thing. Simon showed me a photograph that he said he'd borrowed from Mum and Dad's album some years ago, meaning to get it copied although he never had. It was one of their early colour photos, of Dad and Marie when Marie was about five or six. She was almost pretty then, blonde and bonny and looking remarkably like Katie. Simon and I had been scrawny, skinny kids, in sharp contrast. In the photo she's playing Lego with Dad. She's out in the conservatory-cum-playroom with him on a sunny day. You can tell it's the afternoon by the way the light's falling across the lino. Marie's wearing a bright yellow T-shirt and blue shorts, both of which I later inherited as hand-me-downs. I don't know what's just happened but it must have been funny: Dad must have told a great joke, because Marie is laughing so much she's falling over backwards. Her feet, in the Start-Rite sandals we both used to wear every summer, are waving in the air. The wonderful thing is, you sense her faith in Dad. She knows he'll catch her if she really does fall over backwards. She is completely abandoned in the way she's laughing, because she knows he's there.

Simon passed the photo across to me without saying anything. I swallowed hard when I looked at it, and glanced across at Simon who was staring resolutely at the skirting board. Older brothers live their emotional lives in the gaps between the words that they say, I decided that night.

'Sue always wanted to have children, and I thought I did. Couple of years after we got married, I saw that photo again and I froze. What happened? I didn't want kids if they're only going to go and kill themselves.' Pause. 'So I went off to Marie's old university and tried to track down some of her friends. I wanted to find out if it was something Mum and Dad did wrong.' He was finding the skirting board incredibly interesting. 'Eventually I got the head of her department on my side, and I managed to find this bloke who Marie had gone out with a few times. Asked him if he had any idea why she'd killed herself, and he said, "She was just that type."' Simon poured us both another brandy, although I'd so far only managed one mouthful of mine. 'God, I don't know.' He shrugged. 'Those words: "She was just that type." What can you do?'

It was my turn to shrug. 'I don't know.'

'You know she left some books of her poems?'

I nodded.

'Did you know there was one about me? It was called "Lines for my brother".'

'Was it crap?'

Simon actually laughed. 'Yeah, kind of. I think it was supposed to be a sonnet or something – fourteen lines?'

Simon's degree was in civil engineering. I nodded.

'Anyway,' he said, looking at me for a brief moment, 'I memorised some of it. It really annoyed me.' He turned back to the wall, fixing his stare on the phone socket, and started reciting: ' "He's fixed, secure and stubborn, content in his rose-hued world. I could never be, would find it shallow." Then, near the end, there was this whole diving imagery thing going on. The final lines were, "But we plumb different depths: Mine, uncharted, lost and difficult; his, sensible, well-defined and satisfying." '

He left it there, assuming I'd understand what he meant from his tone of voice. And I did, sort of. 'Simon,' I said, taking another medicinal gulp of brandy, 'Marie killed herself because I wouldn't watch *Dallas* with her when she came home for the weekend.'

Daniel Green, the college boyfriend who slept with my flatmate Caroline, once said something very cruel to me. It was during one of our phone rows, after I'd caught him with Caroline and dropped out of university. 'The thing is,' he said, 'everyone tiptoes around you being all sensitive because of this great tragedy in your past. Mustn't upset Justine, don't you know her sister killed herself? But frankly, having got to know you better, I can understand why she did it.'

It's the kind of cruel remark that sticks in your head because you think it might be true. Or maybe you think it might be true because it sticks in your head. Anyway, lying in my old bedroom at my mum's house, I remember that remark and I start to wonder if I'm somehow the reason not just for Marie's death but also for Nicky's.

14

Nicky Bennet is standing on the beach.
The warm glow of the low, late-
evening sun has cast a bronze hue on his
normally pale skin. His hair is long, down to his
shoulders, more strawberry blond than ginger,
and matted in grungy dreads. He's dressed in surf
gear, his wiry, muscular torso encased in a black
and orange neoprene zip-up jerkin, and he holds a
surfboard upright beside him. He smiles down at
the cute, feisty woman who has just run up to him.
His large hand fondles her cheek affectionately,
with a jokey tug at the silver ring in her nose.
Close-up of Nicky's green eyes blinking back a
tear. Anna leans forward and tries to scoop up
home-made guacamole from a bowl with a sour-
cream-and-chive-flavour Pringle, but loses half
the crisp in the process. She giggles, and I elbow
her in the ribs, hissing an angry 'Shhh.'

Nicky pushes the woman's wet hair out of her eyes and begins to kiss her forehead, right on the hairline. He works his way down to her eyes, her nose and finally her mouth, voraciously kissing her as if he hasn't had a square meal in days. The kiss arouses memories in me and I hug the cushion closer. Nicky walks away from the woman without a backward glance. Close-up on his resolute face: knowing him as I do, I can tell that it would have taken him at least a week to grow that much stubble. He tosses his surfboard down on the beach and begins to unzip his jerkin. At which point Gray walks into the room with a bottle of beer. He tousles my hair, leaving traces of wet clay that I know will be hell to wash out. He kisses Anna, sits down on the settee, stares at the TV screen and says, with a note of pride in his skills of recognition, 'Is that Keanu Reeves?'

I nearly choke on my Pringle and I start to have a coughing fit. Anna sighs. 'No, love, that's Nicky Bennet. Remember, I told you that Justine and I were going to watch Nicky Bennet films tonight?'

'Nicky Bennet,' he says ruminatively. And then his face clears. 'Nicky Bennet . . . that's the chap you used to know, Justine, isn't it?'

I nod.

'And that's him?' he says, still a little confused.

I nod again.

'That isn't who I thought he was,' says Gray. 'Not at all.'

I managed to pull myself together after Monday's weird scene at work. The papers were all still full of stories about Nicky Bennet but there wasn't much new to tell. One story revealed that he had deleted all the files on the computer at his Los Angeles home, as if tidying away his life, while another quoted a friend saying Nicky'd had serious doubts about his future as an actor and had talked about escaping from 'all this bulls***'.

Gavin rang me at work on Wednesday to check up on me, and he came round in the evening with two Meat Feast pizzas and a video that we couldn't watch because my machine's broken. Instead we snuggled up together on the settee to watch some home make-over show. It must have been the DIY that aroused him, because about ten minutes into the programme he started stroking my hair. The hair-stroking gradually turned to neck-nuzzling and a little gentle ear-nibbling. By the time the make-over victims were oohing and aahing over their hideous new bedroom Gavin and I were full length on the settee, snogging with tongues. He fumbled for the inevitable safety pin that was holding my too-big second-hand skirt together while I started unbuttoning his short-sleeved shirt. It was as he reached into the pocket of his grey work slacks to pull out the condom that I knew would be there (he's always well prepared, is Gavin) that I came to my senses. God, this could be my life. Crap TV, takeaway pizzas and sex on the settee. I pulled away from him, sat back on my heels and pulled my T-shirt down over my knickers. 'Gav, no, I'm sorry. This is stupid. Sorry. We shouldn't. I don't . . . just . . . oh, you know.'

I tailed off, shrugged and picked up my skirt. Gavin sighed deeply: 'Hell, Justine, I don't believe this.'

He looked annoyed, then stomped upstairs to the bathroom. He was there for about ten minutes, during which time I cleared away the pizza boxes and rinsed the plates under the hot tap. When Gavin came downstairs he looked less annoyed and smelled strongly of soap. He gave me a goodbye peck on the cheek while I carried on apologising vaguely with lots of shrugs and 'you knows'. 'It's okay. I understand,' he said.

'Wish I did,' I replied unconvincingly. It seemed the least hurtful thing I could say.

I wanted desperately to see a Nicky Bennet film. I phoned Anna and told her about Gavin, about how I didn't know whether I wanted to sleep with him or not, about how my video was broken, the crap TV we'd just watched, how I cruelly sent Gav home with nothing, even though he had paid for the pizzas. 'It's clear to me that you're in limbo,' said Anna crisply, immediately reading my mind. 'You need to grieve for Nicky Bennet, but first of all you need "closure".'

Even over the phone I could hear the inverted commas she put around the word. 'Closure . . .' I repeated.

'Tell me, what's the first thing that normally happens when a film star dies?'

'They have a season of their films on the telly, of course.'

'Exactly,' she said. 'But with Nicky, there'll be no tribute season until they know exactly what's happened. So what we need to do is to organise our own.'

Perhaps unsurprisingly, I have all Nicky Bennet's films on video, either bought at great expense or recorded off the TV with the tail end of inappropriate weather forecasts, out-of-date news bulletins or old adverts on the beginning of the tape. I watch them fairly often, usually when I'm feeling down. The best bits have the power to arouse a faint, nostalgic tingle between my legs, a kind of distant echo of our passionate past that makes me hug a cushion. The films usually make me feel a little better: there's comfort in knowing I've been there, I've had him, it was good.

For tonight's video marathon I narrowed it down to these four: the John Grisham courtroom thing, because it's the only one of Nicky's films in which he employs his full-scale Southern accent; *Summer's Lease*, memorably described by one critic as '*The Big Chill* with surfboards', because he looks gorgeous in his wetsuit; *Trust Me*, for his famous kitchen-table sex scene involving Olivia Ross and some overripe tomatoes; and finally that

FBI comedy thriller for Anna, because while Nicky doesn't do much for her, she really fancies Reuben Scott who plays his wisecracking partner.

We're not even halfway through the tribute season when Gray bumbles in. I take advantage of his Keanu Reeves faux pas to tell Anna something I have a hunch she won't much like. 'I'm going to be interviewed about Nicky Bennet.'

She raises one eyebrow suspiciously.

'It's okay, it's only in the local paper.'

She raises the other eyebrow. 'But you think I'll disapprove and that's why you didn't tell me straight away,' she says.

'No, not really.' She's exactly right.

'How did they know about you? You didn't ring them up and offer, did you?'

I throw a cushion at her. 'Of course not. What do you think I am? The guy rang me. He knows someone who knows someone at the shop. He heard about me. He seemed really proud of himself for finding me. He asked if he was the first journalist to call me. He sounds like a nice bloke. I don't know, maybe he caught me off guard. Anyway, I said I'd do it.'

'What are you going to tell him?'

'I don't know. I don't know what he's going to ask me.'

'Will you tell him about the note, about how much like your sister's note it is?'

I look hard at Anna, trying to work out her tone of voice. She's looking back at me with a strange expression on her face that I can't read. 'Why? Do you think I should?'

'Justine, of course you shouldn't. It's not just your tragedy, you know. It would break your mother's heart.'

She gets up, picks up some empty glasses and goes out to the kitchen. I follow her. 'What?' I say. 'What's up with you?'

A frown darts across her forehead. 'Justine, I love you, but sometimes it's all about you, you know?'

'What?' I say again, and do a kind of exaggerated shrug with my shoulders. 'Tell me.'

She laughs, and puts her hand on my cheek. 'Do you know why I really asked you round tonight?'

I look at her closely. 'I'm guessing not to talk about Nicky Bennet all night?'

'I have something to tell you, and I've been waiting to find the right moment.'

'You mean, you've been waiting for me to stop talking about me and ask you about you?'

Anna laughs again, picks up a tea towel, turns away from me, and then turns back to face me. She is smiling, broadly. 'I'm pregnant.'

I scream, look at her, and then scream again. I put my arms around her and hug her, and together we jump up and down. Gray and Anna have been trying to have a baby for ages. She's had two miscarriages. Thinking about that, I stop jumping up and down and say, 'How far along are you?'

'Ten weeks. I know I shouldn't really tell anyone until twelve weeks, but I think this time it's going to be okay, I really do.'

I hold Anna and hug her, and just for a moment nothing else seems to matter.

15

'Is this where Nicky Bennet lived with you?' says the child reporter, who can't be much more than eighteen and is wearing a too-big shirt and jacket. He looks around my front room from his perch on the edge of the settee as if he's looking for evidence that a film star once lived here. I look with his eyes and see badly painted terracotta walls, an untidy pile of video-tapes behind the TV and a stack of rolled-up posters gathering dust in one corner. It's so obviously a single person's house. I tell him about the bedsit I used to have and he puts something down in his notebook. 'Oh, okay, when was this?'

'In the eighties,' I say vaguely, not wanting to disappoint him too much by telling him it was nearly twenty years ago.

'And, sorry, you'll have to excuse me, I don't

know much about Nicky Bennet, but was he famous then?'

I feel sorry for the reporter. He thought he had a scoop and all he gets is how Nicky once lived in this city with me for a couple of weeks. He tries lots of different angles: did I realise he was going to be a star, do we keep in touch, have I ever been to Hollywood to see him? All he gets from me is 'No' and 'Not really'. I try to tell him how exciting Nicky was even before he was famous, and how we used to love to go to the beach. The reporter perks up a bit when I mention playing pinball on the pier; he says he might try to interview the amusement arcade manager for an angle, to see if he remembers Nicky Bennet. I haven't the heart to remind him how long ago it was. I tell him the address of my old bedsit so he can organise a photo and try to talk to some of the residents. Then he asks me the question that he should have asked me at the beginning: 'What do you think has happened to him?'

I take a deep breath. 'I think he's killed himself.'

The reporter looks interested all of a sudden.

rag. I'm at Gavin's house, reading the paper at the table in his kitchen-diner while he cooks me dinner. He's bought five copies so he can send one each to his mother, his Nan and his aunts, just because there's a picture of me on the front cover. In the photo I have a shiny forehead and untidy hair, frowning at the magazine in front of me, looking as if I'm in the middle of some kind of shrine to Nicky Bennet. The story's straight-forward and largely true. It describes me as thirty-six (I told the reporter that I was the same age as Nicky Bennet). It mentions where I work but not my home address (I asked him to leave that out). It says I'm his ex-girlfriend, that I've known him since the 1980s and that I fear he might be dead. 'But,' says the paper, 'Miss Fraser denied rumours that the movie heart-throb has a serious drugs problem. "I don't believe it," she said. "The Nicky I knew was never into drugs."'

Inside there's a centre-page spread all about Nicky's time in the city, and it's a triumph of imagination over content. There's a large photo of the pier, captioned, 'Nicky Bennet enjoyed playing pinball here,' and an interview with the arcade manager, who for the sake of the news-paper has pretended that he remembers Nicky.

There's a photo of the house where my bedsit was, and a picture of a young blonde girl with a baby who now lives in the flat I used to rent. It claims that she's a fan of Nicky Bennet and is delighted to discover he used to live there. 'Maybe they'll put up a plaque' is the comment next to her photo.

'Oh Gavin, look,' I say, and he wipes his hands on a tea towel and comes over to the table. 'They've even got a picture of the chip shop.' By the way he grins at me I can tell he is, bizarrely, aroused by the whole thing.

D inner is lamb chops marinated in redcurrant sauce and cooked in one of those ridged grill pans, served with oven chips and every man's favourite vegetable, coleslaw. Gavin's laid the table with a thick linen tablecloth and matching napkins. The plates are heavy dark blue earthenware; they match the bistro-style cutlery. There's a bottle of ice-cold Riesling and a jar of Hellmann's mayonnaise in the centre of the table and the Lighthouse Family are playing quietly on the CD player. 'Gavin,' I say, as I savour the taste of the crispy fat of the lamb chop and run a piece of bread around my plate to soak up the last of the flavour, 'that was lovely.'

He says nothing, just grins at me and crinkles up his eyes. Then he pulls his chair closer to me and starts kissing me. I can taste lamb and chips and mayonnaise, and a hint of toothpaste. His teeth feel clean against my tongue. I close my eyes, run my hands through his hair and smell the sharp piny tang of his aftershave. What the hell. Everything's been so weird recently, I decide to give in to the moment. I kiss him all over his smooth face. He starts to nuzzle my neck and my shoulder blades. He kicks his chair away and with a slight pressure on my shoulders we're lying on the kitchen floor, on the cushioned terracotta-tile-effect lino, almost under the table. He undoes my bra, pushes my T-shirt up around my neck and starts sucking on my breasts, an intent look on his face. I watch him, and think how soft and clean his hair is. We're starting to ebb and flow together, then he catches me looking at him, grins a cheeky grin, says 'Stay right there,' and goes to the fridge.

He pulls out another bottle of Riesling, even more icy cold than the first one, and touches the bottle to each of my nipples in turn. They stand to attention, distracting my attention while he fumbles with a condom. By the time he puts his penis in me I'm writhing so much that I hit my head on the leg of the kitchen table and don't even notice how much it hurts.

The following morning I wake to find us lying together like spoons, his arms wrapped protectively around me. Gavin has muscles in the right places and thick blond hair on his arms. If he weren't only five foot seven he'd be extremely attractive. He's awake already, and kisses me on the back of my neck. 'So,' he says, 'am I your boyfriend?'

Fuck. How did this happen? It's been years since I last slept with him. 'Oh Gavin, I don't know. Everything's strange at the moment. Just, you know, I don't know, maybe we should go with the flow' – whatever that's supposed to mean.

16

The PR woman, Pippa, is blonde, bustling, scary and a good few years younger than me. She takes a long look at me, her eyes narrowed as they scrutinise me from head to toe. I am wearing my best dress, a shop-bought one, which I got last year in the Monsoon half-price sale. It's long and silky, with a batik-style print in shades of blue and sea green. My hair is twisted up at the back of my head and caught there with a silver and turquoise clasp. I'm wearing silver earrings in the shape of dolphins looped back on themselves, some blue mascara and a smear of pink lip-gloss. On my feet are my favourite flat leather sandals and for luck I've painted my toenails iridescent sky blue.

Pippa weighs up the effect, tilting her head first to one side, then the other. 'Yeah,' she says finally. 'Kind of artsy intellectual. I think we can work with that.' Then she digs into her handbag, pulls out a compact and is dabbing at my face with a grubby sponge before I can stop her.

'What's that?' I say, as she smears something into the sides of my nose.

'One-touch cream-to-powder foundation. Max Factor. Ivory.' She's brisk with the details, as if I was asking because I wanted to buy some.

'I don't really wear make-up.' I'd like to object more strongly but I've lost the power.

'Well, first time for everything,' Pippa says brightly as she takes a pencil to my eyebrows. 'Okay, now your hair . . .'

My skin feels tight from the make-up, my hair feels tight from being twisted into a chignon and sprayed until brittle. I'm sitting behind a long table in the conference room of a business hotel just off the motorway. In front of me are a microphone, a glass, a carafe of lime cordial and a bottle of fizzy water. All I can think is how much I want a drink of the water, but I know if I try to open the bottle my hands will shake and the water will squirt everywhere. Pippa is introducing me and I'm trying to make eye contact with some of the people in the room, as she told me to. I'm trying to remember her instructions. 'Don't lean forward into the microphone. Focus on the person asking the question and speak to them. If you don't know or don't want to answer something, just say so. Relax. Be yourself.' Although it's going to be pretty difficult to be myself when my face is plastered in make-up, my hair is so tightly pulled back that my neck hurts and I'm sitting at a table facing about a hundred journalists and photographers. I can feel them all looking at me, curiously. What are they thinking? Not what we expected. Far too old. How could she be Nicky Bennet's secret lover? God, she looks like a librarian.

A lot of people think I'm mad to do a press conference but I have to. I owe it to Nicky. Gavin agrees with me, my mother's given her blessing, but Anna's not so sure. A new angle on the story has broken: the producer of the film that Nicky was working on has accused him of trying to sabotage the movie. 'Of course he's still alive,' the producer told journalists. 'He's a spoilt movie-star brat who's just trying to get out of a film he doesn't want to make. He'd better have disappeared for good, because if he reappears alive I'm going to sue his goddamn ass.'

I wasn't sure what to do, how to let everyone know what I know: that Nicky Bennet has killed himself and that's why he wrote that note. But then I arrived at work after a couple of days off to find Paul looking stressed. 'We've had every tabloid newspaper in Britain on the phone, looking for you. They've picked up on the story in the *Echo*. They all want your reaction to the Nicky Bennet case. What are you planning to do about it?'

I looked at him and had a sudden inspiration. 'Paul, do you think someone from head office PR would organise a press conference? I mean, if the papers keep calling me here it will disrupt everyone, won't it? So it'd be good for the company to get it over with. And if I do a press conference then I could talk to all the journalists at once and stop them calling the shop.'

Which is how I found myself sitting here with too much make-up on, facing a roomful of journalists.

'How did you first meet Nicky Bennet?' Thank goodness, an easy one to start with.

'At university in America. I was on an exchange programme . . . 1984,' I say as the next question is fired. 'Then he came back here the following summer and we spent a while living together.' The questions are coming thick and fast now. 'We just drifted apart eventually. We were both students when we met, but then – you know – real life got in the way. Whatever. No, no, I never saw him again. Or heard from him. No, no Christmas cards. I mean, not from him. In love?' That question comes from a woman a couple of rows back and stops me in my tracks for a while. All I can think to do is shrug. 'In love? Yeah. I don't know. Who knows?' I can feel little red circles forming high on my cheekbones and suddenly I'm glad of the cream-to-powder foundation.

'Any regrets, love?' I simply shake my head in response to that one, and then comes the question I've been dreading: 'The note he left. If you know him so well, do you understand it? And if so, what's happened?'

It's a young guy, far to the left in the front row, with a face like a monkey's. I make eye contact, take a deep breath and lean towards the microphone, then pull away again. I pick at the label of the bottle of fizzy water. 'It's a suicide note,' I croak, my voice suddenly sounding like it's coming out of my boots. I clear my throat and try again. 'I *think* it's a suicide note. I think it means he's killed himself. And I think he thought that I'd understand what he meant.'

'Why?'

I've prepared a kind of answer. 'Just, well, the words he used. It was a phrase he knew I'd recognise, just, you know, something private we used to say to each other?' I can hear myself putting the question mark on the end as if to say, you do believe me, don't you? I'm clasping my clammy hands together between my knees, twisting them until the joints are sore. There's a pause. Everyone's writing something down.

'Does it have anything to do with your sister's suicide?' The question comes from the far corner of the room. Sharp intake of breath. That's the right cliché, isn't it? I breathe in so sharply that it hurts my throat, and I can hear everyone else doing the same. The thing is, I knew the question was coming; Pippa told me she'd planted it so I wouldn't have to raise the subject myself. But still it sits there, blunt and unanswered.

I try to reply and no words come out. I look blankly at the reporter concerned, and wonder who he is, why he was picked, how much he knows and how much he's guessing.

'I was just wondering if the words he used reminded you of your sister's suicide note. Maybe something about the phrasing?'

I take a deep breath, pray that my mother will forgive me, and launch into an answer. 'My sister killed herself when she was eighteen. Nicky Bennet's note is an almost word-for-word copy of part of her suicide note. That's why I'm sure he's dead.' Remarkably, my voice stays level right until the end.

Hubbub. Almost uproar. More questions. 'How would Nicky know what your sister's suicide note said?' is the first one I hear.

'I told him.'

'Why? Did he ask?'

'Yes.'

'Why?'

'He was interested.'

'You're saying Nicky Bennet was interested in your sister's suicide?'

'Yes.' I'm answering like a robot, I know. They want more, but what more can I say?

'How interested?'

'Very interested. Interested enough to ask what her note said.'

'Would you say that he was obsessed with your sister's suicide?' The query comes from the woman who asked if Nicky and I were in love. I look at her, make eye contact, and see that she's trying to wheedle something out of me. Quite unexpectedly I find myself giving a shriek of laughter. 'No! No, you can't have that as your headline. Nicky Bennet was not obsessed with my sister's suicide, merely very interested.' The mood in the room has lightened perceptibly. I hold my hand up like a traffic cop. 'Very interested. And that's as far as I'll go.'

Pippa clears her throat. 'Time for just a couple more questions.' The monkey-faced guy puts his hand up, Pippa nods at him, and he says, looking at his notebook, 'You say that you first met Nicky Bennet in 1984. By my calculations, he would have been sixteen at the time.'

I shake my head. 'Twenty. Same as me.'

'That would make him three years older than the official biography from his agent.'

I shrug.

'So you're saying he's been lying about his age?'

I remember something I once said that got a good laugh at a dinner party. I widen my eyes innocently and plaster on a straight face. 'Oh no, I'm not saying that. I think it's quite possible that there's some kind of wrinkle in the space-time continuum somewhere in Hollywood that enables Nicky Bennet to be genuinely three years younger than me.' Gratifyingly, the whole room laughs.

'What would you say to Nicky if you could see him one more time?' The question comes from somewhere in the middle of the room. What would I say to Nicky? For a brief moment I see myself slapping him round the face, yelling obscenities at him. How dare you do this? How dare you steal my sister's note? I put my face in my hands, pressing the heels of my hands into my eyes to wipe out the picture. I look up. The room's still waiting for an answer.

'I'd say I hope he's happy. I hope he's finally got what he wanted.'

I'm wiping at my face with a tissue trying to get the make-up off while Pippa tells me how well I've done, and then I turn and there, of all people, is Daniel Green, my old college boyfriend, looking at me intently. He's wearing a tatty old faded corduroy jacket that looks like the one he used to wear at college. 'Daniel,' I say by way of greeting, but he's still staring at me so I say, 'What?'

He smiles. 'I was just thinking how much you haven't changed. I always liked you in that dress.'

'You've never seen this dress. It's new.'

'Oh. Well, you've got another one like it, haven't you?' He pecks me on the cheek and says, 'Do you fancy a drink?'

17

Of course, I shouldn't be surprised that Daniel's here. I knew he was a journalist, one of those who specialises in being clever and funny about popular culture. He writes articles for magazines like *Q* and *Mojo* and *FHM*. He sometimes pops up on television, on those reminiscence programmes, remembering the 1980s or the top one hundred films. He had a book out a few years ago, a compilation of his magazine pieces about dead pop stars, called *Dead Good*. There was a chapter in it about Gram Parsons. I'm surprised he's not published a mega-hyped bloke-lit novel yet. Maybe he's getting too old. But of course he's here. The Nicky Bennet story is right up his street.

I look at him across the table in the hotel bar. Daniel has bought us each a Scotch, without asking me. I hate Scotch but I don't like to say.

Each sip burns the back of my throat and makes me shudder involuntarily, like childhood cough medicine. I have the beginnings of an evil headache. He lights a cigarette and says, conversationally, 'You know, we're thinking of moving down here, me and Caroline.'

Maybe I look surprised because he says, 'You do know I married Caroline, don't you?'

I nod. I didn't know, but I don't want him to know that. 'I can't imagine you leaving London.'

'No, I can't imagine it either. But then, you know Caroline. What Caroline wants, Caroline gets.' He shrugs, looking faintly pissed off. 'She thinks it would be better for Pid.'

'Pid?'

'Perdita, our daughter. Sorry, I thought you were still in touch with Caroline. Obviously not.'

He clears his throat and rests his chin on the hand he's holding the cigarette in. He looks at me deeply. I stare back into his familiar light brown eyes. I look at his big bony nose, his wide funny mouth and the three little freckles dancing across his Adam's apple and into the hollow at the base of his throat. He hasn't changed a bit.

'Anyway,' he says. 'Let's talk about you and Nicky Bennet. Let's try and get this straight. I remember you sending me a strange letter from America, when you were at college there. It was kind of a Dear John letter. You'd met someone there. I'm guessing it must have been Nicky Bennet, right?'

I nod.

'Anyway, you sent me a letter dumping me.'

I open my mouth and try to tell him that it wasn't a Dear John letter, I hadn't meant to dump him and that he just took it the wrong way. But no words come out. Instead, Daniel just carries on talking. 'I have to say, it was a pretty weird experience, being dumped by someone who wasn't actually my girlfriend.'

I look at him hard, trying to read his eyes. But he chooses that moment to take a long drag on his cigarette, do a practised Clint Eastwood-style squint and gaze around the almost empty hotel bar. I'm trying to think what to say. I want to be cool, to seem as if I know what he's talking about. But I have to ask. 'What exactly do you mean?'

'Well, we were friends, weren't we? I remember that. Me, you and Caroline. And you had that other flatmate, didn't you, the Bible-bashing one? You were all a good laugh. I had some good times at your flat. But it was always Caroline I was after. I remember being quite relieved when you went away because it meant we didn't have to pretend to be a threesome. That's why it was so funny getting that letter. But – hey – I guess I should be flattered that you dumped me for Nicky Bennet. Anyway, so that's what got me wondering, you know, about what really went on with you and Nicky Bennet.'

I look at him, hard. He's talking bollocks. What on Earth is he on about? He was my boyfriend. Wasn't he? I play scenes back in my head. Daniel playing the spoons in our kitchen. Watching *Hill Street Blues* together, sharing a pizza. Me and Daniel and Caroline. Daniel, unshaven, greeting me when I arrived back from America, coming out of Caroline's room in just his underpants. I shake my head, trying to clear it. I want to throw up; I want the ground to open up under me. I know he's right; how could I have been so wrong about him?

I look at him again. He's gazing at me across the table with something that looks like tenderness. I'm a bit drunk and I'm trying to understand what he wants from me, what exactly he's wondering about Nicky Bennet and me. He continues to look at me in that curious way. 'What?' I ask, snapping at him.

He reaches for my hand. 'Did I tell you how good you look today?'

I laugh, a loud, harsh, humourless guffaw. 'No, you bloody didn't. You just told me that I hadn't changed, and you totally failed to notice that I was wearing a new and really quite expensive dress. Expensive for me, anyway.'

I think I paid more than twenty pounds for it, an unheard-of sum of money for me to spend on an item of clothing.

'God, I'm crap, aren't I? When I said you hadn't changed, what I meant was, seeing you standing there in those beautiful colours, that wishy-washy sea green, I remembered what it was I always liked about you. You have your very own kind of beauty, you know, pale and watery and elusive like a mermaid. I think I can understand what Nicky Bennet might have seen in you.'

As he says this I know my face is turning from pale to blotchy. My very own kind of beauty, indeed. That's a backhanded compliment and a half. For a man who's such a good writer, he's really bad at love stuff. 'Daniel,' I say, 'are you sure you're not drunk?'

'Maybe a little bit, but it doesn't change what I'm trying to say. You look like a sea nymph or a

facing me, with the time blinking in red numbers: 06.34. There's a tray with a kettle and some cups. There's a pinky-grey painting of some flowers on the wall above the TV. Bland hotel-room decor. I turn and see Daniel asleep in the bed next to me, wrapped in a sheet, his faced crushed into the pillow and his mouth open. He's wearing a T-shirt and a pair of boxer shorts and he is snoring, quietly. His hair flops over his face and there's a hint of grey at the point where his cow-lick flips up from his forehead. I can see a hollow at the back of his right knee. I remember that hollow. I think I kissed and sucked him there, as if licking out marrow from the centre of a bone. 'Oh God,' I groan as the shipbuilders increase their work-rate and the flicker of a memory crosses my mind, like a dying man's life flashing before his eyes. 'Oh God, what have I done?'

He took advantage of my drunkenness. That's my excuse. I don't recall much about last night. I think I remember leaving the bar, and then I remember sitting in the hotel restaurant laughing hysterically because the menu seemed so funny, and the next moment I was sobbing because it was all so complicated and there wasn't a single thing I wanted to eat. After that there was a walk to the lift and along the corridor to a room where Daniel appeared to be staying. I think I threw up once or twice en route. Daniel must have all but carried me to the room, and I remember running into the bathroom and being sick all over again. Daniel was waiting for me, and somehow together we managed to take my clothes off. We got into bed and Daniel leaned over to turn off the light. Then it happened. Who started it? I can't remember. I think he held me, touched me, got me aroused. I think I remember kissing him: in the hollow at the base of his throat, in the hollows at the backs of his knees. It was like sex by memory. It had to be; I wasn't capable of conscious action.

The light's starting to come through the gap in the curtains. I go into the bathroom and look at myself in the mirror, pulling my hair back from my face. I stare into the reflection of my eyes, and it's as if I'm seeing the real me for the first time in a long time. From the other room I hear Daniel grunt. Is there any worse feeling than waking up beside a man you wish you hadn't slept with? Every time it happens I feel I've lost a little bit of something; as if something has broken off and crumbled away, like a corner of my soul or my self-respect. Quickly, without giving myself time to think, I splash my face with water. Then I creep back into the bedroom and pull on yesterday's clothes from the crumpled pile on the floor.

In the taxi on the way home, as I struggle to remember the night before, I go cold with fear. Before the sex, before I was sick, something happened. Just a shard of memory. Daniel had a tiny silver tape recorder. A minidisc, he called it. I remember reaching out to touch it, and laughing because the buttons were so dinky and neat. It made a little clicky whirry sound as it started. Where was that? In the restaurant? Oh Jesus, what were we talking about? Nicky Bennet, obviously. Daniel smiling, smugly, and I wanted to hit him. 'Go on, prove it,' he said. 'Prove to me that you really were Nicky Bennet's girlfriend. Why should I believe it? Tell me all about him. You must have a photograph somewhere.'

And because I don't, I haven't, not really, I told him about Nicky, lots of stuff, I can't remember exactly what, but things that no one else would know. I wanted to prove it to him, to prove it to myself. Oh God, what the fuck did I tell him?

18

There are, in fact, at least two pieces of concrete evidence that Nicky Bennet was once my boyfriend. One is the silver ring I wore, the one like his, which clanked against his when we held hands. I tried to flush it down the toilet in the New York hotel room after he stood me up. Needless to say, it wouldn't disappear. It lay there in the characteristically shallow American toilet bowl, glinting at me. When I came back to the hotel room the next day, after it had been cleaned, the ring had been recovered and placed on a face flannel on the imitation-marble basin surround. I wrapped it in some toilet roll, put it in my purse and took it home. Now it lives in a little basket on my dressing table together with a brooch that was my grand-mother's and a Plasticraft four-leaved clover that Marie made.

The second piece of concrete evidence is a photo. Yes, there is in existence a single photo of the two of us together. My parents have it in an old shoebox in their cupboard under the stairs. But it's such a poor, blurry image that you have to take it on faith that it is who they say it is. I never took any photos of Nicky myself. I forget exactly what my reasons were, but I was adamantly against cameras and photographs when I was that age. As well as the Sony Walkman, my parents bought me a really nice camera to take to college in America. I think my brother Simon, who knows about cameras and has a subscription to *Which?*, helped them choose it. It had auto-focus, a kind of zoom lens, built-in flash; everything that was new, expensive and exciting about cameras in 1984. When I was packing I put the camera in and out of my suitcase about five times and eventually decided not to take it. It seemed too heavy, too expensive, too special for me. And besides, I had some weird hang-up about taking photos. I didn't want to be an observer; I wanted to be a participant, to travel light, to experience things, not just record them. Remember, I was twenty and more than a little intense.

So there is just one photograph of Nicky and

me together. We're in my parents' back garden on Live Aid Day. We're sitting on a rustic-style garden bench that Mum and Dad had just bought at B&Q. We're on the far left of the frame, out of focus, overshadowed by the magnolia tree. My parents' decent camera had given up the ghost and they were using Marie's old one. I still remember the heartbreakingly would-be-casual shrug Dad had given when he'd said, as he'd got it down from the attic some weeks earlier, 'Might as well make use of it.'

It was one of those small, cheap cameras that took a cartridge of 110 film, and it was so rudimentary that the viewfinder wasn't even in line with the lens. It was impossible to focus properly on what you wanted to be the centre of the photograph. Mum said brightly, 'Just one film left,' which was Mum-speak for one shot left on the film. So Nicky and I smiled, embarrassed, the evening sun in our eyes, blurred for posterity at the edge of a shot of the magnolia tree.

I guess everyone of our generation remembers what they were doing on Live Aid Day, 13 July 1985: in most cases, glued to the television or the radio, witnessing Bob Geldof thumping the table and saying, 'Send us your fucking money.' I missed the whole thing. It was years before I fully understood the dramatic overnight revival of Queen's popularity, not until I saw the tenth-anniversary showing of the concert on TV in 1995. On Live Aid Day itself I was strolling hand in hand along the seafront of my home town with Nicky Bennet, who had just walked back into my life as dramatically as he had walked out of it more than a year before.

It wasn't what I'd intended to be doing. I'd planned my day carefully. Although I'd been working in the bookshop for only about eight months, I was the youngest person there by some years and had managed to wangle the day off as no one else shared my enthusiasm for watching Live Aid. I had only a tiny black and white portable in my bedsit, with a crap aerial that I had to suspend from the top of my dressing-table mirror if I wanted a decent picture. So I went up to my parents' house the night before, planning to spend the whole of the next day watching the concert on their big colour TV. I'd infected my parents with my enthusiasm, or maybe they were just doing a good job of counterfeiting excited anticipation at the thought of seeing the likes of Wham! and Duran Duran perform live. I'd persuaded my mum to buy lots of picnic-type food from Marks and Sparks, like she had for the Royal Wedding, so none of us would need to stir from the settee all day.

I was still in bed in my old room, complete with its shelf full of stuffed toys, when the doorbell rang. I turned over and looked at the clock. Just gone eight. Must be the postman. I heard Mum open the door and then a gentle hum of murmured conversation and a happy, surprised noise from my mother. I heard two sets of footsteps going down the hallway, and the sound of the kettle being filled. More low-level talk that went on for some minutes. Obviously not the postman. Then Mum called up the stairs. 'Justine! Are you awake? There's someone down here to see you.'

Some warning would have been nice. It would have been nice not to be wearing my dad's smelly old dressing gown. It would have been nice not to have morning mouth, bed hair and crease marks across my face. It would have been nice not to have the sleep still in my eyes for the reunion.

Mum and Dad were sitting at the table,

surrounded by remnants of their breakfast, grinning like Cheshire cats. An extra place had been laid; an extra teacup was half-full of tea. The extra person was standing with his back to the east-facing window. The sun was streaming in over his shoulders, picking up the strawberry-blond highlights in his hair. His face was in shadow but I knew it was him because his Nudie jacket was draped over one of our dining chairs. He walked towards me, his hands up, palms towards me in a curious gesture of surrender, like a bank cashier in a hold-up. 'Justine Fraser,' he said.

I fiddled with the tie belt on my dad's itchy dressing gown and took a deep breath. I closed my eyes, and then opened them again. 'Oh my God. Nicky Bennet,' I said, but my voice twisted up involuntarily at the end, making it sound like a question.

'Yes, it's me,' he said, as he took hold of my shoulders and leant forward to kiss me. I turned my head away suddenly. No one's allowed to kiss me in the morning until I've cleaned my teeth. His mouth made awkward contact with my left ear, so I flung my arms around him and held him as tightly as I could so he would know I was happy to see him even if I wouldn't let him kiss me properly. As we stood there in each other's arms I looked at my mum and dad and tried to will them to disappear. Their Cheshire cat smiles had grown even soppier. The hopeful look on their faces made me want to cry. I didn't know what Nicky had told them, but it must have been enough for them to forgive him for breaking my heart.

19

A traffic jam. He'd been stuck in a traffic jam. Gridlock, that was the word he used. On Labor Day 1984, as I sat forlornly on a brick wall in Brooklyn, Nicky Bennet was stuck in hot holiday traffic on the New Jersey turnpike, in the car he'd borrowed from his mother.

We were sitting on a bench on the old sea wall down by the docks, looking across the Solent at the Isle of Wight shimmering in the hazy sun. He gripped my hand and held on to it. I was imagining him driving all the way from Savannah in a borrowed car, probably a convertible with the top down, listening to his favourite Gram Parsons tape, only to hit a traffic jam just a few miles outside New York. Better to travel hopefully than to arrive a few hours late and discover your girlfriend's got pissed off with

We walked along the prom towards the pier, swinging our clasped hands. I showed Nicky the ice-cream kiosk where I worked the summer after I'd done badly in my A levels. I introduced him to my old maths teacher who happened to be sitting in a deckchair on the prom, fanning herself with the local newspaper. She smiled politely but obviously had no idea who I was. I took Nicky Bennet onto the pier and we played pinball and chanced our arm on the tuppenny falls. We bought chips and a jar of cockles and ate them as we walked. Seagulls, sun, crashing waves: it was like a falling-in-love montage from a soppy 1970s film. The only things lacking were a syrupy ballad on the soundtrack and a zany photo-booth moment. There've been many times in the last eighteen years when I would have given almost anything to have a strip of photo-booth pictures of me and Nicky pulling stupid faces while wearing Kiss Me Quick hats.

Nicky told me how he'd tracked me down. Something about contacting my old university, finding out the name of my home town, phoning all the Frasers in the phone book until someone said 'Yes' when he asked if they had a daughter called Justine. He'd hitch-hiked down the day before and had found a cheap hotel. I did wonder why Mum and Dad hadn't mentioned his call. Maybe they were hoping it would be a nice surprise for me. It didn't make total sense, but it was good enough.

We walked along the beach, working our way past the towels and sunbathing bodies and patches of oily seaweed towards the sea. I gave him a huge hug and said, 'Thank you for coming.'

He smiled his half-smile, and then went down on one knee on the pebbly beach. He winced, but stayed in place. I looked at him, surprised. I couldn't work out what he was doing. And then he took my breath away. 'Justine Fraser,' he said, 'I'm asking you to marry me.'

I knew he meant it because kneeling on pebbles is only slightly less painful than kneeling on Lego, or on an upturned three-pin plug. Also, he had a smile on his face that went right across his mouth from corner to corner.

I was stunned. I wasn't expecting a proposal. Here was a man prepared to kneel on pebbles for me. I looked around me. Everything was so familiar. I'd spent my life in this town. The search-and-rescue helicopter was buzzing through the pale blue sky. Kids were screaming at the water's edge as they tried to dodge the waves. I could smell coconut suntan lotion and warm Coca-Cola. On a transistor radio somewhere I heard what sounded like Bob Geldof's voice, raised and angry, complete with a thumping sound. I could feel goose pimples forming on my arms and the back of my neck. I reminded myself how I'd felt when we last saw each other, how much in love I was, how sore and achy he'd made me feel. I put my hands on his head, running my fingers through his fine, straight hair. I cleared a space on his pale freckled forehead and kissed him. It felt cool, dry and reassuringly familiar. 'Yes,' I said, almost in a whisper.

When we got back to my parents' house Dad was lighting the barbecue he'd recently won in a mystery-voice competition on our local radio station by correctly identifying Tom O'Connor. Mum was excited about the new garden bench they'd bought that day in the half-price sale at B&Q. 'I'm afraid we didn't watch your concert after all,' she said apologetically but slightly relieved.

She wanted me to guess how much the bench had cost. I stared at her as if she had gone mad. I shrugged. 'I don't know, Mum. I mean, I've got no idea how much garden benches are supposed to cost normally. I've never really looked at the prices.'

She told me the price and then, as if she'd just remembered Nicky was with me, 'Have you two had a lovely day?'

'Yeah . . .' we said, in unison, and glanced at each other. There was a tiny moment of uncertainty, when one of us might have said, 'And we've decided to get married,' but neither of us did and instead we just shared a smile and a squeeze of a hand. We sat down together on the bench to wait for the barbecue and that was when Mum took the one and only photo of us together.

Later that evening I said, 'Nicky's going to stay with me for a while,' and Dad said, 'In your bedsit?' and Mum said, 'Oh love.'

That could have meant anything but what I think she meant was, you've only got one bed and we really would prefer to think that you're still a virgin and you're going to stay that way. Or maybe it just meant, I'm really happy the love of your life has come back. You look beautiful, and your dad and I love you very much indeed.

20

When he came back to me, Nicky was wearing a pale blue chambray shirt that was so old and faded that the fabric disintegrated as I tried to pull it over his head. It was a difficult manoeuvre anyway because at the time he had one hand inside my knickers and his mouth clamped to my left breast. As I undid the top two buttons of his jeans they fell straight down to his ankles and I was shocked by how much thinner he'd got. His long, erect penis looked unreal and almost comical against his pale, scrawny thighs and concave stomach. He kicked his jeans off across the room and they landed on the army kitbag he'd brought with him. He pushed me down onto the old metal-framed single bed under the sloping attic ceiling of my bedsit and I discovered for the first time how creaky the springs were.

We'd done little more than hand-holding all day, but as I drove my much-loved Triumph Herald back home Nicky had given me his half-smile, licked his right index finger, and run it up the inside of my thigh. As we stumbled up the five flights of stairs to my bedsit he was behind me with one hand in my knickers, the other pressed tightly over my mouth to stop me screaming and his denimed erection hard against my backside.

Afterwards I got a couple of beers out of the fridge and we sat, semi-clothed, at opposite ends of my bed and grinned at each other.

Later, we got into the narrow single bed together and Nicky fell asleep almost immediately, my arms wrapped around him and our legs entwined. I lay awake trying to get comfortable. The rough skin on my heels kept catching on his shins, my right arm had gone dead where he was lying on it and every time I breathed in I got a mouthful of his fine hair. It needed washing. I turned my neck awkwardly, rested my hot cheek on his cool, bony back, and tried to sleep. My heart was beating so fast it felt as if I'd had too much coffee.

On Sunday I woke early and disentangled myself from Nicky. He half-woke, then turned over, pressed his face into the pillow and went back to sleep again. I got dressed and crept out to the corner shop, where I bought a paper, a pint of milk and a pack of condoms. It was a declaration of sorts. The woman behind the till, used to my usual Sunday shopping, raised her eyebrows. I wanted to tell her that my long-lost boyfriend had arrived from America and wanted to marry me, but all I could manage was a blush.

I got back into bed, and that was where we spent much of the day: having sex, reading the paper, talking, just lying there together. I made us Pot Noodles for lunch, telling Nicky that I was going to introduce him to a traditional English delicacy. While he had a bath I checked his kitbag, but he hadn't brought many clothes with him. So I found my dad's old dress shirt that I'd planned to adapt with lace and embroidery but hadn't got round to yet. Nicky put it on, letting the tails hang loose outside his jeans and the long double cuffs flap around his elegant hands. He looked wonderful.

We sat side by side at a table outside the pub down by the docks, the chilly sea breeze lifting Nicky's now clean hair. 'Are you pleased to see me?' he said, staring at the sea.

I watched the tip of his nose move up and down as he ate a mouthful of dry-roasted peanuts. I couldn't remember ever being happier. 'Course I am,' I said, and clumsily kissed his ear.

During my abortive two years studying English Literature at university I completed a module on classic Victorian children's fiction. I'd been particularly struck by how *Alice in Wonderland* was written; how Charles Dodgson had taken the Liddell girls out in a boat on the river and told them the story. Years later, all the girls remembered it as a rapturous, glorious, golden afternoon, and yet meteorological reports for the day in question reveal it was actually grey and overcast. I'm quite prepared to be told that the eleven days immediately following Live Aid were the coldest, wettest summer days ever, but I remember golden evenings at the beach: on the pier or swimming in the warm sea.

Nicky met me most nights after work, materialising silently from the street corner where he waited for me and taking me by the wrist. We'd leave our clothes in a pile by one of the wooden groynes on the beach and wincingly make our way down over the shingle and shells to the sea. I'm not a good swimmer: I can do about five hugely impressive strokes of crawl before messing up my breathing and getting a mouthful of water. What I really like to do is float on my back with my toes pointed and my arms outstretched, with just my face above water. One evening Nicky mimicked my pose, and we floated together end to end, the soles of our feet touching. Then, with simultaneous breaststroke, we swam towards each other and kissed. I laughed. 'What's funny?' he said.

I told him about how Marie and I used to pretend we were synchronised swimmers. It was during a rare summer when we were getting on with each other. I would have been about nine or ten, I think, because Marie was at the age when she was beginning to develop two little rolls of fat high on her chest. She was very proud of them, and kept telling me she'd be wearing a bra soon. We'd seen some synchronised swimmers on television and Marie decided we would work out a routine and perhaps get chosen to represent Britain at a big international gala. We taught ourselves to do backward somersaults in the sea, and spent a lot of time on our pointy foot and hand movements. We each had a horrible swimming cap that we had to wear for lessons in the school pool, and Mum could not work out why we suddenly insisted on wearing these at the beach. One day at teatime Marie said, in her too-loud voice, 'Mum, me and Justine want synchronised swimming lessons. Can we? Please?'

I twisted in my seat, really embarrassed. 'Please,' she wheedled, blundering on.

'I don't think so,' said Mum, kindly. Instinctively, I somehow knew it was something we would never get, something there was absolutely no point asking for, like the year before when Marie had wanted a Sindy doll with hair that grew out of the top of its head. Marie burst into tears, looking ugly and red-faced. 'You never let us have anything we want,' she screamed, and ran upstairs to have a tantrum.

Nicky swam under my legs and emerged with an artificial smile plastered on his face, as if he was trying to impress the imaginary judges. 'You know, men aren't even allowed to dream about being synchronised swimmers,' he said, so we agreed that we would pioneer a new pairs event and become the Torvill and Dean of the swimming pool. For the next ten minutes or so we swam around each other, darting this way and that, pointing our toes and doing elaborate hand movements. Then, still with the same rictus of a smile, he took my legs and wrapped them around him. Pulling the crotch of my swimsuit to one side, he pushed his erect penis into me. With his hands caressing my backside and my legs wrapped around him, we turned round and round as if we were on the *Camberwick Green* music box, while I made balletic shapes with my arms.

Nicky didn't wash his hair much, and it took on the distinctive smell of the sea, a sharp, evocative mix of salt and seaweed and tar. I don't swim in the sea often these days, not since the great sewage-slick scandal of a few years back, so I don't get to smell that smell very often. But even those big bottles of bright blue economy bubble bath, usually called something like Ocean Fresh or Cool Marine, that you get from the supermarket, even that smell is enough to make me remember the precise texture and feel of Nicky's hair against my face.

I used to love the walk back from the beach. We'd be cold and goose-pimply, with the gentle evening sun on the backs of our necks. My hair would start to frizz from the sea water and I'd feel the canvas of my plimsolls rubbing with each step against my still damp, sockless heels. We'd stop for a pizza and eat it sitting on the floor of my bedsit, exhausted, drained and happy.

Before long we were like a proper couple, with our little habits and routines. I'd force myself out of bed in the morning while Nicky groaned and hid his head in the pillow. I'd make a mug of instant coffee and grab whatever came to hand for my breakfast: rock cakes that my mum had made, a chocolate biscuit, yesterday's leftover pizza from the fridge. Nicky liked to watch me get dressed, and sometimes he'd tell me not to put any knickers on so he could think of me while I was at work. On those knickerless days he'd come into the shop during the day and lurk in a corner, pretending to look at books. He'd glance across at me from time to time as I tried to serve customers without revealing that I was in a squirming state of sexual arousal.

Nicky discovered things I'd never known about my home town. He bought us season tickets for the fun fair, took me to a poetry reading at a club I never knew existed, and discovered an art supply shop hidden in an alleyway off the high street where he bought paints and brushes. He'd go on shopping expeditions during the day and proudly show me his purchases later: strange stuff like nipple clamps, a mirror ball and a Hawaiian shirt that clashed spectacularly with his Nudie jacket.

On the days when he wasn't waiting for me after work I'd get home to discover him there with a treat he'd prepared for me. One evening I found he'd replaced my Athena prints of Robert Doisneau photos with some of his own work: shots of the beach, the pier and the tall Victorian house my bedsit was in, all messed up and overshadowed with swirly daubs of orange.

One Saturday evening I climbed up to the bedsit to find it empty. For a moment I thought he'd left. I stood in the middle of the room, hyperventilating. Then I looked up and saw his spurred cowboy boots dangling from the skylight above my bed. He'd found a way to release the safety catch and open the window wide enough to crawl through.

We sat on the roof smoking a giant spliff and drinking bottles of beer, listening to Nicky's

Gram Parsons tape on my tinny portable cassette player. I told Nicky stories about the things we could see. Across the roof of the dilapidated Grand Hotel was the Common where I scored the winning rounder in an inter-schools tournament. The low sun was glinting on the silver dome of the roller-skating rink where Marie lost a tooth, and the light was also twinkling on the gently lapping sea. In the other direction we could see my old school, and the windows of the classroom where I used to have violin lessons. Just across the road I pointed out the corner where the neighbourhood flasher used to ply his trade.

'Sshh,' said Nicky, and put his hand over my mouth. 'None of this matters.' He was sitting behind me, his long legs wrapped around me and his chin resting on my head. With his spare hand he burrowed into my jeans and brought me to an orgasm that had me biting on his fingers as I stared into the windows of my old school.

21

Twice in my life I've gone a little loopy and I'm really scared it might be happening again. When I got back from America, after Nicky Bennet stood me up in New York and I arrived in London to find Daniel sleeping with Caroline, I went back home to my parents' house, shut myself in my bedroom, cried a lot and destroyed things. Later, when I was living in the bedsit, I went through a terrible time. It was after Nicky had left me for the second time, but it didn't happen immediately. It took maybe six months for it to kick in, and more than a year for me to realise that something was seriously wrong. Now I've read enough women's magazine articles to confidently diagnose myself retrospectively as suffering from mild depression.

What happened was this: I could get myself to work okay and do really quite a good job, day in, day out. What I couldn't do was live my life. I was supposed to be a grown-up but I didn't know how. Important-looking letters (bills, bank statements) I would shove unopened into the top drawer of my desk. I started living on takeaways and ready meals because I couldn't get myself organised to do proper food shopping. My hallway was stuffed full of bags of dirty washing waiting to go to the launderette. Because I kept running out of clean clothes I'd started stopping off at the charity shop at lunchtime, just to buy something to wear to work the next day.

Worst of all, the bedsit was a tip: utterly untidy. I had to go out of my way not to make plates and cutlery dirty because I knew I'd never get around to washing them up. The kitchen area looked like a bomb-site. The living area wasn't much better. The floor and furniture was covered with overdue library books, junk mail, magazines and old newspapers with half-finished crosswords in them. Everything just fell where I left it; nothing was in its proper home. There was a me-sized patch of floor bang in front of the TV and that was about it. I'd get home from work, sling my bag somewhere and put on the kettle. I'd find the mug I'd used most recently and rinse it out. I had a way of measuring exactly the right amount of instant coffee into the mug with just a flick of the wrist, which avoided having to make a teaspoon dirty. Then I'd sit in front of the TV, watch crap programmes and eat chocolate biscuits straight from the packet. A couple of hours later I'd still be there. My feet would be numb. I'd have finished the biscuits but would probably still have my coat on.

I could spend hours just staring at the veins on the underside of my wrists or chewing the soft inside of my mouth until it bled.

Once in a while I'd attempt a massive clean-up – dustbin liners, rubber gloves, bleach, the lot – but within an hour or so of starting I would give up, defeated by the sheer horror of the mess. My life was normal in every other respect. I was good at my job, well liked, friendly and funny. I'd go down the pub with my workmates, see my parents on Sundays. But I never invited anyone back to my bedsit. The last guest I'd had had been Nicky Bennet.

I know it sounds trivial. Loads of people live with clutter and untidiness. Lots of people live on ready meals and takeaways. I don't; at least not usually. But when you've been in a state like that once and hated every moment, and then finally managed to get yourself out of it, you live in fear that it might happen again. And here's why I'm scared: at this precise moment I am standing with my forehead resting on the glass of the French windows at the back of my house staring out at the backyard. The weeds have got out of hand but there's nothing I can do about it because I'm still in my pyjamas at three in the afternoon. In my hand I have a mug of tea. The mug has gone so long without a proper wash, with just being rinsed out between cuppas, that there are now archaeological strata of tea stains inside the mug. Earlier today I was curled up on the edge of my settee, watching daytime TV – *Quincy*, followed by *Streets of San Francisco* and a TV movie starring the actress who played Laura in *Little House on the Prairie* as a plucky investigative journalist. Later, if I can pluck up the courage, I might plough through four days' worth of mail and newspapers lying on my doormat unread. I might even plug my phone back in at the socket. What's more likely, though, is that I will lean on the kitchen doorpost, realise there's no food in the fridge, and decide to call for a pizza because that way I won't have to make a plate dirty.

I've been like this since I got home after sleeping with Daniel. After that awful night I arrived back at my house to discover that my answerphone was making a strange, strangled noise. The light that tells you how many messages there are was flashing a frantic red eight, which is the highest number it goes to. I guessed the tape was full of journalists following up the press conference, wanting to ask me one last question; or maybe friends wondering how it went, was I happy with it, did I say the things I meant to say, did I mean the things I'd said. Or, probably, Daniel, wondering why I'd run out on him, asking me for permission to use the quotes he'd recorded. I didn't listen back to the messages. I didn't want to talk to anyone, least of all to Daniel. If I didn't talk to him, it'd all go away.

There was a note pushed through the door. I unfolded the paper with trembling hands. It was from Gavin. 'J – your answerphone seems to be broken. Hope the press conference went OK. Did you forget you were coming round to mine for dinner afterwards? Don't worry about it. Give me a call whenever. G. xxx.'

Jesus. I'd managed to have casual sex with two blokes in a matter of days and in both cases, for very different reasons, I deeply regretted it. I put the chain on the door and before I pulled my phone out at the socket I rang my boss Paul and called in sick. 'Don't worry, Justine, take as much time as you need.'

He sounded so kind and thoughtful that I immediately felt guilty. 'You know, I'm not actually ill, just . . .' I was going to say hung-over but thought better of it. Instead I said, '. . . in a bit of a state.'

'That's okay. It's not surprising. You've got a lot on your mind at the moment. Seriously, don't worry about it. See it as a sabbatical or something. Take as much time as you need. Don't come back until you're ready.'

Gavin came round that evening. He brought me some garage-forecourt flowers and a carton of orange juice. I answered the door in my pyjamas and opened it just a couple of inches.

'I phoned you at work and they said you were ill.'

I automatically put on one of those husky, phoning-in-sick voices, leaned pathetically on the doorpost and said, 'It's just flu or something. I'm okay. I just – you know – want to be on my own, okay?'

'Okay,' he said. 'You do look a bit rough.' Then he shifted his weight from one foot to the other as if wondering what to say next, blew me a kiss and left. I looked at myself in the mirror. Gavin was right. I did look rough. I looked spectacularly pale even by my own standards.

Anna is my best friend, the best person in my life and, apart from my parents, the only person who loves me with anything close to unconditional love. Were she not so blissfully, ridiculously in love with her husband Gray, I'd say she was that elusive one person who loves me more than they love anyone else. She manages to be the most morally upright person I've ever met while remaining almost totally non-judgemental.

We met when we were working together in the bookshop, I'd been there for a couple of years already and Anna was a Christmas temp. The first time I saw her I thought I recognised her. She's very small and very neat, with dark brown hair that she always wears in the same style: immaculately parted in the middle, tucked behind her ears, thick and straight down to her shoulders, like a little girl playing the Virgin Mary in a nativity play. To work she always wore the same basic clothes: a short, straight skirt in navy, black or brown, opaque tights to match the skirt, flat shoes and a plain white blouse with a little round collar. It looked like school uniform, and that's how I finally worked out why I recognised her. 'You were at Holy Trinity, weren't you?' I said to her one day when we were unpacking books in the stockroom. Holy Trinity is the Church of England primary school that educated the entire Fraser family, parents and all.

'Yes. I was in the same class as your sister Marie.'

'Oh.' That made her two years older than me, which surprised me. There was a short pause, and then Anna put down the books she was holding and turned to me decisively. 'I haven't said, "I'm sorry about what happened to your sister," because that's probably not the most useful thing to say. But I want you to know that I know what happened to Marie. I guess losing a sister probably takes a long time to stop hurting. So, you know, I've said my bit now. You can talk about it or not talk about it. Whatever. You have my sympathy. For what it's worth.'

I looked at her, stunned into silence. She has an unexpectedly deep voice, and what she says carries weight. I didn't think about Marie that often, except occasionally to consider idly how nice it would be to have a sister now that I was old enough to get on with her. But perhaps Anna was right. Perhaps it was all right to feel sad about it sometimes. I felt tears prickle in my eyes so I turned away. After I'd sniffed them away I turned back and Anna was smiling at me with a wide, beautiful smile. My heart leapt in the same way it had when Nicky Bennet first smiled a whole-mouth smile at me. I knew I'd found a really good deep-down friend and, having carelessly jettisoned every other friend I'd ever had, I knew she was just what I needed.

We got into the habit of going to a wine bar once or twice a week straight after work, to talk about love, periods and other girly stuff, and generally to make each other laugh. Anna had just got married to the mysteriously named Gray. She told me he was a potter, and she'd given up her job as a primary-school teacher to run his business: to do his books, his marketing, his organisation. She was working in the shop temporarily to get enough money for a new bathroom. I asked her how she could be so sure of someone that she was prepared to change her life for him, and she said, 'Solid love. It's like ordinary, run-of-the-mill love but a hundred times better.'

'How can you tell the difference?'

'A couple of years ago I was absolutely head over heels in love with a fellow teacher called Tony. But then one morning I woke up and realised something had changed. The love had gone. Completely evaporated. It had drained away like bath water. There was absolutely nothing left except a scummy tidemark around the metaphorical bath.'

'Yuck.' I shuddered, thinking about the state of my own bathroom. This was before I'd confided in Anna and got her to sort it all out.

'Indeed. And I remember thinking, was the love real when it was here? Where did it go? Isn't love supposed to be eternal? Then I met Gray and realised the difference. You know when you go to the garden centre and find a plant with no flowers but lots of buds and a really sturdy-looking root ball?'

'Not really. I live in a bedsit. I haven't got a garden.'

'Well, just imagine it. Solid love is like buying the plant with the root ball instead of a showy plant with lots of flowers that dies within a week of planting.'

I liked the image but I didn't know exactly what she meant. I couldn't fit what I still felt for Nicky Bennet into either category. At that time in my life, after Nicky had left but before he became famous, I would have said that my love for him was one of the few facts in my life that I was sure of. And yet I wouldn't have been able to describe it in terms of something as pleasant as a plant. It was painful: it was a hard, solid, shiny thing, like slate or flint or something, a lump that wouldn't dissolve; a heavy weight in a bag with handles that cut into my hands, something that I had to carry everywhere with me even though it annoyed me and made me sore and frustrated. I couldn't imagine it ever being any other way.

I couldn't wait to meet Gray, the man who inspired such love. All I knew about him was that he was a potter. In my mind's eye he was tall and craggy in an Aran jumper, like a young Ted Hughes, with clay all over his hands. I was right about the clay and the Aran jumper. Anna had invited me to his birthday party, and the first surprise was that it was his fortieth, making him half a generation older than us. The second was that he was about five foot six or seven, with a barrel chest; short and thickset with slightly bandy legs and an untidy grey beard. He tousled my hair, said, 'Jasmine, I've heard so much about you,' and poured me red wine into a pint glass. I liked him instantly.

All night I watched Anna and Gray like a

hawk, looking for outward evidence of their solid love. The only manifestation I saw was this: even when they were at opposite ends of the room, every so often they exchanged a look and a beatific smile. Literally beatific: they really were blessing each other.

Anna knocks on my door maybe five days after my night with Daniel. She calls through the letter box. 'It's Anna. Please let me in.'

I feel so guilty. I've hardly spoken to her since she told me she was pregnant. Maybe I'm finding good news difficult to deal with at the moment. But today I've had a slightly better day. I've managed to get dressed properly, and I've even washed and blow-dried my hair. I know resistance is futile so I open the door. Anna follows me into the living room and it's like déjà vu. I wave my arm vaguely at the mess in the room and sit down on the settee, feeling ashamed. I can see a frown flicker sharply across Anna's forehead as she takes it all in: the pile of mail in the hallway, magazines everywhere and, most incriminatingly, a pile of Nicky Bennet videos that I've been

23

Anna has brought a folder with her. 'I thought maybe you were worried about the press conference, about what you said and what the papers might have said.'

I want to cry out of love and gratitude for her generosity. Even though she tells me she's still feeling sick every morning (I have to ask her; she doesn't volunteer the information), she's helped me tidy up most of the mess. Now we're sitting at my dining table. I'm drinking red wine; she has a glass of water. I don't know what to tell her. She doesn't know the worst of it. She doesn't know about Daniel, how I slept with him, and I daren't tell her how stupid I've been. Quite apart from any other considerations, he's married – and I have a feeling that's one thing that would lose me Anna's non-judgemental sympathy. Let her think it's the press conference that's got me acting like this. I put my head in my hands. 'What's the damage?'

'It's okay. Really, mostly okay.'

She opens the folder and spreads out some newspaper cuttings. I pick up one from a tabloid. 'Obsessed With Suicide' says the headline. Another has 'Nicky Copied Suicide Note'; a third reads 'Why I Know My Nicky's Dead, by Blonde Ex.'

'Blonde,' I say, managing a smile.

'Oh yes, you're blonde in quite a few of the stories. Also, "attractive" more than once. The one I like best is this one.' She hands me over a cutting from one of the glossy showbiz weeklies. 'Apparently you're a "slender, elegant blonde".'

'Not a scrawny, mousy-haired ageing spinster? You're right. It's okay. Could be a lot worse, couldn't it?' I wonder again what I told Daniel, and if it'll ever appear in print. 'Was there anything bad?' I ask Anna, not really wanting to know.

'Not really. Not about you. Don't worry about it. Except . . .'

'Except what?' I look hard at Anna. She's doing the same little frown she did when she first walked into my house.

'Is this it now, Justine? You won't do any more interviews, will you? Have you got it all off your chest now? All this Nicky Bennet stuff? Because it's not doing you any good and it's upsetting us all, all your friends, and I'm sure it's hurting your mum too. Will you leave it now? Please? Just try to get back to normal?'

'Oh Anna, I'm so sorry. I've been crap, haven't I? There's you and Gray, all thrilled about your wonderful news and I am too, honestly, I'm really excited for you, it's the best news I've heard in ages.' I've run out of words. I look away. I look at my hands, all dirty from the newsprint. I look at headlines in the newspaper cuttings, at the photos of Nicky Bennet. I look out to my backyard, all covered in weeds. Snap out of it, I think to myself. That's what she's telling me. I take a big gulp from my glass of wine. I know Anna's watching me carefully, waiting for an answer. I put my head in my hands again.

'Justine, is this really all about your sister? Kick me if I'm about to come out with a load of psychobabble rubbish, but – you know – you seem unreasonably upset about Nicky Bennet disappearing. Is it to do with your sister killing herself? Is that why you're so upset? Is it because you still don't know why your sister killed herself and maybe you're still – I don't know – cross with her or something?'

I look across at Anna with narrowed eyes. She has her hands up in front of her as if to say, don't hurt me. 'Fuck, Anna, if it was all about Marie it would be easy, wouldn't it? I'd go and get some counselling, talk to some nice woman in a comfortable room once a week for a few months and everything would be okay. I mean, it's happened, hasn't it? Marie has killed herself. Nothing I can do about it now except talk about it.'

'Is it something to do with me being pregnant? Are you upset about that for some reason?'

'Oh God, Anna, no. Don't think that. I'm so sorry you might have thought that.' I look at her, this woman whom I love so much, and I know that I've hurt her somehow.

'So what's it all about, then?'

'What do you mean, what's it all about? It's about what it's about. It's about Nicky Bennet.'

Anna has her face screwed up as if she's concentrating really hard, trying to understand me. She opens her mouth to say something, but I get in first.

'You see, I know everyone just thinks it's a bit

of a laugh. You know, when people talk about famous people they've met, and I say that Nicky Bennet used to live with me and they laugh, and I have to say, "No, really," and eventually they believe me. Maybe I go on about it too much . . .' I look at Anna and she's got her lips pressed tightly together in a wavy line that's either an unspoken 'hmm' or a stifled laugh. 'But, you see, it's more than that. It's not just an ex-boyfriend who got famous. God, that'd be really sad. Watching all his videos and stuff. No, the thing is, and I'm sure you know this, the thing is, I loved him. Like mad. No big secret. I loved him. I loved him so much and he screwed up my life. Fuck him. He was an arsehole and I hate him, but I love him as well. Still. So much. And it hurts. So much. But at least he was always there, you know?' I'm sobbing, the words are catching in my throat, and Anna has come over to my side of the table, kneeling on the floor to put her arms around me. 'He was always there and I always knew he was there but now he's gone. But the thing is, Anna, I don't know where he's gone.'

'He's killed himself. That's what you think, isn't it?'

I think about how I can explain myself clearly.

'Anna, do you know why I did that press conference?'

'Because you think he's killed himself.'

I shake my head. 'I'm trying to make myself think he killed himself, because then I can just get over it.' I think again. What will make her understand me? 'If Gray died, and you didn't know, do you think you would feel it? Do you think you would know that he was dead even if no one had told you?'

Anna rocks back on her haunches and breathes in sharply. 'I don't know. Yes. Probably. I think so. I think – I'd like to think – that I'd know if he stopped being there, stopped thinking about me.'

'Okay. Well, maybe you'll know what I mean when I say that I haven't stopped feeling Nicky yet. This will sound stupid, but Nicky and I had a connection. A really strong connection. He got under my skin. Almost literally. It's as if he planted some kind of hook, like a fish-hook or something, under my skin or maybe in my heart, and attached it to a long cable. And I've always been able to feel him tugging. You know, whenever I read about him or see a picture of him, and suddenly – yank – there's a sharp sensation. It's painful, but weirdly – nice. Sexy.' Suddenly I remember the nipple clamps that Nicky bought, and I smile to myself. 'It hurts like mad but I like it. One of those things that's really painful, but really pleasurable at the same time. When I read what he'd written in that note I was convinced he must be dead, but I can still feel him yanking at that fish-hook. So now, Anna, I'm wondering. That note. It was so like my sister's that he must have meant something by it. So either he's dead, or he's trying to send me some kind of message and I've got to work out what it is.'

Anna sighs. She leans towards me and puts her arm around me again, then kisses me gently on the forehead. 'Oh Justine, you've got to sort this out. This is going to take more than me hiring a cleaning company for the day, isn't it? You're going to have to do something about this.'

She's right. I love her and she can't help me. This time I've got to sort it out for myself. And after she's gone I decide what it is I'm supposed to do. If Nicky's dead, they'll find his body eventually. If he's not dead, and that note wasn't a suicide note, then it was a message for me. There's something he wants me to do. 'When you know why, you'll understand.' I need to find Nicky Bennet. He wants me to. He wants me to understand why.

A few years ago my father died. It wasn't unexpected; he'd been ill for some time. After he died my brother Simon and I found out he'd left us each some money, quite a nice amount. His will said we should use it on something we really wanted, such as the deposit on a house or the trip of a lifetime. It's been sitting in a high-interest savings account ever since. I know now what I need to do. I don't give myself too much time to think. I go upstairs to my computer and I get on the Internet. Paul told me to take a sabbatical – 'as much time as you need' was what he said. I log on to a travel site that I've used before and I book a flight to America.

a runner. I try to imagine what a sculptor would make of my story. Maybe he'd pose me sitting on my settee, drinking red wine and watching videos, waiting for Nicky Bennet to come back to me, still dreaming about the great lost love of my life.

As I drove in from the airport yesterday past chain motels and fast-food joints I was worried that Savannah wouldn't live up to my expectations. But after I checked into my hotel and walked through the historic city centre it was as if I'd entered a secret garden. It is one of the most beautiful places I have ever visited. Today it feels like I'm walking through a film set. The streets are lined with what must be ante-bellum houses, and lead to one tree-lined square after another, with benches in the shade of the trees. Every square seems to have a statue of a local worthy posed on a plinth in the centre, surrounded by more trees. Hanging from the branches everywhere is a kind of cloud of green that I assume must be the Spanish moss that Nicky Bennet used to speak about dreamily. Along the riverfront, restored red-brick warehouses are now restaurants; in one of them I have just lunched on crab cakes and two glasses of a very good Californian Sauvignon Blanc. The warm September air seems to be scented with an indefinable Southern perfume. I waggle my shoulders and soak up the warmth.

I may be on a quest but I am determined to enjoy myself. I am wearing a new dress, a shop-bought one. It's linen, a minty-green colour, sleeveless with a slit halfway up my thigh. I've gathered my hair up into a ponytail and fastened it with a covered band that has a big, flamboyant green flower attached to it. I bought it in a shop at Heathrow as I waited for my flight to be called. It made me smile. I'm wearing make-up – one-touch cream-to-powder foundation in ivory, again bought at Heathrow. It makes my skin look smooth and somehow grown-up. I've got my favourite flat sandals on again, and I've topped up the iridescent sky-blue polish on my toenails. In my wildest dreams I let myself imagine I will turn a corner into a shady square and there, sitting on the steps of a beautiful white-pillared house, the kind of house in which I once imagined we'd live, will be Nicky Bennet in his cowboy boots and Nudie jacket. I need to be prepared. I need to look as nearly beautiful as I possibly can.

And so, down to the serious research. You know the scene. It's in every self-respecting thriller. I'm talking about the microfiche scene. Picture a hushed library in a strange town. The intrepid investigator, played by some feisty actress like Sandra Bullock or Julia Roberts (and, of course, didn't Olivia Ross have a microfiche scene in her film with Nicky Bennet, *Trust Me*?) is on the case. She calls up back copies of the local newspaper and scans through them on the screen. Cut to the heroine, close shot. She frowns slightly, a sharp but sexy worry line darting between her eyebrows. Cut to blurry newsprint whizzing through the frame of the microfiche screen. Cut back to the heroine as she bites her lip, deep in thought. She winds and rewinds backwards and forwards, shaking her head in frustration. Absolutely nothing.

Actually, that's not quite true. Nicky's name crops up in reviews of his films, but there's no reference to him being from Savannah. I would have thought that if I'd been the editor of the paper I'd have run a story headlined something like 'Local boy stars in movie'.

I check the dates around the time he was nominated for the Best Supporting Actor Oscar, but there's nothing beyond a simple listing of his name. I don't know Nicky's birthday, just that he's Sagittarius. (I asked him once. I used to read his horoscope, just to see how it interlocked with mine.) So I check birth announcements for November and December 1963, then '64 and '65 and '62 and even '61, just in case he'd started lying about his age earlier than I suspected. I want to find out the names of his parents, a clue to whereabouts he used to live. Again, there's nothing. Not that it necessarily means anything. Not everyone registers births in the local newspaper, do they? And maybe he wasn't even born in Savannah, just brought up there. But the thing is, I don't know very much about investigations, and if I draw a blank with the local newspaper I don't know where to go next.

I push my chair back, stretch out my arms and neck. I feel hot and dizzy and there are spots dancing in front of my eyes. I've been in the library too long, looking at microfiche too long, trying for too long to find some evidence of

Nicky Bennet. 'This is stupid,' I say to myself, and stride over to the woman on the desk.

She's large and pretty, around my age, with white powdered skin and dark red hair. Her badge tells me she's called Lanyon Slidell. While she finishes her phone call I find myself trying to work out what it's an anagram of. She puts the phone down and turns to me with a dazzling smile. 'Can I help y'all?' she says in a voice dripping with mint juleps, Scarlett O'Hara and memories of Nicky Bennet.

'Yes,' I say, all English, polite and hesitant. Little red ovals are already forming high on my cheekbones. 'I wonder if you can.'

I ask her if there's some kind of computerised index of old newspaper stories, something I can check by subject rather than by date. 'Was there a particular subject y'all are interested in?'

'Yes. It's a person, actually. Nicky Bennet?'

'And how are you spelling tha-yat?'

I spell Nicky's surname. 'One T,' I say.

Lanyon Slidell's face brightens. 'Oh, like the movie star?'

'Yes. I mean, it *is* the movie star.'

She frowns, almost a mime of puzzlement. 'Now, forgive me, but why would y'all be particularly interested in what our Savannah papers have to say about Nicky Bennet?'

And there's a cold flash high across my chest. A creeping doubt that I'd been trying to put behind me suddenly takes concrete form and settles there.

'Well, because he's from Savannah?' and by putting a question mark on the end of my explanation I voice the doubt for the first time.

'Jeez, I wish,' she laughs as I feel my knees go wobbly and I have to put a hand out to her desk to steady myself.

Lanyon Slidell turns out to be a huge fan of Nicky Bennet. She's seen all his movies, read all the articles, probably even has the T-shirt. 'Believe me, I'd know if he was from Savannah, sugar. Baby doll, we all would be so proud.'

'But where is he from?' I say, and as the words leave my mouth I realise that I'm asking a chubby Deep South librarian called Lanyon to tell me where the man I once thought I would marry was born.

'Y'all know what he always says. "A godforsaken steel town in the industrial heart of this country." That's how he put it in *Vanity Fair*, you remember, the one with that rodeo photo on the front cover.'

The cover I tore off and kept in my underwear drawer for many months. How could I have missed that?

25

I have felt like this twice before in my life. Once was when I was six and I fell awkwardly on the climbing frame during PE. I landed across the bar with an audible thump as it made contact with the bottom of my ribcage. I was so badly winded that I couldn't speak for an hour or more. The second time was ten years later, when I was summoned out of triple history on a Tuesday afternoon so that the headmistress could tell me that my sister had killed herself. I sat in her office fighting for breath, as if someone had just punched me in the stomach.

Now I feel as if the whole middle part of my body has been knocked out sideways by someone wielding a giant mallet. I'm breathless, winded, just about hanging together, like the blocks in a game of Jenga when it's about to collapse. If I sit still for a while with my arms wrapped around my body I just might hold myself together. The thing is, I know what I've just heard is true. I even remember reading those words in *Vanity Fair*, about the godforsaken industrial town. It just didn't register when I read it, so strong was the memory of Nicky's voice telling me about Savannah.

After a while, when I get my breath back, I start fiddling with my hair. I undo my ponytail, wind the flowery elastic band around my wrist, gather my hair up back into a knot, wind the band around it, then undo it again and repeat the whole process. Why does it matter so much where he comes from? That's what I'm asking myself, trying to be logical, to make some sense out of how I feel. Why does it matter? Because of a dream I'd once had of living in a beautiful white-pillared house with my gorgeous Southern husband and our little daughter, whom we'd probably christen Emmylou. Because of the world's most seductive voice, all slow and husky and twisted. Because of the way Nicky spoke to me: Justine Fraser, I love the crazy way you dance. No, not dance. Dayyance. That's how he said it.

It was early one evening down at the swimming dock that Nicky first told me all about

Savannah. I remember the midges biting and the gentle lapping of the river against our ankles as we dangled our toes in the cool water. I began telling him about my home town by the sea: about the tang of salt in the air, the sound of seagulls, the melancholy beauty of the beach out of season, the way the old faded ice-lolly wrappers would stick to the tarpaulin stretched over the stacks of deckchairs. I told him about drinking pints in the pub down by the docks and watching the ferries arrive from France and the Isle of Wight. Then I asked him, 'Where are you from?'

'Have you heard of Savannah, Georgia?' he said dreamily, his beautiful voice meandering, as if it wasn't in a hurry to get anywhere. I half-nodded. It sounded familiar. He told me about the squares and the houses, the Spanish moss hanging from every tree and about General Sherman presenting the town to Abraham Lincoln as a Christmas gift at the end of the Civil War.

How did he do it? How did he know so much about Savannah? But I know the answer even before I finish asking myself the question. Nicky Bennet had seen the same tourist information film I had. I think back to this morning. In a spirit of discovery, I'd visited the tourist centre in the old railroad station on the edge of the historic district. The introductory video (award-winning, apparently, but rather dated and full of actors with 1970s facial hair playing the parts of Civil War heroes and other worthies) told me all about the city, in almost the same words that Nicky had once used. I realise the truth: all he had ever told me about Savannah were the standard tourist clichés. He'd never told me anything about his life here, where his home was, the smell and texture of day-to-day living. He'd simply picked a city off the shelf and learned a few essential details.

I go back to the hotel, get in my hire car and drive out of the city, heading for the coast. The road takes me over a kind of causeway onto a flat, marshy island. It's a frustrating drive. I guess I'm looking for a beach to walk along, to be melancholy on, but the landscape just seems to peter out towards the sea while never quite getting there, liked a frayed piece of fabric that needs hemming. I pull off the road at some kind of historic fort and hand over some money to a man in a wooden hut, who gives me a leaflet in return. I park the car and walk along a planking footpath towards the sea, and then I sit on a bench looking out at the ocean across yards and yards of marshland. It's almost impossible to tell where the sea begins. I guess it's funny, really: the excitement of booking my flight, of arriving in Savannah; remembering Nicky Bennet's accent, the way he used to speak to me. And of course the whole thing's just a joke, a lie. Nicky Bennet's not from Savannah.

It's early evening, I'm drinking beer in a waterfront bar and I'm telling a version of my story to a fifty-something businessman. He's skiving off early from a conference; his suit jacket, complete with a laminated name tag clipped to the breast pocket, is lying at his feet, folded over a sponsored conference bag. He has a full head of curly grey hair, crinkly eyes and a wedding ring. He's funny and perceptive and interested in what I have to say, which I like. I tell him I'm travelling round the States and came to Savannah to look up an old friend who turns out to have moved away. 'Old boyfriend?' he says.

'Yeah.'

'And you were hoping maybe to rekindle something?'

'Kind of. Not exactly. It's just that he used to tell me all about Savannah, and I always imagined coming here with him, so it's strange, you know, just being here . . .' My voice tails off. I'm not sure exactly what I'm trying to say.

He reaches for my hand, just to pat it in a friendly way. 'A beautiful woman alone in a bar on a beautiful evening in a beautiful city. You'll have dinner with me?'

I smile a kind of yes.

The following morning I pick up the phone and call Anna. She answers within two rings. 'Hi, it's me,' I whisper, and remember to ask her how she is, how she's feeling and whether she's stopped being sick yet. Then I catch my breath and I can feel tears starting. 'Nicky doesn't come from Savannah.'

'Ah,' she says, and leaves space for me to cry. She knows exactly what I mean and why it matters. 'I know, I know,' she says as I quietly sob myself dry. Once my tears have subsided she says, 'How dare he tell you lies?'

'Yeah, I hate him.'

There's a long silence. Then Anna says, 'You sound strange.'

'It's nothing,' I say. 'Just really hung-over.'

'Well, be careful,' she says. 'Don't do anything you might regret.'

I flash back to that night with Daniel and shudder. I came close to doing it again last night. After the bar, after the restaurant, the fifty-something man walked me back to my hotel. He seemed to be expecting to be invited back to my room. I stammered some excuse, I'm not sure what. He was disappointed, angry even, as if I'd made a promise that I'd then reneged on.

I was sorry to disappoint him. He was a nice guy. Really kind. He listened to me properly. There was something he said, something that made me realise what I needed to do next. Where were we? In the restaurant, I think. What were we talking about? Nicky Bennet. Oh my God, I told this strange man that I was looking for Nicky Bennet, that I'd been at college with him, that he was the ex-boyfriend I was hoping to hook up with. And it turned out that he'd been at Lowell too, years earlier. 'The Lowell Alumni Net,' he said. 'I'm surprised you've never heard from them. They're real big on organising reunions. I bet you could track down some of Nicky Bennet's old college friends. Find someone else who knows him from way back.'

'Justine?'

It's Anna's voice. I'm still on the phone. 'Sorry.'

'Where are you? You sound really distant.'

'I'm in Savannah.'

She laughs. Then she stops laughing. 'You're in Savannah.'

'Yes.'

'In America?'

'Yes,' I say, in a tone of voice that suggests she's very slow on the uptake.

'Justine, what on Earth are you doing there?'

'You told me I had to do something about Nicky Bennet. So I've come to find him. Only I'm not doing very well.'

'Oh Justine, that wasn't what I meant. I didn't mean that you should go and find him. I meant – oh, whatever. Just be careful, okay?'

'Thank you. Sorry. And Anna?'

'Yes?'

There's something I have to say. 'You know I love you, don't you? It's just that I'm really crap at showing it.'

As I drive out to the airport I'm trying to remember what accent Nicky had when he came back to me. Do I just remember him speaking in his seductive Southern voice because that's how I want to remember him? Or had he changed? Was he planning to tell me he wasn't from Savannah, Georgia at all but from some godforsaken steel town in the industrial heart of America? Pittsburgh, maybe, or Milwaukee or Akron, Ohio. He got stuck in gridlock en route to New York. He came on the New Jersey turnpike. Perhaps that's a clue. I remember going through a grim industrial town called Trenton, New Jersey on the train from Lowell to Washington DC; it stuck in my mind because it had a wonderfully proud sign on a bridge that said 'Trenton Makes, The World Takes.'

Maybe that's where Nicky's from. Trenton makes, the world takes. It would make a great title for a magazine feature about him.

It suddenly becomes overwhelmingly important to remember how he spoke when he came back. If he asked me to marry him in a fake Southern voice then he didn't mean it. If he said it in a standard American accent, he did. From the airport, just before my flight to Boston is called, I

26

I've always loved the romance of American place names, ever since I was about fifteen, a time when I had a big map of America on my bedroom wall and dreamed one day of living somewhere with a name like Roanoke, Grand Rapids or Nantucket. It seemed to me that American place names were invented specifically to put in songs about love and heartbreak. San Antonio. Winslow, Arizona. Amarillo. Galveston.

Driving up the Interstate through Massachusetts and New Hampshire I'm trying to write my own song in my head. I'm watching the road signs, reading some of the names out loud: Nashua, Concord, Lake Winnepesaukee. Contoocook, Sunapee, Cornish Flat. Comfort Inn, Motel 6, Taco Bell. It's a sunny autumn Tuesday, in what the Alamo car-rental man at Logan Airport told me was the slack period between the end of the summer and the start of the leaf-peeping season. If I were a proper traveller I'd be on a back road, a blue highway, seeing the real New England and eating a blue-plate special of eggs over easy at a roadside diner, served to me by a waitress called Myrtle. As it is, I'm nervous about the long drive and anxious about getting to the Lowell Inn before they let someone else have the reservation I made from a payphone at Logan. So I'm sticking to the Interstate: the 93 from Boston, then the 89 across New Hampshire towards the Connecticut River and Vermont. In the distance to the north I can see the outline of mountains I never noticed when I was here as a student.

I come off the I-89 at the turning for Lowell University and the two-lane road is suddenly steep and dark, bordered by tall trees, a few orange leaves amongst the dark green mass. The road twists and turns downwards for about five miles, a scattering of white board houses amongst the trees. All at once the road flattens, the landscape levels out and in front of me is the Lowell campus: broad and flat with ivy-covered red-brick buildings and a white-painted cupola peeping above the trees. The road takes me round three sides of the green in the centre of the campus, where I lost my virginity to Nicky Bennet. The sprinklers are still there.

So much for my worries about time: having left Boston about two, it's only half past five as I pull into the parking lot of the Lowell Inn, haul my suitcase out of the boot of the car and go to check in. It's posh, with comfy armchairs and spindly antique furniture in the lobby and hardly anyone around. A porter carries my suitcase up to my room before I can stop him and I awkwardly hand him a dollar. He leaves, and I look around me. I have an excellent view of the parking lot and the shops just beyond it, a sofa, a huge television and a coffee machine. The bathroom has shampoo, body lotion, a shower cap and a shoe-cleaning kit but no bubble bath. I kick my shoes off, sit down on the vast bed and suddenly and inexplicably burst into tears.

Later, a little after six, I go out into the town for a walk and to find something to eat, unable to face the prices or the starched linen of the hotel restaurant. The town consists of a few blocks of shops and houses, a kind of appendage to the campus. Maybe there are people living there who have nothing to do with the university, but I never met them the last time I was here. It's quiet, still early, just a handful of students milling around. I guess it gets busy later in the evening.

I remember walking down the main street with Nicky Bennet, idly filling Saturday afternoons when we had nothing better to do. All the shops are closed now so I window-shop for a while, surprised and pleased that almost nothing's changed. Lowell Hardware still has an impressive display of hunting knives in leather sheaths. The windows of the Lowell Co-op are still full of university baseball caps, button-down shirts and expensive leather deck shoes. Ivy Garden is new, with its display of scented candles and upmarket body lotion: maybe I'll buy some bubble bath tomorrow. And then the Lowell Bookstore, which I remember being good for recipe books of down-home New Hampshire cooking but remarkably weak on any kind of book you might possibly need for studying. One Saturday I browsed the cookery shelves looking for a present for my mother while Nicky stood behind me, pressing his erection hard against my backside. In the double-fronted glass windows of the bookstore are photos from next year's Ivy League Men calendar: black and white shots of clean-cut big-jawed hunks playing sports. Years ago I bought copies of the 1985 calendar as presents for my flatmates Katie and Caroline, but things being what they were they stayed in my suitcase and eventually got ripped up.

There are half a dozen restaurants and bars, all in a cluster, all named after someone. I remember Sam's and Molly's, I think, for long intense conversations with Nicky in dark booths at strange times of the day. We'd go out drinking at four or five in the afternoon some days, when the only other person in the bar would be the bartender wiping glasses and laying tables. We'd sit in corners and sometimes just look hungrily at each other, or talk about the sex we planned to have that night.

The other restaurants could be new. Most of them are open, but empty. I look non-committally at the menus in the windows. I'm still feeling a bit shaky and tearful. I'm scared to death of being the only customer, accidentally ordering a huge mound of food I don't like and then having to hide it under my cutlery while the owner and the waitresses all glare at me.

Outside the ice-cream parlour (closed) I sit on a wooden bench and soak up the last of the evening sun. The faint whiff of vanilla reminds me of something: I sat on this bench with my new friend Nancy on a Saturday afternoon, just a couple of weeks after arriving at Lowell. When I told her I'd never tasted Oreo cookies, let alone Oreo cookie ice cream, she bought me a cone. I remember the rich, creamy vanilla and the unexpected chewiness of the dark chocolatey cookie bits. I was wiping ice cream off the tip of my nose when I looked up and saw the tall ginger boy in the strange jacket walking rangily past us on the other side of the street. He was oblivious to my gaze. Nancy nudged me, smiling. She must have seen the way I was looking, because she shook her head and mouthed a long, exaggerated 'No.'

I duck down a side street with no pavements and with grass growing out of the cracks in its tarmac. I'm trying to find a funky dark café I remember, which had picnic tables and paper plates: the kind of place where no one will mind if I don't finish my food. A crisp, clever girl who wrote for the campus newspaper brought me here for what she described as a hero. 'Maybe you know it as a hoagie?' she said, 'Or a sub?' I had no idea what she was on about. It turned out to be a delicious long bread roll stuffed with shredded beef, fried onions, bits of red pepper and mayonnaise. I was having difficulty eating it, struggling to keep the filling inside the roll, and then I saw Nicky sitting at a table across the room. I'd left him in bed just a couple of hours before. He looked straight at me, twitched the right-hand corner of his mouth, then turned away again and ignored me. I must have given off some kind of aroused signal, because the girl I was with put her hand on my knee, worked it up towards my thigh, and asked me if I wanted to go back to her room to watch *Valley of the Dolls* on video. Shocked but a tiny bit flattered, I shook my head and carried on eating the hero, making embarrassed 'this is delicious' noises while she pretended nothing had happened.

The café's closed but at the end of the street, lit up like a beacon, is the open-all-hours Lowell Grocery that I remember so well as the place where we used to buy our emergency post-sex rations. I buy a six-pack of Samuel Adams beer, a large bag of sour-cream-and-chive crinkle-cut chips and some nostalgia-laden Pepperidge Farm Mint Milano cookies, Nicky Bennet's favoured cure for the munchies. Back in my hotel room the

between harsh, staccato sobs, almost hiccups, that made my throat hurt; as if the fact that he wasn't from Savannah was the worst thing in the world.

I make myself a list, the only sure-fire way I know to fight off nagging worries. I'll start by having breakfast. But where? Room service means worries about tipping. The hotel restaurant's wildly expensive. Will Bob's Diner open for breakfast, or is it a lunch and dinner only kind of place? Maybe coffee and a muffin from a street-corner stand. Then I'll buy some bubble bath, the panacea for all ills. That achieved, I'll revisit some old haunts – Nicky's old room, if I can remember which one it was – and then go to the registrar's office and search the college records for anything about him that I can find. I'll try this alumni net thing (I don't actually know what 'alumni' means but I'm sure I'll find out). I'll look through back copies of the college newspaper, maybe on microfiche. I'll talk to the people in the admissions office. Main priority: to find out Nicky Bennet's place of birth and old home address and anything that will give me a lead on where he might have disappeared to. Simple.

At Bob's Diner they give me a seat at the counter. I eat about half a gigantic mound of

French toast, which is served with maple syrup, strawberries and four slices of bacon fried so crisp that you could snap it in half. The waitress who tops up my coffee mug from time to time looks like she could be friendly, just not today or with me. I'd imagined myself striking up conversations with people in restaurants who'd turn out to remember Nicky Bennet when he was here; maybe they'd have some kind of amusing anecdote or insight into his character. Instead, I perch nervously on the counter stool, move the food around my plate to make it look like I've eaten more than I have, then work out a fifteen per cent tip and leave the money under the coffee mug. 'Thanks!' I say to the back of the waitress as I get down awkwardly from the high stool. 'That was great.'

'Uh-huh,' she replies.

Two girls in clean pressed jeans and pastel sweaters dart curious looks at me as I walk through the double doors of the dorm building where Nicky Bennet used to live. 'Hi, can I help you?' says one of them over-brightly, as if talking to a young child or an idiot.

'Um, I'm just visiting a friend,' I say, and she says, 'Okay! Have a nice day,' but as she and her friend leave I'm sure I hear them giggling. I don't know if it's my accent or my age that they find so funny.

Nothing much has changed. The noticeboard in the foyer is still full of posters for frat parties ('Rage 'Til Dawn with Rho Tau Delta!') and handbills from students planning road trips and looking for people to share the cost and driving duties, each one fringed at the bottom with tear-off tabs with a phone number. I climb two flights of stairs and wander down the corridor, trying to remember which was Nicky's room. He had a wipe-clean memo board on his door – we all did – and he'd leave me messages if we hadn't made plans. Brief, to-the-point messages, like 'Meet me in the bar, 9 p.m., 2morrow.'

Orders, places to be, delicious anticipation.

This is the door, I think. Now there's a Limp Bizkit poster dotted with neon-coloured Post-It notes. 'Rho Tau Delta, 10 p.m. – if not, Thayer Bar.' I wonder who the message is for, if there's a love story behind it or just a group of mates going out drinking. I knock on the door and I'm not quite sure why I'm here. After a few minutes a very pale guy with spiky hair and a pierced lower lip puts his head round the door and I splutter out some kind of explanation. 'Cool,' he says and invites me in.

His name is Bryce and he's wearing a striped towelling bathrobe that I guess his parents bought him. His girlfriend lounges on the bed in a T-shirt and jeans. 'You mean Nicky Bennet lived in this room?' she says, saucer-eyed. 'Bryce, did you know this and not tell me? Jeez, you mean Nicky Bennet probably slept in this very same bed. Hey Bryce, NICKY BENNET.'

She prods him with a languorous finger as Bryce taps cigarette ash on the floor and does his best to look mildly impressed. The girlfriend does a mock erotic shimmy. 'Nicky Bennet,' she repeats, this time to herself, and then suddenly the penny drops. She stares straight at me and says, 'You mean you were Nicky Bennet's girlfriend?' and she puts all sorts of shades of disbelief into the last word. 'When was this? Are you sure? I mean, I thought he was only about thirty or something.'

And then maybe she sees something in my eyes because she quickly says, 'Shit. Sorry. That was like, so rude. Listen, my girlfriend Susie is sooo into Nicky Bennet. She's been virtually in mourning since he disappeared. She would just die to meet you. Come to the bar tonight, yeah? And tell us all about him.'

I wander down Frat Row towards the river. Down at the river bank there's a new dock with lifebelts and a built-in barbecue. There's no one else there. I sit down on the edge, take off my sandals, dangle my feet in the cool water and wonder how old I really look. I close my eyes, take long deep breaths and think myself back all those years. Nicky, comparing prehensile toes with me. Nicky, kissing me with his dry lips. Nicky, asking me about my sister. And for a moment I can almost feel him sitting next to me. I shiver, and suddenly I imagine something with such conviction that I almost believe it's true. He killed himself here. That's what his note was trying to tell me. He killed himself here, on the swimming dock, where he talked to me about suicide. He secretly made his way back here and slipped silently into and under the dark water.

I wonder if I could get the police to drag the river. But maybe his body's floated downstream by now. I try to work out where the current would take it. Maybe it will turn up on a deserted New England beach, unrecognisable but for the tattered rags of his Nudie jacket. Maybe I'll be called to identify it. I allow myself another shiver, then open my eyes and watch the water gently lapping my toes.

28

I know what I'm scared of. I'm scared of walking into the admissions office, blushing and saying 'actually' about a million times as I ask my question, and then a woman with a name badge, New Hampshire's equivalent of Lanyon Slidell, frowning and saying, 'Nicky Bennet the movie star? What makes you think he was ever at Lowell?'

Except what the woman with the name badge in the office says to me, once she's finished frowning, is, 'Are you a journalist? We're not allowed to talk to any journalists about Nicky Bennet.'

I smile – almost laugh – with a huge sense of relief. I'm not making it up. I didn't simply imagine the whole thing. Nicky Bennet really was at Lowell. I'm not the first person to ask. I collect my thoughts. 'No, no, I'm not a journalist actually, just an old friend. I was here – eighty-four – here at Lowell, on an exchange term. I'm just driving through New England, on holiday actually, I mean, on vacation. I thought it would be fun to, you know, come and look around and see what I could find out about my old friends. Not just Nicky Bennet, but, you know, the others too . . .'

For once my stammering, blushing English-ness serves me well. How can I be a journalist? A journalist would have a smooth, convincing line of patter. The lady with the badge, whose name is Dorothy Farriss, warms to me. 'An exchange student?' she says, in an almost English New England accent. 'What college were you from?'

I name it, and her face breaks into a smile. 'Oh my dear, do you know something? That exchange programme is still going strong. We've only just said goodbye to a charming girl from London, an Indian girl but quite delightful, who was with us here for the summer.'

She offers me the services of the alumni database. 'I do know there's nothing about Nicky Bennet on it, but if any of your other friends are likely to have joined the Alumni Net we'll be able to trace their whereabouts for you. Would you like to give me some names to check?'

And that's where my plan breaks down. What other friends? Of the other friends I had at Lowell the only one whose name I remember is Nancy, and once I took up with Nicky I hardly spoke to her again. I have no idea of her surname; in fact, I don't think I ever knew it. Dorothy's waiting for me, still smiling. If I don't come up with a name she won't believe me, and then I'm almost sure I won't be able to get access to the library or any college records. She's my only hope. I trawl through my memory, and suddenly a name comes to me from nowhere. Not someone I knew, but a name that stuck in my mind because it was so extraordinary. The name I once thought belonged to the tall, beautiful ginger boy with the strange, garish jacket. 'Alexander Esterhazy?' I say, and Dorothy gasps with pleasure, clasps her hands together and smiles at me with her head on one side.

'No need to search the database for Alex,' she says. 'I know exactly where he is. He organises all the alumni events for your year. I often speak to him. I'll give you his number. He'll be delighted to speak to you.'

*

The next morning I wander around the town and campus, walking off my hangover and finding things to do while I summon up the courage to ring Alexander Esterhazy at the restaurant Dorothy tells me he owns, 'way down in North Carolina.' I could leave now, go back to England and forget the whole thing. I could fly down to North Carolina, walk into Alexander's Bar and Grill, fling my arms wide and say, 'Alex! Darling! Long time no see!' Or I could ring him up and say, 'Er, maybe you remember me, maybe not, but anyway, you know, whatever, I don't suppose you know anything about Nicky Bennet, do you?'

My stomach is in turmoil and my mouth is so dry that I have to stop at every water fountain I pass. I didn't intend to have a hangover. I'd meant to have a quiet night in my hotel room, eating room service and watching TV. But around nine my phone rang and it was the girl I'd met that morning, proud of herself for tracking me down. I found myself out drinking with a bunch of students, in the selfsame bar where I first spoke to Nicky Bennet. I kept saying that to people as they plied me with questions and drinks. 'The selfsame bar. The selfsame banquette,' and what a silly word that is when you say it out loud. Bonkette.

29

Nicky Bennet is still missing. The free copy of *USA Today* that I am given on the plane confirms it. America is still baffled. In a way I'm pleased. At least it makes me feel better about my own lousy detective skills. Last night, looking at my road atlas, I realised that I was about to retrace my steps virtually all the way back to Georgia. The driving-time chart on the back page of the atlas revealed I could have driven from Savannah to Alexander Esterhazy's home on the North Carolina coast in about a day. I've been in America for five days, travelled thousands of miles, and what have I found out? That Nicky Bennet doesn't come from Savannah and that I'm a drunken slapper. I've managed to embarrass myself in front of a bunch of students half my age and spent a large part of my inheritance on flights up and down the eastern seaboard of the USA. I've discovered one other thing: that a man I don't even remember meeting has such fond memories of me that he's invited me to stay for as long as I like. 'Cool,' he said when I eventually rang him. 'Jesus, it's so good to hear from you.'

Alexander Esterhazy. I push my seat back, eat airline pretzels, drink my miniature can of Diet Coke, and try once again to remember if I ever met Alexander Esterhazy. What would he look like? Tall, exotic, mysterious. Where's the name from? Eastern Europe somewhere – wasn't there an Esterhazy involved in something we studied in history at school? The Austro-Hungarian Empire, maybe. He'd be thin and dark, with smouldering eyes. I remember Dorothy's reaction. Oh, he's probably gay if middle-aged women like him so much. A tall, exotic, effete restaurateur, probably with designer stubble.

A fat bloke with dark sticky-up hair, a goatee beard and a bright blue shirt worn untucked to cover his paunch greets me at the arrivals gate. He hurls his arms around me and I'm enveloped in a bear hug, my feet off the ground. 'It's you!' he says. 'I can't believe it. I was thinking about you just the other day.'

I'm still getting my breath back as he leads me to his car. He's dragging my wheeled suitcase with one hand and his other hand is firmly holding mine. He looks at my fingernails. 'Thank God,' he says, mock dramatically. 'You've recovered from that tragic condition that turned them green.'

And then he catches sight of my sandaled feet, still with the chipped remains of the iridescent blue polish. 'Uh-oh. Spoke too soon. It's spread to your toes.'

He hurls my case into the back of his car, leans on the roof, his chin in his hands, and stares at me. He's smiling and shaking his head. He says things like, 'My God' and 'I can't believe it' and 'You look great,' and all the while I'm thinking, I have never seen this man before in my entire life.

'I was thinking about the last time I saw Nicky Bennet,' Alexander Esterhazy says. 'He was here filming a couple of years back.'

I look out of the car window at the sprawl of fast-food places, motels and malls, and then at Alexander in disbelief. 'Here? Filming?'

'Hey, wait until we hit town. You'll understand. There's a lot of filming goes on here. They make *Dawson's Creek* here. You can tour the studios. *Blue Velvet*. *Teenage Mutant Ninja Turtles*. All made here. Honestly.' He turns to me and I realise that his eyes precisely match his blue shirt. Honest eyes. Eyes I have no recollection of ever seeing before. 'Anyway, he was here filming that FBI thing, you know, the one with Reuben Scott? He came into the bar with some of the team, posed for photos, signed some stuff. Just thought it might make a good piece for your book.'

Ah yes, my book. My little white lie. My alibi. Alexander thinks I'm writing a book about Nicky Bennet. On the phone I thought it sounded much less weird than my real reason for coming: obsessively revisiting the past to find out where Nicky Bennet has disappeared to. 'So you keep in touch with him?' I ask.

'Yeah, we talk most weeks on the phone. E-mail all the time. Great friends.'

'Really?'

He turns to me with those blue eyes and roars with laughter. 'No! Jesus, I've never known a guy so keen to forget his past. Try getting Nicky Bennet to a class reunion. But, hey, we were room-mates once so I figured it was worth trying to get him to come to the bar while he was in town. He stayed – ooh – thirty minutes maybe? Big star.'

He stares ahead at the road, shaking his head and smiling to himself. Then, 'Shit. So you've just realised that you've flown all the way down here to talk to a guy who's seen Nicky Bennet once for thirty minutes in the last twenty years.'

'It's okay. It's his past I want to talk about.' Because that's where I think I'll find the answer to the clues in his note.

We drive through a neighbourhood of attractive old houses, with porches and pillars and circular towers, and then turn on to a cobbled back street. Alexander makes a sharp, difficult turn into a tiny alleyway at the back of a weathered clapboard building and then leads me up a narrow wooden outside staircase to the first floor. Second floor, of course: I'm in America. 'Go on through while I go get your case,' he says, pushing me forwards. I walk through a tiny galley kitchen with saucepans hanging from the ceiling and pots of herbs clustered together on the cramped windowsill, across a small landing cluttered with coats, boots and a mountain bike, and into one of the most beautiful rooms I have ever seen.

Beautiful. Actually, maybe that's not the right word. More like comfortable. Likeable. Instantly liveable-in. Just how I'd like my own living room to look. It's big and white and tall, with a floor-to-ceiling bay window at the far end, half-obscured by white wooden shutters. There are two squishy dark brown leather sofas facing each other across the wooden floor, a faded ethnic rug between them. There's a widescreen TV in one corner, an impressive-looking stereo system in another. I sneak a quick look at the CDs on the rack. Wilco. Matthew Sweet. Neil Young. And, unexpectedly, Echo and the Bunnymen. 'You see?' says Alexander's voice, suddenly behind me. 'You've had a great influence on my musical tastes.'

He pulls open the shutters, hauls up the sash window and instantly the room is full of sea air and the sound of seagulls. I look out. We are on the waterfront and the view goes on for ever.

'I've put your case in the spare bedroom upstairs.' He interrupts my reverie. 'I've got to go downstairs and get started. I guess you'll want to wash up and stuff. Make yourself at home, then come on down to the bar when you're ready and I'll fix you something to eat.'

Alex sits me at the bar and pours me a beer, pushing a dish of peanuts towards me. A young blonde waitress with a silver ring through her eyebrow drifts in from the kitchen, tying a little white apron round her short black skirt. 'Kirsten,' he says, 'here's someone I want you to meet. Remember I was telling you about the girl with green nails, the weird British student who was in love with Nicky Bennet?'

Kirsten throws such a cool glance at me that I wonder if they're sleeping together. 'Yeah?' she says, as if she doesn't have the energy to feign interest.

'Well,' he says with a flourish. 'Ta-da!'

'Cool,' she says, and sniffs. 'Do you want me to do the specials board?'

30

'I need to ask you something,' says Alex as he cooks me breakfast in his tiny kitchen the next morning. 'You don't actually remember me, do you?'

I squirm.

'Go on, it's okay, I can take it. I guess I'm simply not that memorable.'

'Um, I don't know,' I say. 'Didn't we meet at a frat party or something?'

It's bound to be true, since that's where I met most people at Lowell. Alex tosses his head back and laughs, a big, booming, boisterous laugh. It occurs to me that he looks like he should be a lumberjack, or maybe the guy you always get in an American high-school-reunion movie; the one who never left his home town and took over the family plumbing business from his widowed alcoholic father. He looks like he should be married to his childhood sweetheart.

Last night he sat me in a prime seat at the bar, at right angles to the room so that I could watch the comings and goings in the restaurant. He kept me topped up with beer and brought me plates of food. 'I remember you had one of those birdlike British appetites,' he said, and kept me supplied with little plates of starters: nachos, chicken wings, chillies stuffed with cream cheese and deep-fried in batter. I watched him, Kirsten and another waitress serving the customers, and sat in a mellow trance as I realised how choreographed and balletic they were as they moved among the tables with their huge trays of food. For a fat bloke, Alexander was very light on his feet. The restaurant was by no means full, but it was buzzing. Every time Alex brought me a plate of food we had another snatched conversation, and I tried to put the clues together to remember the circumstances under which he'd come to know so much about me.

'You still really into music?' he said. 'Are Echo and the Bunnymen still together?' And, another time, 'I guess you've got some cool job in London?'

I fumbled some replies together: 'Yeah,' 'No, I don't think so,' and 'Er, not quite.'

I was about to say, well actually I work in a bookshop. In a small city. On the coast. It's quite *near* London, I suppose. Well, near in American terms, anyway. But before I could, Alexander flung his huge ham of an arm around me, squashed me painfully, and said, 'And now you're here writing a book about Nicky Bennet, the Hollywood star who broke your heart. Good for you. You show him what he's missing.'

'Tri-Bete,' says Alex as he pushes a red and green pepper-flecked omelette onto my plate, and for a moment I think he's saying, 'Try to eat.' 'I think it was one of the legendary Tri-Bete parties. You know, Beta Beta Beta?' he explains to my blank face. 'We sat on the porch outside the frat house in the early hours one morning and you told me this great story all about your freaky shoes. Then you made me promise to playlist Echo and the Bunnymen on WLWL.'

'Oh.' A memory leaps into my head. A fat no-hoper in khaki shorts. Stout, hairy, bare legs. I was explaining my shoes to him. I had this pair of shoes that summer that I really loved. I'd bought them at Camden Market and they were white leather, completely flat, with long pointed toes. They'd started to fall apart but because I loved them so much I'd started mending them with silver gaffer tape, winding it around them to keep the soles attached to the uppers. I'd worked the story of the shoes into a kind of comedy routine, and I remember it made Alex laugh – guffaw – so much that he nearly fell off the porch.

'You were head of music on the radio station, weren't you?' I say, delighted at the memory. It all becomes clear now. He was a nice guy. I used to talk to him quite often at parties if there was no one else there I knew. But like all the guys who worked on the campus station he was a little intense and nerdy, as if he should have been in the chess club but had got lucky.

'Yeah. Now we're getting somewhere.'

'Did you ever tell me your name?'

'I dunno. I guess I thought maybe you knew it. But why would you? You only ever had eyes for Nicky Bennet. There was one night. A group of us were in the bar. Nicky Bennet was there too, and you were trying real hard to pretend you hadn't even noticed him. You spent all night talking to me. I thought you were really cool and funny. Kinda strange and "London".' He does inverted commas with his fingers. 'I don't know what we talked about, but I remember your face was flushed and I think you let me kiss you. When I got back to my room that night I figured that maybe I stood a chance. Next thing I knew, you were spending your whole time slavishly following Nicky Bennet around and obviously I'd blown it.'

I stare at Alex, slightly open-mouthed. He tells the story well, with a kind of droll self-deprecating look on his face. Of course I remember that night: it was the first time I ever spoke to Nicky. I can remember the feel of the worn velvet banquette through my thin hand-sewn skirt, and the way I squirmed in my seat to hide the wetness in my knickers. 'Oh,' I say, and 'Sorry,' because I feel the need to apologise: not for not recognising him but for the misunder-standing all those years ago. Alex was right. I had flirted with him just to make Nicky notice me. I can remember leaning on a solid chest that was covered by a brushed cotton shirt, maybe even playing with a bristly beard. 'Did you have a beard then?' I say, and he looks embarrassed and says, 'Well, sorta. You know, stubble. I thought it made me look cool.'

And I wonder why, if he's embarrassed by his stubbly past, he has a goatee now. Does he not learn from his facial-hair mistakes?

'I've done you a list,' he says and, seeing my puzzled face, he adds, 'Source material. People you might want to talk to, magazines you could try.' Obviously I'm still looking baffled. 'You know, for your book?'

Ah yes, my book. And as I sit on Alex's soft brown leather sofa in his beautiful airy living room, as the motes of dust dance in the autumn sunshine and I read the list, in bold, surprisingly flowery handwriting on a page of cream writing paper, I think: why not? It's obvious. Of course I should write a book. I'm sure I can write as well as the next person. I'm literate. I know about books. I even have contacts in publishing, albeit of a very tenuous sort. It wouldn't be a biography but a 'memoir'; one of those short, sharp, slim books that are so popular these days, the ones that sit by the till and get snapped up as an impulse buy. I can even imagine the blurb: 'The bitter-sweet true story of a fairy-tale romance that spanned two continents and two summers.' It could be a huge surprise hit: this year's *Longitude* or *Nathaniel's Nutmeg*. Perhaps I'll get invited onto a Radio 4 programme like *Start The Week* or *Woman's Hour* to promote it. I can't believe I didn't think of it before.

Alexander Esterhazy will have to have an acknowledgement in the book. I find the first item on his suggested source list exactly where he says it will be, in a cardboard box under the spare bed. Back copies of *The Lowellian*, a publication that I never even noticed in my entire three months at college there. I settle down to read every edition for 1984. Scene-setting is an important part of any memoir, and I'm looking for indicators of the *Zeitgeist*. I discover over the course of the next couple of hours that there is a whole side to Lowell life I never even noticed. This is a world where men play lacrosse while wearing masks, the wimps. At my school, girls were always getting their noses or jaws broken playing lacrosse, and no one ever suggested wearing masks. This is a world where there could be serious debate about the rights and wrongs of a woman, Geraldine Ferraro, standing for vice-president. The piece in favour was written by someone called Nancy Marshall, and it occurs to me this could well be my campus feminist friend. The listings for the campus station WLWL reveal that Alexander Esterhazy presented the weekly Alt Rock programme as well as a show called *Britscene*, which sounds too dreadful to contemplate. I speculate on whether my London insights steered his musical choice beyond playlisting Echo and the Bunnymen; and then I wonder indignantly why he never offered me a guest-presenter slot. Perhaps because he was so miffed that I dropped him for Nicky Bennet.

I pay special attention to reviews of art and photography exhibitions and college drama productions, wondering if there's any mention of Nicky Bennet, but he might as well not have existed. I scour any group photographs and any casual shots of the campus, looking for a glimpse of Nicky or his jacket. Nothing. Just one little paragraph catches my eye, though, a notice of a forthcoming gig at one of the bars in town. The band third on the bill are called The Grievous Angels. Nicky's hero Gram Parsons made an album called *Grievous Angel*; I bought it a few years back when it was re-released on a double CD. I look through the next couple of editions of *The Lowellian*, searching for a review of the gig, but find nothing. It's a tantalising fragment. It

31

'The Grievous Angels?' says Alex, yawning hugely. 'Oh yeah, God, I'd forgotten them. The worst band of all time.'

He's lying full-length on his sofa, his big sausage fingers interlinked and resting complacently on his paunch. It's late, long after closing time, and we're drinking beer in mellow companionship.

'Was Nicky Bennet involved in the band?'

'He *was* the band. Well, him and his girlfriend. What was her name? I forget. She was short, looked like a boy, had this aggressive punker haircut.'

'Did she have a big fifties car?' I can see the car with the shiny sci-fi fins pulling up at the Greyhound station, and Nicky offering me a lift. It feels as if I'm filling in pieces of a jigsaw.

'Yeah,' he says, delighted by the memory. 'I loved that car. But as a band, God, they were awful. I don't think either of them could play a note. He would stand at the mike and kinda declaim lyrics while she played maracas or something. I think he thought that he was a male Patti Smith. That's why it's so weird he became such a big star because he was always pretty much a laughing stock on campus.'

Alex heaves himself upright and goes to get more beer from the kitchen. 'Martha,' he calls.

'Um, I'm Justine?'

He's laughing as he comes back in. 'No, I mean that was *her* name. Martha. Martha Johnson. Jansen. Jensen? Anyway, I'll check it out for you. I'm bound to have her details on file. Maybe you should talk to her? She's probably the person who knew Nicky best. I think they went off to Europe together one summer. I think it was quite serious between them at one point.'

I try to stifle an involuntary shiver. Alex doesn't seem to notice. He stretches out and runs one hand through his thick hair and makes it stick up in another direction. The motion lifts his shirt a few inches, revealing an ample and darkly forested belly. 'I shouldn't have said that, about

Nicky Bennet being a laughing stock. I mean, that's pretty insensitive if he was the love of your life or something.'

'Scarcely. He was just a guy who seemed special for a while,' I say, reminding myself of the pretentious prat, the coward, the up-his-own-arse poser. The trouble is, ever since he disappeared, I've been thinking more and more about the Nicky I was in love with, the Nicky who wanted to marry me. 'Alex, how well did you know him?'

'Ah,' he says. 'Now there's a question. How well did any of us know him?' He leans forward, clutching his goatee, as if he's a hard-hitting TV interviewer.

I sigh. 'Yeah, yeah, but how well did *you* know him?'

'I knew him when he had two Ts in his last name. Nicholson Bennett. A strange, shy boy from the Midwest. He was my room-mate for one semester in our freshman year. We both liked music, neither of us played sports. We had stuff in common.'

I don't know what to react to first. Nicholson? Two Ts? The Midwest? *Shy?* 'So, what happened?'

'I dunno. He changed his name, turned up in that strange jacket and the cowboy boots and started lying. Fantasising. Whatever. One whole semester he'd been brought up on a Wyoming cattle ranch. Full of tales about castrating bulls and eating prairie oysters. Girls seemed to like it. Lowell gets a lot of students from other colleges, maybe just doing one semester, transferring credits, whatever. So there was always plenty of fresh blood, new women to fall for his stories. What was his line with you?'

'Savannah. Savannah, Georgia. Shit. I thought he had the most beautiful accent in the world.' I'm sitting on Alex's leather sofa with my arms wrapped around myself, feeling almost as bad as I did on the park bench in Savannah. 'I've just been to Savannah,' I say, my voice starting to crack, 'and ever since then I've been trying to remember what accent Nicky had when he came over to England to find me. It's like it's really important to me, you know?'

I look across to Alex and he's staring at me with his mouth open. 'England? He came to England to find you?'

'Yeah. A year later. He turned up on the doorstep. We lived together for a while. We were going to get married. He knelt on the beach and proposed to me.'

My own voice sounds incredulous as I say this. How can it be true? I know it is true, but how can it be? Alex looks flabbergasted. 'God,' he says, and then for greater emphasis, 'Jesus. Nicky Bennet flew to England a whole year later and proposed to you? Jesus. That's, like, a whole new ball game.'

I hate that expression. 'Alex, you're a bloke . . .' Another expression I hate: I only ever start sentences with those words when I'm drunk.

He laughs. 'A "bloke".'

'What's so funny?'

'Nothing. I love your voice, that's all.'

That rings a bell. 'What you really mean is, it's so British and toneless and couldn't-give-a-shit,' I say bitterly.

'Is that what Nicky told you?'

I nod. It still hurts. 'But anyway, Alex, you're a guy . . .' I say 'guy' with an exaggerated American accent.

'Yeah. Sure am.' He proudly pats his belly.

'Would you fly all the way to England to propose to someone unless you really loved them?'

He leans forward on the sofa, deep in thought. 'First of all, I'd like to point out that I am not, nor ever have been, an expert on love. I'm a divorced guy in a casual relationship with a twenty-two-year-old Gen X waitress with a ring through her eyebrow, God help us. But I can't think of any other reason but love for flying to England and proposing to someone.' He laughs. 'I love the fact that Nicky Bennet fell in love with you. Makes me feel much better. I guess you really got under his skin.' He smiles to himself and tugs on his hair again. Then, 'So, what happened? Why didn't you get married?'

How can I answer that? I don't know. It all seemed to be going so well and then he just walked out on me, leaving a message scrawled in lipstick on the mirror. 'Thanx 4 evrything,' it said, and at least the way he spelt it helped ease my heartbreak. Over the next few weeks the ghost of the message reappeared every time I took a bath and the mirror steamed up. Just before I got tearful I would steel myself and say, 'Justine, in your heart of hearts, could you really live with the kind of man who writes "thanx 4 evrything"?'

To Alex, I give the only reason I've ever given anyone. 'It was real life,' I say. 'I was a different person, a grown-up. I was holding down a job, paying rent, cooking meals, trying to be responsible. I think he was too immature to cope with real life.'

32

Despite my advanced age I have a kind of standing agreement with my mum that I will phone her regularly every time I go abroad, just to let her know that I'm okay. Alex says I can ring her from the restaurant, so I call around three on Sunday afternoon, while I'm earning my keep wiping tables. A man answers, and it takes me a few seconds to place the voice. 'Simon?'

And before I can ask him what he's doing there on a Sunday evening he launches into a tirade against me, his voice full of self-righteous older-brotherliness. 'Where have you been? Mum's out of her mind with worry. How could you do this to her?'

'Do what?'

'Disappear like that.'

'I haven't disappeared. I told her I was going to

America for a few weeks. That's where I am.' A cold thought strikes me. 'Simon, she's not going senile, is she? She hasn't forgotten I was going away, has she?'

'No, of course she hasn't. But she doesn't know where you are. All she's heard from you is one strange phone call from a call box. Where are you staying?'

'Oh, now, Simon. Don't be stupid. I'm travelling in America, I'm a grown-up and I have a credit card. I'm perfectly safe.'

Alex has come out of the kitchen and overheard the last few words. He catches my eye and we do a 'Tsk! Parents!' shrug at each other. Simon says, 'I'm putting Mum on. She'll tell you why she's so upset.'

'Oh love,' she says. 'It was all over the paper. It was all about that thing you said Nicky Bennet did, and then it said you'd disappeared as well.'

I sit down suddenly on one of the bar stools. Daniel. It must be Daniel. He's sold a story about me to the paper. But for some reason I visualise the local paper, my mum's usual newspaper of choice, always full of tragic tots and local traders up in arms. 'Assistant manager of local bookshop in Nicky Bennet scandal,' it would say, and then a picture of the shop and maybe Paul, my boss, looking scandalised. But what scandal? What thing that Nicky Bennet did? What story has Daniel sold?

My mum's still talking. 'You could have told me, love. Is that why you went all quiet and never talked about him again? You should have said. I'm much more open-minded than you might think.'

And of course, I can't ask Mum to tell me exactly what it says in the paper. I can't let her know that there's more than one thing I could have said about Nicky Bennet that, in the hands of a tabloid journalist, could be shocking and scandalous. Simon comes back on the phone. 'You need to ring your boyfriend Gavin,' he says curtly. 'He wants an explanation.'

'Simon, there's no need to be like that. If I'd known I'd disappeared I would have called sooner.'

I've never heard Gavin so angry before. His voice is quiet, completely flat and monotonous, but it sounds as if it's being forced out through clenched teeth. I can imagine him holding the phone so tight that his knuckles are white. He tells me that he's disappointed in me, horrified at what I've done, that I'm a bitch, a thoughtless cow, not a nice person at all. It seems that he's most concerned about my apparent betrayal of a past love. 'How could you sell out Nicky Bennet like that?' he says, and I still don't know what I'm supposed to have said.

'I think it was when I was drunk,' I say. 'I think Daniel stitched me up.'

'Yes, well,' in an icy cold voice. 'Well, that would figure. I think it's about time you realised you drink too much.' And then we get to the real reason why Gav is so cross: 'It was in the *Sun*. One of the guys at work was reading it when I went into the coffee room. There he was, holding up a copy of the *Sun* with you on the front page and that headline. Imagine how I felt.'

'Gav, what headline?'

'Come on, Justine. You can't have been so drunk that you don't remember what you said. Do you have Internet access where you are? Check out the *Sun*'s website, and you'll see exactly why I'm so upset.' Then he pauses, takes a deep breath, and in something closer to his normal voice he says, 'Justine, I've made an important decision. I don't think I want to see you again.'

Alex's computer is upstairs, perched on an old table in a corner of his bedroom. He turns it on for me and logs on to the Internet. Then, discreetly, he makes himself scarce while I sit on the corner of the bed hyperventilating and trying to summon up the courage to check out the article that Gavin was talking about. To put off the inevitable, I nose around. The bed is one of those huge wooden sleigh-style beds, curved up at the head and bottom and covered with a big fringed tartan blanket and proper white sheets. The room is directly above the living room and there's the same endless sea view from the window. There are some photographs on the windowsill. One is a wedding photo: Alex in a tuxedo and bow tie and one of those horrible cutaway stand-up collars that snooker players wear. He's standing next to a strong-faced dark-haired woman with a heavy fringe and a severely elegant wedding dress. Then there's a picture of a tiny premature baby in an incubator, with a crocheted hat and bootees that are far too big. I hold the photo, wondering if this is the story behind Alex's divorce, and then I say to myself, 'Come on, Justine. Get this over with.'

I take a deep breath and open the website. There's a list of stories to click on, one called 'Nicky Bennet latest'. I open it, but it seems I've accidentally clicked on the second page first. There are a couple of short paragraphs under the heading 'Nicky Bennet's Secret Life', obviously a continuation of the front-page story. I can make out one line in bold near the end: **Now she too has disappeared**. I take another deep breath and click on the first page.

I'm holding my hands like a cage in front of my face, obscuring part of my field of vision, the way I used to watch scary bits of *Doctor Who*. The first thing I see is a photo from a few years ago of Nicky with long hair, round about the time of *Summer's Lease*, I should think. Then there's a picture of me, sort of. It's me a long time ago. I'm nineteen or twenty, maybe second year at university, and my hair's all spiky and pushed up at the front like Kim Wilde's. I'm wearing my dad's old dinner jacket over some kind of cut-off T-shirt, and dangly earrings in the shape of fuchsias. My blusher, in diagonal lines that take no notice of the natural contours of my face, looks like it's been applied with a paint roller. I'm holding what looks suspiciously like a bottle of Blue Nun, and I'm pouring some into a glass. I think the photo was taken by Caroline at one of our occasional girls' nights out. I think maybe I gave it to Daniel myself, back when he was my student boyfriend.

It's when I take my hands from my face and look at the whole page, including the headline, that my blood runs cold. I know blood doesn't really run cold; I know it's a cliché. But how else can you describe that feeling when your whole body does an involuntary shudder and you get goose pimples on the backs of your hands and the back of your neck?

The headline's in huge black letters, almost filling the entire page. What it says is this: **KINKY NICKY BROKE MY ARM**. And then a smaller sub-headline: **Sordid Sex Secrets of Missing Star**. The story begins with these words: 'A former girlfriend of missing film star Nicky Bennet has revealed the actor enjoyed violent sex sessions, and once beat her up so badly that he broke her arm.'

I stuff my knuckles into my mouth as far as they will go and I hear myself make a funny high-pitched noise somewhere at the back of my throat. Oh shit. The thing is, it's almost true. Not quite true, but almost; like a Chinese-whispers version of what really happened. I can't believe I was so drunk, so off guard, that I chose to tell Daniel about the night when Nicky broke my wrist. My wrist, not my arm, but that's about the only factual error in the story. That, and my participatory role in the incident. I stare at the computer screen, at that unforgiving headline, so crude and so black and white, so brutally ignorant of any possibility of subtlety, and I feel angry, confused and sweaty with guilt. Nicky trusted me enough to leave me a special clue in his note, one that only I would understand, and this is how I repay him.

Alex comes into the bedroom as I'm closing down the document. He's holding a steaming mug of something. 'I made you herbal tea,' he says, pronouncing it 'erbal'. I hate herbal tea. It's nothing but warm coloured water. But I take the mug anyway, warming my hands around it. I follow him back down into the living room. 'Shouldn't you be at work?'

'Sunday night,' he says. 'We don't open Sunday nights.' He looks across at me, sharply. 'So, was it bad?'

'Yeah, pretty bad.' I explain as well as I can. 'It's like one thing I said has been blown all out of proportion and now the whole world thinks I've done the dirty on Nicky Bennet.'

I say this in a really casual voice as I slump onto Alex's sofa, but there are tears in my eyes before I finish the sentence, and pretty soon they're running down my cheeks. Alex puts a CD on, some kind of woozy, sad American alt-country stuff. He turns and sees me crying, and then comes to sit next to me. He puts his arm round me and pats my shoulder gently. 'Hey,' he says.

'And now it's out there I can't get it back.'

Alex's hand moves to my head, brushing my hair away from the right-hand side of my face with delicate, circular movements. He repeats the motion again and again, almost subconsciously, as I think about Daniel and about Gavin. 'Oh fuck,' I say with feeling, full of self-disgust and irritated regret. 'Oh fuck. What am I going to do?'

He jumps up suddenly. 'Something everyone should do when they've had a shock. We're going for a walk on the beach.'

33

There's a cold wind off the dark grey sea as we tramp along the beach through the damp sand. I'm wearing a cagoule and boots that almost fit me, magicked somehow from the pile of coats on Alex's landing. There's no one about, just a band of giant seagulls circling and calling. The sound reminds me of home. The sun is setting over the town, which now looks tiny against the huge streaky orange sky. We walk companionably towards the dark outline of a pier, which is rickety and crooked like an arthritic finger pointing out to sea. Alex turns, walks backwards and talks to me. 'We used to come out here at weekends, me and my wife. We were both in corporate law in Raleigh. We'd get out of town on Fridays, get down here and just walk along the beach and breathe. We used to talk about opening a restaurant here together.'

'So what happened? Why did you get divorced?'

'We had a kid. A little girl. She was premature.' He turns away from me, walks forward again. 'She only lived for seven weeks. She didn't even live long enough to reach the day she should have been born. We just didn't know what to say to each other after that.' He shrugs, turns back to me. 'So we moved on. Whatever. It happens. No big deal.'

I shiver. My hands are freezing. I rub them together, trying to get some feeling back into them. Alex grabs them both with one big hand and winks at me. 'I know how to warm those up,' and before I know what's happening he's lifted up his coat and his shirt, and my hands are on his stomach, nestling in the thick dark hair that feels almost like a carpet. And the strange thing is, it feels nice. His stomach is much firmer than I'd expected and the hair is soft and warm. I stand facing him, my hands warm inside his shirt, his arms around me pulling me closer, his goateed chin resting on the top of my head. I nestle my head against his chest and feel very comfortable.

I'm not a great believer in the road not taken. I think I believe in fate, that what happens to you is the only thing that's meant to happen, and it always happens for a purpose. But a phrase comes into my head, a line from that George Michael song about turning a different corner. Suppose I'd taken a step sideways at Lowell, looked the other way, dated this guy instead of Nicky Bennet: what would have happened? Would we be living here in this town, walking on this beach, kids and the restaurant and the whole thing? Alex kisses my forehead and we snuggle closer together. 'So, here's the thing,' he says. 'If Nicky Bennet hurt you so badly, why are you still chasing after him?'

And the moment's gone. He just doesn't understand. A sharp gust of wind blows, stinging my cheeks and making my eyes water. I pull away. 'Listen. I think maybe I need to be on my own for a while?'

And so I go down to the water's edge. The gentle grey waves make shifting soft shapes on the sand. It feels damp through my jeans as I sit with my hands around my shins and my chin on my knees, licking my lips to feel the salty tang.

I used to take Nicky down to the beach in my home town. It has always been part of what I am.

There's nowhere you can go in my city and not be reminded of the sea. The very air tastes of salt and wherever you go you can hear seagulls. As you drive in from the north and west you see great rusting hulks and grey battleships; from the east you pass salt marshes and hundreds of yachts, their masts clanging in the slightest breeze. I have always thought it a beautiful city, clinging to this belief in the face of all empirical evidence to the contrary.

When I went to university and told people where I came from, the first thing they usually asked was, 'Do you sail?' Some of my school friends sailed, the ones whose dads were lawyers or accountants or high-ranking naval officers. I had my own way of sailing. I'd come down to the seafront on a windy day, stretch out my arms and run, feeling the wind lift and carry me. Nicky Bennet understood. When I showed him how to do it, he smiled right across his face and his eyes lit up. He stretched out his arms and ran, tacking diagonally from side to side of the prom, narrowly missing pedestrians and laughing like a maniac. He got it. He understood.

I wanted to give my city to Nicky. I wanted him to feel about my home town what I felt about

Savannah, Georgia. In his slow, twisty voice he had told me about Spanish moss and ante-bellum houses and I had felt myself swept away. I wanted him to listen to my stories and be swept away too. I wanted him to dream of one day living there, to love the taste of the salt in the air and the feel of the shingle under his feet and his knees. That was why I brought him down to the sea on the day he came to find me.

After my sister Marie died I went to the beach a lot when I should have been at school. I remember sitting there trying to work out if I was sad. I didn't think I was. I couldn't make myself cry, so I probably wasn't sad. In fact, I couldn't see the point of being sad. Marie had been alive, now she was dead and it didn't seem to make much difference to the world either way. But then I worried that if the death of my sister meant nothing to me, then maybe nothing would mean anything ever again. I felt as if I was falling into a hole and maybe going to Hell but probably it didn't matter because even the flames wouldn't hurt me. I was impervious to pain.

The first thing that did mean anything to me after Marie's death was the love of Nicky Bennet. I brought him to the beach and showed him what it meant to me. We sat on a bench by the sea wall, sideways on, at opposite ends of the bench, our feet touching sole to sole. It was windy and we were laughing. I had a tissue in the pocket of my jeans and I remember tearing a corner off and secretly twisting it round and round the ring finger of my left hand because I wanted something tangible to represent the closeness that we were feeling. I remember looking at his face and feeling an intense, pleasurable pain. I loved him so much it hurt. I was almost totally happy.

If Nicky Bennet hurt me so badly, why am I still chasing after him? Because nothing ever has or ever will feel better or truer or deeper than the peculiar brand of pain he made me feel.

34

'Oh Anna,' I cry as she picks up the phone. 'I've really screwed up this time. Gavin's furious. He never wants to see me again.'

There's a pause. I look around Alex's living room, thinking again how much I like it, and wondering how much money I should leave him for all the phone calls I've made. Then, in her curtest, most English voice, Anna says, 'This would be Gavin who's not your boyfriend?'

'He said I wasn't a nice person and that I drink too much.' Anna, bless her, laughs.

'Justine,' she says, 'if I were asked to write down the qualities that I love you for, niceness and sobriety would be nowhere near the top of the list. It doesn't matter. No one who knows you well expects you to be nice or teetotal. You wouldn't be you if you were.'

I'm disconcerted but also a little comforted.

'Now,' she says, 'it doesn't matter about Gavin, does it?'

'I don't think so, except . . .' My voice is cracking. 'The thing is, I don't want to keep hurting him. He's a really nice bloke and it's not his fault that he's too good for me.'

'Talk to him.'

'Who?' For a moment I think she means Alex and I wonder how she knows about him.

'Gavin. He's moping around like a wet weekend. Just tell him. Put the poor bloke out of his misery. He loves you. Tell him you're sorry and for God's sake let him down gently.'

I call Gav at work. They track him down to the bathroom section and he picks up the phone and answers it – 'Bathrooms?' – before he realises it's me.

'Gavin,' I say really quietly.

He says: 'Justine,' in a voice completely and carefully drained of feeling.

'Gav, I'm really sorry I've upset you. Can we talk about it?'

'There's nothing to talk about.' His voice is

very quiet and even. 'You've played around with me all these years, you've had me on a piece of string. And I've finally realised what you're really like: the kind of bitch who would betray a former lover for a cash handout from a tabloid news-paper. What did you get, anyway?'

'Nothing!' I can hear my voice squeak with indignation.

'How could you do it? I mean, can you blame me for being upset? There you are, making out you're so worried about his disappearance, and then suddenly you stick the knife in and tell the world he's a sadistic, brutal thug.'

'I didn't say he was a brutal thug. What I think I actually told Daniel was that Nicky accidentally broke my wrist while we were having sex.' Gavin clears his throat, about to say something. I cut in, angrily. 'And anyway, what the fuck do I owe Nicky Bennet? Why shouldn't I stick the knife in?'

Gavin drops his voice to a hiss. I'd forgotten he was in the middle of the store. No doubt he's surrounded by customers trying to look at bath-room fittings or simply listening to the argument. 'He was the love of your life,' he squeezes out between his teeth.

'Some love,' I mutter. Then I tell Gavin something I've never told anyone before. 'Do you know what he did to me? Do you know how he left me? He broke my wrist, and while I was in hospital having it plastered he walked out on me. He left a crappy note written on my bathroom mirror and I never saw him again.'

Silence. Then, 'I thought it was all hunky-dory and romantic.' Gavin sounds as if I've just told him that Father Christmas doesn't exist. 'You always give the impression it was the love affair to end all love affairs.'

'Suppose you'd gone out with Julia Roberts,' I say. 'You'd tell all your mates, wouldn't you? But you'd miss out the bit about how she walked out on you because she got bored, wouldn't you?'

Gavin gasps, as if I've hit the nail on the head, as if he suspects that's exactly why Julia Roberts would leave him. Suddenly I feel exhausted and overwhelmed. 'Shit, Gavin, it's over. I'm fed up with having to justify myself to you. I'm sorry. It's never going to happen, is it? You deserve someone much nicer.'

I can hear him swallowing hard at the other end of the phone. 'There's a song, isn't there?' he says. 'If you love somebody, let them go.' My

35

It's true. Nicky Bennet left me on the day he broke my wrist. Ironic, really: my wrist and my heart broken on the same day by the same person. And for a while the pain of my broken heart was overshadowed by the discomfort and annoyance of having my right wrist sealed in itchy, heavy plaster in the middle of the summer. I concentrated on tasks like getting dressed, cooking for myself, taking baths with one arm wrapped in a plastic carrier bag. Under normal circumstances I would have rung my mum, gone to stay with my parents for a while. But instead I had to do all these difficult domestic tasks for myself because I knew I couldn't tell my parents Nicky had left – not without breaking down in tears, and I didn't want to upset them all over again. In fact, I still haven't told my mother he's left, although I think she may have realised by now. I couldn't even tell them how I'd broken my wrist.

Nicky didn't mean to do it. It was a Monday night. He was waiting for me on the corner of the street as I walked home from work, and we went for a swim and then had fish and chips on the pier. When we got back to the flat he grabbed me by the hair and kissed me, and we collapsed onto my bed with our lips locked together. We started to pull each other's clothes off, and I caught a look in his eye that gave me a frisson of excitement. Inspired by the look and what it seemed to be telling me, I ripped his shirt off with such violence that it tore. Then I straddled him, pinning him down by the wrists. He wriggled free, biting me on the arm. He pushed me up against the wall and slapped me round the face. I grinned at him and slapped him back. 'Harder,' he said, so I did.

'Again,' he said. 'But much harder. Go on, use your fist. Try and break my nose. You really hate the sight of my face. You want to smash it in.'

I was suddenly uneasy. 'Come on, Justine. Hurt me. Draw blood,' and he took my wrist tightly in his hand and started bending it backwards so that my hand would connect with his face with real force. 'Come on, you know you want to. You know you like it.' And I said, 'No!'

I didn't mean 'No, I don't like it', but something closer to 'No, I don't know whether I like it or not,' or even 'No, I don't want to know whether I like it or not.' I twisted my hand away as he tried again to make me hit him, which was when we heard the bone in my wrist crack. For a split second we looked each other in the eye as if we were both about to laugh, and then I realised how much it hurt and I screamed instead. At which point Nicky did laugh, while simultaneously saying, 'Oh God. Oh shit. Oh God.'

In the taxi on the way to casualty we rehearsed our story. 'You were getting out of the bath when you slipped,' he said.

'But I'd be wet. At least, my hair would be. It takes ages to dry properly.'

'Okay, you fell out of bed. You put your hand out to break your fall.'

'Ah – but what was I doing in bed at this time of the evening?' I grinned and nudged him, feeling comfortable with him again now that strange moment had passed. He put his hand at the back of my neck and kissed me long and hard all over my face, with tongue, teeth and everything.

After we told our story to the nurse in the cubicle she asked Nicky to go and sit in the waiting area. She pulled the curtains around the cubicle and asked me to tell her the story again. Then she said, 'I see,' with a weird look on her face.

They wouldn't let Nicky come down with me when I went to be X-rayed and plastered. After they put the plaster on, I was taken to a little room with floral curtains and a settee. A woman in a blouse with a bow at the neck came in and sat down beside me. 'Is there anything you'd like to tell me?' she said.

'About what?'

'About how you broke your wrist.'

How did she guess? I thought, and I shrank up small in the corner. I didn't want to tell her about my boyfriend's sexual proclivities. 'What about how I broke my wrist?'

'There's no need to be scared. You're safe here.'

'I'm not scared. What do you mean?'

She looked at me with a real social worker's face and said, 'Do you want to talk about the other bruises? The finger-shaped bruises around your neck? The bruise here on your cheek?'

My left hand automatically went to my face and then I realised what she was trying to say. 'Oh, *those*. No, that's not, you know, honestly. I mean, it's nothing to worry about. It's fine. It's just, you know . . .'

I think 'consensual' was the word I was searching for, but I started to tail off as I realised that she was someone I vaguely recognised from when I used to go to church with my parents. That's the trouble with my home town. It's the kind of place where you find yourself having to explain your sex life to someone who's probably taken communion with your mum and dad. 'Um,' I said, blushing like mad. 'It's just something we do.'

'Well,' she said, only semi-satisfied. 'You do know you don't have to, don't you?'

By this point it was more than two hours since Nicky had been banished to sit in the waiting area. After half-listening to the nurse's instructions on how to keep the cast dry, when to stop wearing the sling and when to come back to have the plaster cut off, I couldn't wait to run out into his arms. I walked through the swinging doors ready to say, 'You'll never guess what they thought . . .' I had a smile already prepared on my face to go with the anecdote. It stuck to my face, redundantly, as I surveyed the waiting area. Nicky wasn't in the first row of chairs. He didn't seem to be in any of the chairs. I looked again, carefully, along each row. Maybe he had his head in a magazine. Maybe he was over by the drinks machine.

'Miss! Miss!' called the woman on the reception desk. I went across to her. 'If you're looking for your brother, he said he had to leave, but he's left you the money for a taxi.' She brandished a fiver. 'Would you like me to call you one?'

'My brother? My brother's not here.' Stupid cow. 'I'm looking for my boyfriend.'

'Oh, I'm sorry. I assumed he was your brother because you look like him.'

'But he's American, for God's sake. How could he be my brother? And anyway, he looks nothing like me!'

I think I must have shouted at her because she put her hands up defensively and said, 'I'm only the receptionist. Now, would you like me to call you a taxi?'

I had to stand outside to wait because I didn't

want anyone to see me cry. I told myself Nicky had gone out to buy flowers or some food for supper, and would be waiting back at the bedsit ready to help me have a bath and get undressed. My bag kept falling off my unaccustomed left shoulder as I climbed the five flights of stairs and awkwardly put the key in the lock. The light was on. Thank God, I thought, and called his name. No answer. I went into the bathroom to have a pee and there, on the mirror, written with my one and only pink lipstick, was the message: 'Thanx 4 evrything'. On the shelf above the washbasin, by the soap, was the spare door-key that I'd had cut for Nicky eleven days ago. I cried quite a lot when I saw it.

All I could think was, why? Why the fuck did Nicky Bennet go through the whole rigmarole of finding me, coming back, tracking me down, only to break my heart again? Why couldn't he have left me alone on the brick wall in Brooklyn and never bothered me again?

I had never felt so abandoned. It's frightening to remember the depths of my desolation. It was grief compounded by the 'why?' factor. Why had he left me? Why had he come back in the first place? Who was I going to marry now? Could I have done something to make him stay? Should I have slapped him harder? Could I have worn nicer clothes or more make-up? Was it simply the subsistence diet of pizza and Pot Noodles that he didn't like?

The evenings seemed too long without him. Even weeks after he'd gone I'd be sitting on my bed watching my little black and white portable TV, eating a ready meal out of the plastic tray to save on washing-up, and then suddenly I'd find myself screwing up my mouth as if to stifle a sneeze and the tears would start in jerky, involuntary shudders.

It seemed crucial to keep my grief private, as if Nicky had never even existed. Other than the key and the ghostly mirror message he'd left nothing behind. He'd even taken his pictures, his defaced photographs, with him. I allowed myself quite a few black nights of the soul alone in my bedsit; evenings of sobbing and teeth-grinding and rocking backwards and forwards, keeping the crying quiet because the walls were thin. In public, well, for a while there was my broken wrist to concentrate on, and the short, curt, functional little phone calls that I made to my parents every week to tell them everything was okay. Then there was work, learning to use the till with one hand, and keeping up the usual level of banter with my colleagues. 'Where's Scarecrow Boy?' said Paul, the dapper second in command of the popular-reference department in the coffee room one day. 'I haven't seen him lurking on the street corner for a while.'

'Oh,' I said, gesturing vaguely. 'You know, he's had to go back.'

'What? Back to stand in the middle of a field?' I laughed weakly at Paul's joke. 'D'you know,' he said, 'I thought he was your brother until I saw the way he kissed you,' and then, 'Oh Christ, I've really put my foot in my mouth, haven't I?' he said as he looked at me and saw my face crumple.

My only other public relapse came on the day when my cast was taken off. I was looking forward to seeing my wrist again. I felt it would be a symbolic transition, a moment of wholeness and healing. The saw whizzed through the plaster and the technician split it apart. Nothing could have prepared me for the shock. There, in the nest formed by the split-open cast, was a hideous greyey-white thing, a grotesque alien foetus, something you'd expect to see leap from John Hurt's stomach. It was no longer my wrist. My wrist was no longer mine. I started crying, and my sobs were so long and loud and embarrassing that I got taken once again to the little room with the settee and the floral curtains and someone brought me a cup of tea.

36

Martha Jansen Mayer still has the wonderful 1950s car. It's up on bricks in the three-car garage of her large suburban home at the northern end of one of the Finger Lakes in New York State. She pats the car affectionately on one of its sci-fi fins. 'She's gathering dust now. We're trying to decide whether to restore her or sell her. Our eldest has just turned fifteen so I guess he'll be getting a car next year and we'll have to make more room in the garage. So maybe we'll have to say goodbye to Audrey.'

Martha hasn't changed much. Her hair is still short and fair, although now it's cut in a bob that's pushed behind her ears, which have delicate little diamond earrings in the lobes. She's as small and slim as ever. She's wearing a pink hooded sweatshirt and grey Lycra jogging bottoms, as if she's just come in from the gym. She makes me feel like a galumphing great giant beside her. She's pretty and neat and pert, and the only flaw is a heavy smear of make-up under her chin where she has presumably applied foundation in a hurry. I wonder if she did it especially for my visit. I could have told her not to bother.

I don't think that Martha really wanted to see me. Alex rang her and explained about my book, and judging from his end of the conversation it took all his considerable powers of persuasion. I said goodbye to Alex and wondered if I should sleep with him, just the once. If it hadn't been for Gavin and Daniel perhaps I would have done, but I'm too well brought up to have three one-night stands in the space of just a few weeks. Alex tousled my hair in a fond way as we said goodbye, and we touched cheeks and promised to keep in touch. Then I caught another plane, hired another car and drove up through New York State, through towns full of Victorian houses basking in the crisp northern sunlight and long, thin lakes glistening invitingly against the blue sky. 'I remember you,' said Martha when she saw me, and she didn't look particularly happy about it.

'Do you still think about Nicky sometimes?' We're sitting in Martha's kitchen, drinking decaffeinated coffee and squinting in the afternoon sunshine. She looks at me as if it's a stupid question. Probably it is. 'Yeah, obviously. Sometimes. You know.' She takes a sip, both hands around the mug. 'Actually, my husband gets a real kick out of it. Telling people that he's married to Nicky Bennet's ex-girlfriend. It makes a good story at parties.' She smiles slightly. Actually it's barely a smile and more of a wince, as if the hot coffee has hit a sensitive nerve in one of her teeth.

'Do you ever think about what might have been?'

'Like what?'

'Well, suppose you were still with him now that he's famous?'

The stupid-question look again. 'Of course I don't. I mean, that's the thing about Nicky Bennet. There's no might-have-been. Once it's over with him, it's over. Once you're dumped you stay dumped.' She does another wincing smile. 'You know, I've got photographs and souvenirs down in the basement, old boxes of stuff, things I did with my high-school boy-friends, other guys I used to know. I didn't keep anything from my time with Nicky. I threw it all away, long before he got famous.'

'Do you regret that?'

'No. No, absolutely not.' Martha shakes her head in a very determined way.

I run my finger around the ring left by my coffee cup on her kitchen table. I'm trying to think what to ask her next. 'Did you hate me at Lowell?'

'Hate you? Why would I hate you?'

'For taking Nicky away.'

She laughs. 'Listen, honey, unless I've got my chronology wrong, you didn't take Nicky away. You were at Lowell – when was it? – summer of eighty-four?'

I nod.

'Okay, that was my sophomore year. I dated Nicky through my junior year as well. It wasn't until the summer of eighty-five that he dumped me. I didn't hate you, I felt sorry for you.'

'Why?' My throat feels tight all of a sudden.

'Because you were so blatantly obsessed with Nicky. It's like you were stalking us. It seemed like everywhere we went, you were there too. We used to wonder how you knew where we'd be, and then Nicky joked that maybe you came and read the notes I used to leave on his door.'

Martha looks up, straight into my eyes, and she smiles at me. There's a question in her smile, as if she's asking, 'Tell me. I've always wanted to know. Were you reading the notes on the door?'

I don't know what I feel. Cold, definitely. Hot at the same time. I can feel red patches starting to form on my cheeks. My throat contracts even more. I lean over and stare into my coffee mug. I'd like time to stop still, just for a moment, so I can work out what she's telling me and what I feel about it. The notes on Nicky Bennet's door, telling me where I should meet him. They were from Martha. From Martha to Nicky. I clasp my hands together and rest my chin on them, studying the table. But Nicky was always pleased to see me. He would smile at me when he saw me. Then he'd ignore me, but in that deliciously provocative way. Later we'd have sex. That was the thing. It was all deliberate. He knew I was going to read the notes. He knew I'd be there. He was planning it all because he wanted to see me. He was playing a game with Martha. I look straight at her. 'You do know Nicky was sleeping with me, don't you? He was sleeping with me all through that summer.' I guess I'm trying to regain some ground.

'It wouldn't surprise me,' she says, giving a cynical shrug.

I remember something that Alex had told me. 'Did you go to Europe with Nicky?'

'Yes. Summer of eighty-five.'

'What happened?'

She smiles. 'You know, I can still remember the precise moment, the precise thing I said, the exact moment it was all over. We were in London. It was the day before Live Aid. We had tickets. I was so excited, but we'd had to cut short our stay in Paris to get there in time. We were sitting in some café and talking about it and I said, "Maybe next year we could . . ." and I didn't even end the sentence because his face just closed up completely. We had a huge row. I was trying to force him to commit and how dare I make assumptions, and God knows what else. And that was it. He stormed out and I didn't see him again till I got back to Lowell.'

'Martha, the day before Live Aid? Are you sure?'

'Yes. Why?'

'On Live Aid day he came to my house. Right out of the blue. He knelt at my feet and proposed to me.'

As the words come out I realise I shouldn't have said it. It sounds like I'm trying to score points but I'm not. I look at Martha's face. Several odd expressions wash over it. It's as if she's trying to swallow medicine. She takes another sip of coffee, stands up, walks over to the kitchen sink and pours her coffee away. 'Well, whoop-de-doo,' she says finally. 'Congratulations. You win.'

I apologise. She shrugs. The moment passes and it's kind of okay again. 'That wasn't why I wanted to see you,' I say, and she does a wry smile.

'I guessed not. Alex Esterhazy says you're writing a book about him.'

'You don't approve?' I'm guessing from her dry, detached tone of voice.

'It's not for me to approve or disapprove, is it? I guess to me it seems a bit like you're jumping on the bandwagon, cashing in on his disappearance, but it's up to you. If you can square it with your conscience, then good for you. Take the money. Maybe you need it.'

I could almost swear that Martha looks at my clothes when she says that.

'What I can't work out is why you've already told journalists about Nicky being violent. I would have saved that revelation for when the book was published. Boost sales with a killer headline. But what do I know?' She shrugs.

I decide to trust her. She once loved Nicky. She'll understand. 'Martha, I'm not actually writing a book. That's just what I told Alex. I'm really just trying to understand what's happened to him. Really, it's all about the note he left.'

'Which one?'

'You know, the one in the trailer on the film set. When he disappeared. Did it mean anything to you?'

'It read like a suicide note.'

'Do you think it is?'

'No, if only because Nicky's not really the type to kill himself. Kill someone else, maybe. Himself? No.'

'There's a phrase in the note that made me think his disappearance has something to do with the past. Something I should know about.'

Martha sighs deeply and leans her forehead on the palm of her hand. 'I get it. You're actually looking for Nicky Bennet. You think he might still be in love with you or something. You really think you'll find him by looking at the past? Listen, Justine, one thing I know about Nicky Bennet is this: he has no past. He never did. I dated him for two years. I never met his family. I think he once mentioned a mother in Ohio – or was it Illinois? – but he is the least pin-downable person I have ever met. If there's a reason for his disappearance beyond mere publicity, it won't have anything to do with his past. Nicky Bennet never believed in the past.'

She looks at her watch. 'I think you should go now. The children will be home soon.'

As Martha watches me reverse out of her driveway she taps on my car window. I wind it down. 'I need to say something, for your own good. Nicky Bennet was – probably still is – a violent, self-obsessed fantasist. He was the most emotionally brutal man I've ever known. I let him do stuff to me, stuff I deeply regret. I told myself I was being modern and daring, and that it was a way of showing how much I loved him. I realised later that it was nothing of the sort. As soon as I

37

I wish I hadn't told Martha about Nicky proposing to me. It's made me feel something I haven't felt in a long time: a kind of empty feeling around my left ring finger. Funny how you can miss something you never even had. After Nicky left I yearned for a ring. The silver ring I had, the one I used to wear on my thumb so it'd clank against Nicky's ring, was too big for my ring finger. So sometimes I'd wind a ponytail band around my finger instead and wear it all night.

I wrote to Nicky a couple of times after he left. Little, non-committal notes in line with the tone of his bathroom-mirror message. I waited until my wrist had healed well enough to write, and then I agonised over the precise words for a week or more. 'Thank you for a great summer – maybe see you again sometime?' was what I came up with for the first communication. I made sure I included a question so that he would have a reason to write back. I wrote it on a carefully chosen postcard, with a gaudily tinted picture of the pier and the beach, hoping he'd realise that I knew it was naff, and I posted it to Lowell University. Every student had an individual post office box at the university but I didn't know his box number, so I had to hope he was the only Nicky Bennet. I didn't get a reply, but I comforted myself with the thought that it was probably still the summer vacation, and he wouldn't be back at university until October. I told myself to be patient.

I wrote to him again a few weeks later, this time at greater length. I wrote a chatty letter, telling him how my job was going and what my home town looked like in the autumn. I mentioned some of the places we'd been together, and how I hoped maybe we could do it again sometime. I suggested we could meet up in New York at some point in the future, given that our last attempted meeting there had been a disaster, but I put lots of question marks and exclamation marks at the end of this bit of the letter so that he didn't have to take it seriously. I included my address, in case he didn't know it, and my phone number complete with international dialling code, and I told him to keep in touch. I sealed the envelope and wrote his name and the university address on the front, and in case of any confusion I put an asterisk by his name and added this at the bottom of the envelope in brackets: 'The Nicky Bennet who's a History of Art major.' Then I went straight to the post office before I could change my mind.

Getting your post is not always a reliable business when you live in a bedsit. All the letters simply lay on the doormat in the communal entry hall until they were picked up. Once in a while, if we were lucky, the bloke on the ground floor who was first to leave each morning would sort them into vague piles and prop them against the wall, resting on the dado rail. We'd had problems in the past with letters being stolen, particularly thick, interesting-looking letters or mail from the bank. I was afraid that something from America, perhaps addressed in the dashing handwriting that I imagined Nicky would have (apart from the note on the mirror and the notes he used to leave me on the door of his university room I'd never seen his actual writing), would prove tempting for the mail thief. So I began getting up early each morning, pulling on a T-shirt and some tracksuit bottoms and scampering down the five flights of stairs the minute I heard the postman. It took at least two months to realise that Nicky wasn't going to write to me.

I wrote a third time, although I hadn't meant to. It was probably a mistake. I had just started tentatively going out with a bloke from work called Colin. He was quite clever and about my age, and played keyboards in a local band. He was almost good-looking: his hair didn't really fit his head properly, and his features were a bit inexact and blurry but if you half-closed your eyes he looked okay. It was all going fine until Nicky Bennet ruined it. I was in the pub, sitting in a corner with a pint and watching Colin play with the band. At one point he looked up and winked at me, and I was filled with such a warm rush of affection that my face went blotchy. Afterwards he put the palm of his hand flat on the back of my neck and said, 'I don't half fancy you.'

My knees trembled and I wondered if perhaps I was falling in love. Maybe this was what it was supposed to feel like: warm and comfortable and quite sweet. Col walked me home and we stood on the steps outside the house. He took off his glasses and kissed me, gently to start with. I opened my mouth slightly, so did he, and our teeth clattered together in the cold. He somehow burrowed his hands inside my heavy winter coat and inside my thick jumper and I could feel one of his cold hands work its way inside my bra and begin tweaking my right nipple. It felt nice and shuddery, and I knew the next step was to ask him in for coffee. But as I half-closed my eyes to look at him I caught a look of Nicky Bennet, just something about his mouth, the way Nicky had looked at me that night on the green with the sprinklers. I pulled away, said something like, 'Anyway, thanks . . .' and let myself into the house, quickly closing the door behind me and leaving poor Col standing on the doorstep.

I lay in the bath for ages and the mirror steamed up, and even then, months after Nicky had left, I told myself I could still read his message. I hated myself for leaving Colin out in the cold, for not being able to love him properly, for still thinking about Nicky. I reached a resolution: I had to sort this, once and for all. That night I wrote to Nicky and told him how I felt: how I still loved him, how sorry I was for anything I'd done wrong. I poured out my heart to him, pages and pages of stuff. I told him I'd tried to forget him and couldn't, I offered to change if that was what he wanted, and told him that the two summers we'd spent together had been the happiest times of my life. I told him I'd even come to America to be with him. I put the letter into an envelope and scrawled his name and address on it, this time adding 'Please forward to home address if necessary.' Next day at work I stuffed the letter deep into the pile in the out-tray and put the cost of a stamp to America into the petty cash tin in the office, so I wouldn't have second thoughts about sending it.

He never replied.

It was months – years – before I finally worked out why Nicky had walked out on me. It wasn't that he didn't love me, it was that he loved me too much. He was afraid. I was afraid. The intensity of emotion that had leapt between us on that night when he broke my wrist: that was why he had left. That was why he never got in touch again. He needed to put thousands of miles – a whole ocean – between us. We were dangerous together. We were going to keep on hurting each other. He loved me too much and he was scared of hurting the one he loved most in all the world.

38

It was three years later that I first saw Nicky Bennet's name in a newspaper. By that point I'd finally realised that I wasn't going to hear from him again; that there wouldn't be any Christmas cards or phone calls or letters explaining why he had to leave; in short, that he had completely and utterly disappeared from my life. It was okay. I was pretty much over him. I had my job and my bedsit and a few friends. I'd had a couple of short-term boyfriends; there was no reason why I shouldn't have more. I was an independent, relatively happy woman living an independent, relatively happy life – until I read Nicky Bennet's name in the paper on a cold, wet Sunday afternoon.

You know how when you're skimming through a paper a word or name can catch your eye even if you're not reading that story properly? It was like that. I'd already turned a couple of pages further on before the name registered. I turned back, searching for what I couldn't believe I'd seen, and there it was, buried in the depths of a report on some artsy film festival.

The report, in the *Observer*'s review section, was describing one of the independent films on show, described as 'a quirky, minimalist Western': 'The big buzz this year is about a New York-based artist called Nicky Bennet, who makes his screen debut in *The Cruel Sand*. Director Josh Lunes said, "He was on set taking some photos when I realised what an iconic look he had. I figured he was born to be in a Western." Bennet himself isn't at the festival. Lunes said, "He's probably in a loft in SoHo, painting. He's not too interested in all this film-star stuff."'

I knew it was him. It had to be. That description: 'iconic', 'born to be in a Western'. I remembered his Clint Eastwood swagger, his stupid, show-offy Nudie jacket. Well, well, well. Nicky Bennet in a film. Jesus. Shit. I didn't know quite what I felt.

It was around two o'clock in the afternoon,

pouring with rain outside, so cold and dark that I had the light on in my bedsit and the fan heater going full blast. The newspaper was spread out across the carpet as I read it. I'd had a very late night and I was easing my way out of a hangover with toast and Marmite and instant coffee, dressed in the same clothes I'd been wearing the day before. I hadn't washed my hair yet, simply tied it up in a ponytail with an elastic band. The bedsit was a tip. I'd told myself I would tidy the place up once I'd finished reading the paper, but I knew that I probably wouldn't.

I went into the bathroom and stared hard at myself in the mirror. Sometimes if you stare hard enough it's as if you can see through your eyes into your brain, see the person you really are swim into focus. I used to dream about being famous, about being a film star. Every year I'd watch the Oscars and then stand in front of the mirror delivering my acceptance speech, even using my watch to make sure that I kept it to the allotted length. I'd always had an elaborate fantasy somewhere in my head, a fantasy of being spotted in the street and given a part in a film. Even then, at the age of twenty-four, I still had faint hopes that my chance of stardom wasn't quite over. Until the moment I read Nicky Bennet's name in the paper.

I looked in the mirror and saw a miserable twenty-four-year-old woman whose life was a complete waste of time and space. No wonder Nicky had left me. Having seen what I was really like, no wonder he put thousands of miles between us at the earliest opportunity. Maybe I had been feeling this wretched for months, but reading about Nicky's success in the newspaper jerked me into realising it. I curled up into a ball on my bed, the newspaper on the floor still open at the review section. I allowed myself a few tears and my favourite self-indulgent whinge: wishing that Marie hadn't killed herself so at least I'd have that option left open to me.

After a while I pulled myself together, had a bath, made myself a cup of tea and phoned Anna.

'Do you want to go and see this film?' she asked.

'I don't know. Maybe. But it's probably not going to come here, anyway. It'll probably only be on in London. It sounds a bit arty. So never mind. You know, maybe they'll show it on Channel Four in a couple of years.'

'I'd like to see it,' said Anna, crisply. 'I'd like to

see what the infamous Nicky Bennet is really like. We could go up to London to see it, maybe go up for the day and do some Christmas shopping while we're there.'

'Yeah, maybe.'

The week that the film was released in the UK I bought all the quality papers and read all the reviews. Almost every article mentioned Nicky Bennet by name, and in several there was a photograph, a still from the film, the same picture every time. It was black and white and not very clear, but it was definitely him. I cut the picture out of *The Times*, which had the best-quality print, and stuck it in the border of my dressing-table mirror. I took a day off work and slunk up to London by myself, not sure I could face seeing the film with anyone, even with Anna. I didn't want to tell anyone where I was going. I bought a copy of *Time Out* at the station and read the review on the train on the way up. I felt furtive, almost guilty, as if I was going to see a porn film, when I bought my ticket for the afternoon showing at a tiny independent cinema in Mayfair. 'One for *The*

Cruel Sand, please.' What a stupid thing to have to ask for.

There were only three other people in the cinema, and two of them spent the whole film kissing and panting in the back row. I sat right in the middle of the cinema and braced myself, wrapping my arms around my body and trying to breathe properly. But nothing could have prepared me for the sheer erotic shock that went right through me when Nicky appeared on screen astride a huge black horse. I gasped audibly before I could stop myself. My eyes watered and all I could do was take deep breaths and twist my hands together tightly in my lap until Nicky was shot dead two-thirds of the way through the film.

And although he'd never replied to my letters, and although he'd probably forgotten who I was, I felt it was only polite to write to Nicky and congratulate him. I found out the name and address of the film production company and I bought a card with an arty black and white American landscape photograph on it. I wrote a brief, careful message: 'Congratulations on your performance. It was nice to see you again, albeit on screen. Thinking of you, your friend Justine Fraser.'

I resisted the temptation to add any kisses. I wrote my address on the back of the envelope and at the last minute scribbled 'Remember me?' in brackets after it.

I followed Nicky Bennet's rise to fame avidly but not obsessively. I subscribed to *Empire* magazine, who were early supporters of his, but that was because I like films in general. Sometimes if I saw Nicky's face or name on the cover of a magazine I'd buy it to read, but not always. It wasn't as if I had a shrine to him in the corner of the bedsit or anything like that.

I daydreamed about Nicky quite a lot, but not to abnormal levels. It's perfectly normal to daydream about your college boyfriend, isn't it? That's what Friends Reunited is all about. And loads of women have fantasies about their favourite film star, so fantasising about your college boyfriend who also happens to be a film star must be okay. Besides, the daydreams I allowed myself were always specifically rooted in the here and now. For example, it was only when I knew that Nicky was actually in England that I would allow myself the bookshop dream, the one in which he'd saunter into the shop to find me. I'd see him on the Parkinson show promoting his new movie and then I'd let myself imagine that maybe he had a day off from his busy press tour. He'd have a sudden impulse to see me, and he'd play a hunch that I was still in the same job, and then . . . well, I could fill whole idle hours and days with that particular daydream.

Of course I went to see all his films, but I didn't go on my own any more; I took Anna with me. Her job was to remind me how much Nicky had hurt me, and how much I hated him. 'Who's the star of this film?' she'd say as we queued for our tickets.

'I don't know, Anna. You tell me.'

'Isn't it that ginger poser who broke your heart?'

'Oh, you mean the tosser who dumped me just before I dumped him.'

During the film she'd keep up the insults, remembering everything I'd ever told her about Nicky. If I showed signs of looking really moony during Nicky's love scenes she would lean over and hiss in my ear: 'Ginger pubes!'

It worked every time.

When Nicky's first film came out I told a few

people at work that I knew this guy who was in some arty movie and there was a moderately interested response. When he started to get really famous I honed my anecdotes more carefully. I told the story about meeting him on the Greyhound bus at Boston, about the first time we met properly, and about how he lived in my bedsit and proposed to me on the beach. I even told a few selected people that I had lost my virginity to Nicky Bennet on a patch of muddy grass in New England. I'm not sure everyone believed me.

I was going out with Lucas the ponytailed mandolin player at the time. I met him in the shop; he was a regular customer and he used to hang around whichever counter I was working at until he eventually asked me for a drink. He was about ten years older than me, which I thought would be good for me. He was, inevitably, slightly shorter than me, balding, and with a really quite horrible greying little ponytail, although in fairness I should add that at this point in time all self-respecting musicians had to have a ponytail. He was impressed by my enthusiasm for drinking pints of real ale; I admired his vinyl collection of obscure 1970s music: he even had a

Gram Parsons LP. On about our third date we were walking home from the pub when I said something about how I'd once been to the same pub with Nicky Bennet. I turned to look at Lucas, and he had a half-amused, half-worried look in his eye. 'Babes, stop with the Nicky Bennet routine. It's not funny any more,' and he grabbed me in a headlock from behind and then began tickling me mercilessly. We ended up in a clinch underneath a street light.

It wasn't until one night we went down the pub with Paul and his wife, and I finally got Paul to remember meeting Nicky, that Lucas actually believed me. I think he was impressed for a while. He dumped me after a few months, though; I'm not exactly sure why. I think maybe he felt he couldn't live up to Nicky. I was briefly upset, but then consoled myself with the fact that Lucas had grubby fingernails, didn't clean the bath out properly and was actually a bit whiffy when you got to know him better.

39

I'm beginning to discover that the world of journalists is like a great worldwide echo chamber or a huge game of Chinese whispers, or like that theory in which a butterfly flaps its wings and sets off a tidal wave on the other side of the world. A couple of weeks ago I had a drunken, whispered conversation with an old friend in the bar of a nondescript business hotel near a motorway junction in the south of England. (Yes, I know, I know, Daniel told me he was taping it; it was all totally above board; it's my own stupid fault, this mess I've created; I should have just kept my mouth shut.) Tonight I am sitting in a room at a Super 8 motel somewhere in upstate New York and — as a direct result of that conversation — the TV screen is filled by the red-eyed face of an actress best known for her roles in direct-to-video erotic thrillers, telling how Nicky Bennet used to beat her up regularly. Once, she tells us haltingly, a mascara-smudging tear easing its way down her semi-familiar face, he broke her nose the night before she was due to have a screen test for what, her implication seemed to be, would have been her big movie breakthrough. I can imagine that the headline for her story would read 'Nicky Bennet Ruined My Career'.

It's one of those blaring tabloid-TV news shows that they have in America, and I am riveted in spite of myself. It's all about the Nicky Bennet mystery, and specifically the claims of sexual violence sparked by my conversation with Daniel Green and the newspaper story he wrote as a result. Our erotic-thriller woman is the main interviewee, but there's a string of others, most of them women on the fringes of celebrity, happy to get exposure by crying on TV and telling the world about the brutality of Nicky Bennet.

And then, freakishly, there's me – kind of: a still shot of me from the press conference I did, looking glazed, scared stiff and unnaturally glossy, my hair neater than it's ever been. A voice-over with an exaggerated Julie Andrews accent reads lines from the interview I apparently gave Daniel. 'It was out of the blue. I was scared. I didn't know what to do,' the voice-over woman over-enunciates. Finding myself looking at my own story from the outside, I can begin to understand the sneery way Martha spoke to me: 'Nicky Bennet broke your arm and you thought it was some kind of symbol of love?'

I can see what she meant. That's what it looks like, isn't it? I'm just one of the many, many women Nicky Bennet has had his brutal way with, only I'm trying to make it sound special. But it wasn't like that. I want to scream at the TV – in fact, I *do* scream at the TV, actually out loud – 'It wasn't like that.'

Me and Nicky, it was different. Honestly and truly, it was different. It was an accident. It was horseplay. It was just part of a game that we were playing. Consensual. Partners in crime. Whatever. I've never hated Nicky for breaking my wrist; I've hated him for leaving me like that, for walking out on me when I was in hospital and never telling me why. I've often thought back to that moment, that look in his eyes, when he said, 'You know you want to. You know you like it,' and I know that was when he left me, when I lost him, when we lost each other. I hesitated. He challenged me and I hesitated. He challenged me with what he knew about me. He knew me. He knew me inside out. He knew that I had – what can I call it? – an undercurrent, a leaning, a propensity to be corrupted. He had looked right into my head and had seen what I wanted, what I really wanted, the reason why we were so good together. And then I denied him, denied myself and lost him. If there was ever a moment in my life, a moment I'd give anything to live again, it's that one. 'You know you like it,' he'd say, that challenging look in his eye. And what would I do? I'd smash his face in with my fist.

I am sitting on the bed in the motel room, eating a Chinese takeaway out of a moulded plastic tray and drinking Bud Light from the bottle. There are still another three full bottles stuffed into the ice bucket that's sitting on the cabinet next to the TV and I will probably drink them all before I go to bed. Outside my window there's a parking lot and the ugly backs of a row of chain restaurants. Beyond that, there's the rumble of the interstate, big trucks passing through on their way to God knows where. I am trying to decide what to do next.

My search for Nicky Bennet has been a dead

loss. I know virtually no more about him than when I started. I don't know where he's from, who he is or even if he's really dead. I thought he wanted me to unravel the clue in his note but I don't know how. I'm pathetic, a failure. I've set about the search all wrong, I can see that. Savannah. Why the hell did I start in Savannah? What a stupid place to start. And Lowell – what on Earth did I expect to find? I should have gone to LA or maybe out to Canada, to the film set he disappeared from. I could have talked my way in, pretended to be from the BBC or something, found clues, chatted to producers and make-up girls and gaffers, whatever they are. I could have persuaded someone to let me look round Nicky's trailer. Somehow I would have unravelled the mystery. What have I done instead? Piddled around in the shallows, self-indulgently revisiting the past. I think about how much money I've spent so far, then try hard not to think about it. I feel a nervous catch in my throat. My dad's money, left to me for the trip of a lifetime, frittered away – and for what? To discover that Nicky Bennet was two-timing me with Martha. (Although ultimately he must have loved me more: why else would he have proposed to me?)

To discover Nicky originally spelt his last name with two Ts. To discover some great big hairy goatee-bearded lunk I can barely remember is still carrying a torch for me after nearly twenty years.

I let myself think about Alexander Esterhazy. I could cut my losses and go back there, back to the North Carolina coast. I could marry him; learn to love his goatee and his paunch and his hairy back. I know I have no proof of the hairy back, but I'm sure he has one. I could spend my time in that beautiful room overlooking the ocean and I could help him run his restaurant. I could learn to cook, or I could do the front-of-house stuff: greet the customers, sort out the bookings, tart up the decor. We'd go for long walks on that beautiful sandy beach and nurse our private sorrows and get through them together; we'd listen to music together and eventually we'd both learn to be happy with what we had left. It could be a good life. It might suit me.

Or, and here's another possibility: I could go home and marry Gavin. I could move into his starter home, or maybe we could both sell our houses and buy something nicer, bigger together. Maybe an old house that needs lots of work: I could do the arty designy stuff; Gavin could provide the DIY expertise. We could have a couple of children: I've still got a few child-bearing years left in me. I could work part-time in the bookshop, perhaps write a best-selling children's book in my spare time. We'd be the envy of all our friends. Gavin would enjoy telling people, 'Did you know, my lovely wife used to go out with Nicky Bennet, yes, *the* Nicky Bennet?' We'd be – what? – content? Maybe.

And then on the television, just as I'm surrendering to an imaginary future as Gavin's contented wife, there's Clio Callahan. She's tall, painfully thin, with her hair in an untidy knot on top of her head. She's wearing a T-shirt with a slogan that must be obscene, because it's been pixilated out. 'Was Nicky Bennet ever violent to you?' a journalist shouts as she comes out of a building and tries to walk down a street. She says nothing, just scowls and sticks up her middle finger. Another reporter shouts from the scrum:

'What's happened to Nicky Bennet? Do you know? Is he dead?'

Clio turns and faces the reporters, and I realise with a shock that she looks a lot like me – a much younger me, a me who's regularly been told she's beautiful. 'When you know why, you'll understand,' she shouts, then turns and walks towards her car with a brisk, angry spring in her step. *When you know what's happened you'll understand.* That's what Nicky's note said. All at once I know who I'm supposed to talk to next.

40

There's a fine line between plainness and beauty, and Clio Callahan balances right on that line. She's skinny, of course, with dirty blonde hair pulled back – uncombed and apparently unwashed – into a ponytail. I imagine she's got the perfect bone structure for a model. I bet photographers love it, all the planes and hollows reflecting and absorbing the light in really interesting ways. But up close, in real life, it's too much. The bones in her face are so sharp, so exaggerated, you feel that they're being thrust at you, that they might snap through her skin, that her face is almost too naked. Looking at it is painful, in a weird way. She has purple circles under her greyish eyes, eyebrows that look like they were aggressively plucked a few weeks ago, and a small crop of spots in the horizontal groove immediately under her lower lip. She walks up to greet me, and her cropped khaki combat trousers fall almost to her crotch, revealing sharp hip bones and a concave stomach. She takes a step towards me and it's clear that we're exactly the same height. She puts her hands on my shoulders and air-kisses me, once each side. 'Justine Fraser,' she says, in a matter-of-fact manner, as if she's often said my name before. Then she holds me at arm's length so she can look at me.

The intense way she's looking at me, I expect her to say something like 'Does Nicky have a type, or what?' Or maybe 'You and I could almost be sisters,' although I remind myself that if the papers are to be believed she's seventeen years younger than me. In fact, I could almost be her mother. But she says nothing, just stares at me for a while without smiling, then turns and leads me into the house. She stops as she enters the main room, turns back to me and vaguely gestures with her right arm as if to say, 'Well, here it is,' and that's when it hits me with a painful thud in the pit of my stomach: she is in my place.

In one of the daydreams that I've allowed myself from time to time, Nicky comes back to England to find me and whisks me off to Vegas to get married (as if it's something that had simply slipped his mind, something he'd always meant to do; as if on the plane back to America he slapped the palm of his hand on his forehead and said, 'Shit! I knew there was something I'd forgotten! I meant to get married to Justine!'). Then he takes me to his home in the Hollywood hills and we live together happily ever after. I've tended to imagine a house in a canyon, the sort of house Joni Mitchell might have lived in with one or more of Crosby, Stills and Nash back in the late 1960s or early 1970s; a beautiful house built by a wildly famous film star in the golden age of Hollywood, allowed to go to seed in the hippie era and now funkily glamorous and tatty around the edges. I'd carve my own niche in Hollywood by writing acerbic screenplays and being caustically witty at the fabulous parties we'd throw, and people would envy Nicky for having such a cool, independent, out-of-the-ordinary English wife.

And here is Clio Callahan standing in the huge, beautiful living room of exactly the house I'd imagined Nicky and I living in.

Nicky Bennet's house is built at the top edge of a curved canyon in the hills high above the city. As I followed the route to his house it was as if my daydreams, my imaginings, were coming to life. The road wound down, corkscrewing into the shady darkness of the canyon, and then curved up so high that I could see the ocean in the distance, hazy and shimmering like a dream. I pulled into the driveway and parked next to a kind of pink jeep-type car, half-hidden by lush overhanging dark green fleshy foliage. I climbed a set of rickety, narrow, twisting wooden steps, the foliage still hiding any sign of what was ahead.

And then, oh my God, Nicky Bennet's house. The house is pink, that's the first – the only – surprise. Pink stucco, I think the material's called. It's actually a bungalow, large and low and somewhat tatty. There's a wide, arched wooden door and windows blanked with wooden shutters, fastened with heavy black cast-iron bars in what might be called Spanish Colonial style. I knocked, using the cast-iron knocker. The door creaked open theatrically and there was Clio, tall and pale and thin, standing in the doorway like the ghost of the younger me.

The front room is wider than it is long, with a white wooden floor and white walls. There's

barely any furniture, just a big old leather couch,
a couple of armchairs that don't match and a
1970s-style chrome coffee-table with a smoked-
glass top. In the far-right corner there's a kitchen
area, gleaming stainless-steel units around a
heavy dark wood table and chairs. In the back
wall to the left there's an archway, leading to what
I can see is a long thin annexe to the house. But
the main glory is the rest of the back wall of the
room – entirely glass, huge glass doors, floor to
ceiling. Through the windows I can see a tiled,
dark blue Moorish swimming pool half-full of
murky water, and then beyond that is the edge of
the hill. Stretched out along the horizon, as if
miles below us, another world entirely, is the
silvery hazy flat grid of Los Angeles.

I would have known at once that it was
Nicky's house: not just because it was the house
I'd always dreamed of, but because of the
pictures on the walls. They're canvases – not
framed or glazed or anything – just the raw
canvas with black and white photos printed onto
the surface, photos of desert highways, deserted
motels, cacti, mountains, road signs. Then of
course, characteristically, those photos have
been daubed with apparently random streaks of

paint: pink, green, white and pale blue. Over the fireplace is a photo of Clio, naked, and it's more heavily paint-streaked than the rest of the pictures. In fact, so is the wall behind it: someone has taken a can of blue paint and hurled it at the photo, allowing the paint to drip down the wall and onto the fireplace surround. I look at the picture and look again at Clio Callahan. It could have been me. It should have been me.

I guess I've always wondered what Nicky Bennet's girlfriends might be like. I don't mean what they look like; that's easy. They're beautiful, all of them, and mostly blonde. They're all willowy and tall with sharp cheekbones and shoulders, and long, slim arms without a hint of flab. You see the pictures of Nicky posing on red carpets at Oscar ceremonies and premieres, a gorgeous woman in a shiny, slinky satin dress standing slightly behind him so as not to over-shadow him or get in the way. Of course they're all beautiful; he's a film star. What I've always wondered about is what his relationship with them might be like, what there is beyond mere beauty that makes him want to be with them. I suppose I'm always looking for a clue: trying to find out what I didn't have, why Nicky didn't stay with me. Looking at Clio now, I firmly believe that I could have been regarded as beautiful if I'd lived in Los Angeles and had been groomed and waxed and perfected. I think I had the raw material once. What I'm wondering is this: what in particular did Nicky see in Clio? Did she make him laugh? Did she share his obsession with Gram Parsons? Was she prepared to go down the dark scary sexual route with him? Did she understand his photographs? Is it because she looks like a younger me?

41

I'm so proud of myself for finding Clio Callahan. I found her on the Internet. I googled her name and got an e-mail address for the model agency she works for. I holed up in a hotel near Newark Airport, ready to fly anywhere, coast-to-coast, at a moment's notice, and sent her a carefully worded e-mail, complete with my Hotmail address and the hotel phone number. I used my real name, which was a calculated gamble. I knew that Clio would have read the newspaper stories, I guessed she would be aware that I was the one who started all the stories about Nicky Bennet being a serial girlfriend-beater. Maybe she'd hate me, want nothing whatsoever to do with me, but at least she'd be intrigued. As least she'd know we had something in common. But I was still surprised to get her reply, which began with these words:

'Hey, Justine Fraser. I was wondering when I'd hear from you.'

Clio and I are standing in the front room of Nicky Bennet's house, staring out at the pool and at Los Angeles beyond. There's so much I want to ask her, starting with 'Where's Nicky? And what did his note mean?' but the time doesn't seem right. In fact, nothing seems right. I've got a weird sense that we're not even in the same place. I mean literally not in the same place; that we're actually figures in some sort of composite photograph, two shots taken at different times and merged together. I don't know how to speak to her. I don't know how I got here. I don't know what the plan is. I think I'm staying here tonight. I think she's invited me to stay here tonight, but I'm not at all sure. I'm basing this on the one garbled conversation that we had when I rang her from LAX. She said something about 'making the most of it before I have to leave'.

I don't want to presume on anything, and Clio's putting me on edge. I think she's on drugs of some sort, but I'm a bit naive about such things and I don't want to show my ignorance. As I'm thinking this, and as I'm trying to think of something to break the awkward silence, Clio suddenly turns to me, takes my hands in hers and stares deeply into my eyes. 'Justine,' she says, and I notice for the first time that she pronounces it as if it's an exotic name, with the emphasis falling French-style on the second syllable. 'Justine, there's so much I want to talk to you about.'

We're drinking ice-cold white wine out by the pool, lying on slatted wooden garden recliners in companionable silence. There are weeds growing up between the stones on the patio, and the dark brown water in the pool, choked with leaves, has a curious, not unpleasant, smell of rotting fruit or compost heaps. Earlier, at Clio's urging, I dragged my suitcase into one of the rooms in the annexe, a room with French doors opening onto the pool, a rough-hewn four-poster bed and an elaborately tiled en-suite bathroom. In the bath there are rust-coloured trails leading down from each tap to the plughole. It's about eight in the evening. It's warm and muggy. The city beneath us looks like another world. I feel as if I'm in Sleeping Beauty's back garden.

I'm trying to guess when this house was built. I'm thinking 1930s. It would have been owned by some impossibly glamorous star, like Rita Hayworth. Cary Grant. Ava Gardner. There would have been parties, with champagne and drugs and hushed-up sex scandals. And then I wonder how long Nicky's lived here, if he had plans to do it up properly, to clean the pool and refurbish this patio area. Once again I let myself imagine being married to him, living here in this house and throwing parties. People would fight for invitations. Johnny Depp. George Clooney. Jack Nicholson. Brad and Jen. And I wonder how long Clio's lived here with him.

'He wants me out by the end of the month,' she says out of the blue, as if she were following the train of my thoughts. At first I'm shocked again at how young she sounds, like a little girl, and then I realise what she's said.

'He wants you out? So . . .' and I tread carefully, not wanting to sound stupid, '. . . obviously he's coming back.' What I really mean is, so Nicky's definitely not dead.

Clio giggles. She's taking a sip of wine and it goes up her nose as she laughs. 'Back from the dead,' she says in a sepulchral voice, once she's stopped spluttering wine out of her nostrils.

She looks across at me with wide, pretend-scary eyes. I'm trying hard to keep my face impassive, not to look shocked or surprised. And I'm not really, am I? After all, I knew he wasn't dead, didn't I? I felt he was still alive. I still felt him tugging at my heart. That's what I had told Anna before I set off on my quest. But Clio doesn't know that. She only knows what she's read about me in the papers. She thinks that I think Nicky killed himself.

'I loved it when you told everyone he'd killed himself. That was so brilliant. I couldn't have planned that better myself. I had no idea that note meant anything like that. It was . . . perfect.' Her voice trails off, and she laughs a little to herself. She's staring into the distance, a dreamy look in her eyes, swirling the wine in her glass. Her voice, her little-girl voice, the laugh, the look in her eyes; the muggy warmth, the alcohol, the rich, rotten smell from the swimming pool; the sound of chirping insects as loud as shrieks in the still, oppressive air: I feel as if I'm on the edge of a revelation.

'Oh, Nicky Bennet,' she says, curling her head

into her arms and making herself into a little ball. 'Nicky fucking Bennet.'

There's a long pause. Then she asks, 'How long did you know him for?'

'Two years.' Or was it nearly twenty?

'And how did he leave you?' Her voice is muffled: she's still curled up inside herself.

'How?' I think back to that day, the day of the broken wrist. 'He left a note. In lipstick. On a mirror.'

'What did it say?'

I feel as if she's testing me, as if she's deciding whether I can be trusted with her story. 'It said, "Thanks for everything." Except he spelt it wrong.' From the curled-up ball on the other recliner I think I hear a snort of laughter.

'Oh my God,' she says, looking at me and laughing. 'That is soooo Nicky Bennet. Okay . . .' She sits herself up, straight-backed, sideways on the recliner, and plants her feet on the ground so that she's facing me. 'It was just a bit over a year ago. Last summer. I met him at a party and I was so excited. I mean, Nicky Bennet! He stood in front of me, really straight, really tall, and just looked at me for a long time. Then he did that weird smile of his and said, "Clio

Callahan." I couldn't believe it. He knew who I was.'

She puts her hands together, interlinking the fingers and fanning them out, staring at them. Then she looks at me again. 'You can guess how good it was. I don't really need to say, do I?' and she gestures around her, at the house, the pool, the view. 'I loved him. I loved him so much.' She hits her chest hard, so hard that I can hear the thump, with the heel of her splayed-open right hand. 'And then it was over. He's gone away. I thought he'd come back, that he just wanted to be on his own for a while, but then he sent me a note.'

'What did it say?'

'Same as yours, really, except that he wanted me to move out at the end of the month. You'd think, wouldn't you, that he'd say something like that to your face, but no. Just a note. Just a fucking note.'

'Clio, where is he? Where's he gone?'

I know that she's about to tell me. I know that I'm about to find the answer I've been looking for. Clio closes her eyes, takes a deep breath. Her voice, when she speaks again, is even younger, even more like a little girl's than it was before.

'Oh, he's just gone to work on this project he's doing. It's "really important" to him.' She makes the inverted commas with her fingers. Then she laughs again, a short, hollow laugh. 'It's about you, the project, sort of.'

I frown at her. What does she mean?

'That's how I know about you. That's why it's all so funny, you saying he was dead and then that other stuff you said.'

'I don't know what you mean. What *do* you mean?'

'Okay . . . here's what was supposed to happen. He wanted out of the movie he was making so he thought he'd disappear for a while, create a bit of mystery, but he certainly didn't mean to fake his death. When you said that stuff about it being suicide I laughed so much. You see, now it looks as if he was deliberately faking his death to get out of the movie, and that's really pissed the producers, big time. They'll probably sue him for millions. That's for starters. And then if that didn't screw up his career enough, then you told everyone he beat up on you. So, even if he manages to settle the case with the production company, nobody's going to hire a star who beats up women, are they? He is completely finished.'

'You really hate him, don't you?'

Clio stops to think about that one, looking again at her fingers. 'That's the thing with Nicky, isn't it? He gets under your skin. I almost think he lays eggs under it or something. Sometimes I want to tear off the top layer of my skin just to see what he's put under there, 'cause there's something, I'm sure about that. He looks at you like he can see inside you and then you're in his power. Look at you, still chasing him after all these years. That proves it, doesn't it?'

I look away, at the bright lights of Los Angeles twinkling in the night sky. I feel sorry for Clio Callahan. She's got it even worse than me, in a way: because now she's seen me she realises that Nicky was just trying to recreate with her what he had with me. He's still thinking about me, still connected to me, still working through his feelings for me. His special project, this important thing he's working on. It's about me. In spite of myself, I feel my heart give a little leap inside me.

'Clio, what's he working on? Tell me.' But it's as if she hasn't heard me. There's nothing but the oppressive muggy silence and those chirping insects. And then I hear myself say this: 'I just want to see him again,' and my voice sounds silvery-clear and English in the Los Angeles night air. I can almost see the words. 'I just want to see him again.' I see them as a tiny silver coin or a shiny piece of shell tossed out into the night sky, skimming across the swimming pool, bouncing through the city lights and out to the sea.

I look across at Clio. She's staring into space, eyes wide, not listening. 'Clio?' Nothing. I do an artificial yawn, stretch, stand up with some difficulty and walk – stumble – to my bedroom. I just want to see him again. Just once. That would be enough for me. That's all I've ever wanted.

she's Marie as well, in that way that characters in dreams can be two people at once. We're on the beach in my home town but perhaps in North Carolina as well, lying on sun loungers, and we're skimming stones into the sea. Except the stones aren't stones, they're shiny silver coins: dimes or five-pence pieces. And where the sea should be, it's Nicky Bennet's swimming pool. The coins bounce onto the weeds and foliage in the pool, and then the foliage stirs and there's something underneath it. It's Nicky Bennet. He sits up slowly and opens his eyes; only instead of eyes there are silver coins. 'You woke me up,' he says, but Clio/Marie is pointing at him and screaming, 'You're supposed to be dead. I killed you.'

And of course I wake up with a start, sweating and shaking. Every hair on my body is standing on end as I go cold all over. I think again about the thick, murky water in the pool and get a flash in my head of the film *Les Diaboliques*, with the body in the bath, and they search the swimming pool, and the woman you least suspected turns out to have done the killing. I remember Clio's voice: 'I loved it when you told everyone he'd killed himself. That was so brilliant. I couldn't have planned that better myself. I had no idea that note meant anything like that. It was . . . perfect.'

Oh my God. That's it. He's dead. She's killed him. It all makes perfect sense to me in the white silence of four in the morning. I try to remember the route back to the city, the winding roads I came along, where I put the keys to the car. And I try not to panic as I wonder where Clio might have hidden Nicky Bennet's body. Oh God, it's in the swimming pool. That's what the smell is. All evening we sat there together by the pool discussing Nicky Bennet, and all along he was dead and she killed him. How could I possibly have been so stupid?

No one knows where I am. No one who cares about me knows where I am. My mother and Anna probably think I'm still in North Carolina. Gavin? I can't even remember if he's my boyfriend or not, but certainly he has no idea where I am. Alex Esterhazy cares about me, I think, but he probably thinks I'm busy tracking down old classmates. If detectives went to see him while they were searching for me, he'd give them all the names and addresses on the Lowell Alumni Net and they'd waste days following up all those leads. I'm here at Nicky Bennet's house in a dark, secluded canyon in Los Angeles, in a bedroom overlooking a creepy, overgrown garden, with a woman I think might have killed him.

I sit on the edge of the bed, feet on the floor, wrapped in a sheet and shivering. I remember what I felt last night: I'm on the edge of a revelation. I'm about to find out what has happened to Nicky Bennet. I've come this far. I can't back down now.

I pull on some clothes, step into my sandals and walk out into the garden. In the early dawn light it looks even more like a scene from *Sleeping Beauty*. Standing propped up against a wall there's a long implement: a pole with something on the end, maybe a garden tool or something to hook people out of the pool with. I look at it carefully, and think hard. I could search the swimming pool. Drag, that's the word they always use in detective stories, isn't it? I could drag the swimming pool. That's sort of what I want to do, I think. I want to take this long pole and see if I can find Nicky's body; I want to search through the weeds in the pool and see what I can find.

I shiver as I stand there, thinking about it. The smell is stronger than ever: like the vegetable section of the fridge when you've left some salad in there for weeks. I kneel down by the pool and dangle my hand in the lukewarm water, feeling the weeds between my fingers, daring myself to look further. Suppose I touch Nicky's hand with my fingers. What would it feel like? All cold and clammy and dead. Suppose his bloated body suddenly floats to the surface, white-faced and virtually unrecognisable. What would I do? And as I make myself shudder even more I hear a noise behind me, the creak of the glass door opening. The hairs on the back of my neck stand on end. I get up, slowly, and turn around. Clio Callahan is standing in the doorway. There's a fierce look on her face. She's clutching – brandishing – something in her right hand: in the dawn light I can see the long silvery blade of a knife. I'm too scared even to scream.

'Justine? What are you doing? Why aren't you asleep?'

I wipe my hand dry on my trouser leg, hoping that she doesn't notice. I struggle to think of something safe to say. 'I couldn't sleep. I was just – you know – getting some air.'

She narrows her eyes and stares at me. I stare back, frozen to the spot with fear. I feel my gaze go involuntarily to the knife in her hand. She notices, looks towards the knife, and looks back at me with an unreadable smile.

'What are you doing?' she asks again.

I don't know what to say. All I can do is stand there, looking from her face to the knife and back to her face, still with its weird smile.

'Have you lost something?'

I open my mouth but nothing comes out.

'You seem to be looking for something in the pool. Can I help?'

Shit. What can I say?

'You're looking for Nicky, aren't you?'

I say nothing, and Clio's smile broadens. 'Do you want to know where he is?'

I nod. It's all I can think to do.

'Come with me and I'll show you,' she says in the sepulchral voice I remember from last night, and then – quite unexpectedly – she doubles over with laughter. 'Oh, Justine,' she says, back to her little-girl voice. 'You should see your face. You look like you've seen a ghost.'

She's trashing the place. That's what the knife is for. She's slashed the cushions of the leather couch and the armchairs, and there's stuffing all over the floor. Every one of the pictures on the wall has been slashed at least once. I wonder if the noise woke me up. Clio says that she's been watching me. She stopped what she was doing when she saw me through the window; she's been trying to figure out what I was up to. 'Did you think you'd find Nicky in the swimming pool?' she asks, giggling.

I don't want to answer. It seems so stupid now.

'Did you think that smell was a decomposing body?'

I shrug, and she laughs again.

'That's so funny. A dead body in the pool. As if. It's the weeds, that's why it smells. Algae, I think it's called. The pool hasn't been cleaned in months. Believe it or not, Nicky actually left me the phone number of the pool man. He really thought I was going to get it cleaned for him before I left.'

She looks at me and she seems to be expecting me to laugh, so I manage a smile. I feel like an idiot.

'Anyway, I was going to go without saying goodbye,' she says, and I notice that there's a suitcase and a vanity case standing by the front door. 'But I wrote you a note.'

She points to one of the pictures on the wall, the photo of an abandoned desert motel. She's scrawled my name in lipstick on it; the lipstick is, I guess, a kind of joke. Sticky-taped to the picture is an envelope. Clio pulls the envelope from the picture and gives it to me. 'It's kind of a map,' she says, 'and directions. I only went there twice so I hope it makes sense. But you're good at finding things, aren't you?'

I open the envelope and pull out a sheet of notepaper. The paper is thick, cream and ridged: good quality. I realise that my whole body is shaking. With Clio watching me, I sit down in a corner of the slashed leather sofa, curling my legs up under me. With trembling hands I open up the sheet of notepaper. I close my eyes, take a deep breath, then open them again and begin to read what Clio has written.

'I think you should go to see Nicky and tell him how you feel about him. I know you want to see him again and I think it would be a really good idea for you to find out about the project he's working on. I think it will be a real surprise for Nicky also. He's staying at the motel that's in the picture. I hope you can find it from my directions.'

The directions. Thick lines scrawled on a map torn from a road atlas. The far eastern edge of Southern California, out there in the desert, near the border with Arizona. A circle with a cross in it. X marks the spot.

'So,' says Clio, briskly. 'I'm going. Good luck with your journey. Say hello to Nicky for me. Tell him I hope he gets everything he deserves,' and she pulls me towards her and kisses me right in the centre of the forehead.

43

Getting out of Los Angeles is the journey from Hell. I'm mostly driving east, so the sharp, harsh sunlight is shining straight into my eyes. None of the roads I choose will behave as I expect them to. They keep petering out or perversely becoming one-way roads going in the opposite direction. Several times I have to pull into parking lots, turn the car around and cross lanes of traffic to retrace my steps. I learn to ignore the hoots of other motorists. I'm tired and shaky and concentrating as hard as I can.

I'm relieved when I finally make it to the freeway, but my relief is short-lived. It's the morning rush hour. The traffic is moving, but it's bumper to bumper. To change lanes you some-how have to persuade your car to move in a sideways direction into a space that seems too small for it. For a while I stick desperately to the inside lane but then I discover that it has a habit of turning into an exit-only lane with very little notice. Twice I find myself swept off the freeway, and I have to drive along the ugly, rutted surface road, past gas stations, motels and chain restaurants, until a small and very missable road sign to my left gives me an opportunity to get back onto the freeway. Having learned my lesson I try to hog the middle lane, but exits seem to go off in all directions. Any lane you choose – left, right or centre – can take you off the road you're on and onto another freeway going in a completely different direction. I'm clinging so tightly to the steering wheel that the tips of my fingers go white and numb.

It takes hours to get out of the urban sprawl. I drive through what I guess must be the San Fernando Valley, and then through smaller, sparser, poorer-looking communities, with hopeful, shabby businesses sprouting like mushrooms alongside the interstate. Then finally the land opens up around me, and to the left I can see ominous mountains rising sharply and casting a heavy shadow. I pull off the interstate and into the parking lot of a gas station that promises clean restrooms. I fill the car's fuel tank, and then, scared by the desolate road ahead, fill the gas can in the boot. I eat a makeshift brunch of gas-station food: tortilla chips, a Snickers bar, Diet Coke. And then I try to work out exactly what it is that I think I'm doing.

When you travel, you are intensely yourself. That's something I'm beginning to realise. You're cut off from the things that you think make you you. It's just you, your core, your soul; on a plane, in a car, or walking across a gas-station forecourt dwarfed by the Californian landscape. When you catch sight of yourself in mirrors or windows, that's when you can actually see inside yourself and see what you're really like. It's a scary thought but a good one to keep in my mind. This is me; this is the core of myself.

I'm on my way to see Nicky Bennet. I just want to see him again. That's what it's all about. I just want to see Nicky Bennet one more time. That's what I've always wanted. All those daydreams about him turning up at the bookshop, all those indulgent fantasies I've allowed myself about being married to Nicky, going to the Oscars with him, showing off our lovely home in magazines. Really what it's all been about is seeing Nicky

Bennet one more time. Closure, I guess you could say. I want to ask him questions: why did he come back to me, propose to me, give me hope for the future, only to leave me all over again? And why did he write that note, so much like my sister Marie's? Did he write it deliberately, knowing that I'd read it, knowing I'd come to find him? Did he call me to him? What does he want to say to me?

I know what I want to say to him. Quite apart from the questions I have for him, there's one thing I've never said to him, something I need to put right. I never told him I loved him. After he left me I used to drive myself mad wondering: would he have stayed if I'd told him I loved him?

I'm going to have to break the habit of a lifetime. I've never told a man I loved him, apart from my dad and the posters of Donny Osmond and David Cassidy that Marie and I had on our bedroom wall when I was eight or nine. I used to kiss them every night, carefully rationing out my affection in even portions so that neither would get jealous. With my dad it was always a casual, throwaway thing: 'Love you!' with a little kiss on the cheek after he helped me top up my brake fluid or hang a pair of wardrobe doors. I realised after he died that that wasn't enough. I didn't tell him often enough or seriously enough that I loved him. Maybe I'm learning my lesson now.

Love. It's a big word, isn't it, but it starts deceptively softly with the little lightweight L. Then it moves to the rich, round mouthful of the O and the long velvety buzz of the V on your bottom lip. Love. It should be said with care. It should have arrows pointing to it and heavy underlining, and maybe flashing warning lights a few sentences before, just to let you know that it's coming. Love breeds hurt and I can't stand the pain. When you really love someone and they leave you, it hurts too much to live.

I've always felt that other people are so profligate with the word love. Pop stars and TV personalities seem to fall in love at the drop of a hat: 'Yes, it's love!' they tell *Hello* magazine. Then six weeks later there's another partner and 'This time it really is love,' they say. Listen to the radio: every day there are dedications – love you to bits, I'll love you for ever. Women meet blokes at nightclubs, two weeks later they've moved in together, she's pregnant and they're buying matching gold necklaces from Ratners to show their love. My father used to sign my mother's birthday and Christmas cards with the words, 'All my love always for ever,' which was touching if tautologous.

I look at myself in the rear-view mirror. I see the violet shadows under my eyes. And I think about the men I might have said 'I love you' to. There've been moments with Gavin, moments when I've felt full of a kind of reassuring warmth that could possibly pass for love, moments when I'd rather be with him than anywhere else. There've been similar moments with other men, too: watching Colin play keyboards in his pub band and feeling myself flush with a kind of pride; kissing Lucas under a street lamp while he attempted to tickle me. Standing on the beach in North Carolina, warming my hands in Alexander Esterhazy's chest hair, I felt something of the same emotion. I wonder if this is when other people might say 'I love you,' and mean it; and then, on the basis of a moment of warm comfort they get engaged and married and live happily ever after. Perhaps that's what Anna means by a root ball.

I think about the sharp, hard, flintlike presence of Nicky Bennet in my life. I imagine him holding my heart in his hands and polishing it like a precious stone, until my heart is sore and bleeding. 'Only love can break your heart,' Neil Young sang. I know that strictly speaking and according to the rules of logic you can't draw this conclusion from that phrase, but somehow I've always taken it a step further and thought: that means it can't be love unless it breaks your heart.

I love Nicky Bennet like crazy. I hate him too, of course. He's the bastard who broke my heart and screwed up my life. Broke Clio's heart, too. I can't wait to see him again. I'm petrified of seeing him again. How will I say it? How will I give the words the depth that they deserve? I'll need to stand up to say it, look him directly in the eye, and perhaps put my hands on his shoulders or on each side of his face to make sure that he's looking at me. I love you, Nicky. I know it's love because it hurts like hell. I will rip off chunks of my own flesh and give them to you, if that's what you want me to do.

He must have known I loved him: it must have shown in my face, my voice, in the way I would do anything he asked me to. Nearly anything he asked me to. But I shudder as I remember the casual, dismissive, deliberately misspelt lipstick message that he left on the mirror when he walked out on me. Justine, why the fuck didn't you just tell him? How difficult could it have been to say, 'I love you'? Maybe that was what he wanted. Maybe the whole of the last eighteen years would have been different if I had.

44

The middle of nowhere. Almost literally. I have pulled the car over to the side of the road and I am half-standing, half-sitting, resting against the warm car bonnet, my sandalled feet half-covered by the hot sandy earth. It is almost unbelievably hot. The sun is high in the sky. I'm not sure what time it is: time seems to have stopped, or at least turned sticky and slow. You could draw a huge circle with me as the centre, go miles in every direction, and there'd be nothing. Nothing but rocks that look like experiments gone wrong, hurled down in the landscape. Actually, landscape's the wrong word. Hurled down in the empty space with no thought for design or grandeur or anything that you could normally find to admire in a landscape. Nothing but me and this rental car.

I'm trying to imagine our encounter, trying to

think myself into the right frame of mind. Nicky will open the door and he'll be dressed exactly as he was when I first saw him in the Greyhound station in Boston, in his faded jeans and cowboy boots and his ridiculous Nudie jacket. For a short while he'll be blinded by the sun. He'll see nothing but a halo of light around my fair hair but then, after blinking for a while, he'll simply smile his twisted smile and say 'Justine Fraser' as if he isn't in the least bit surprised to see me.

'Nicky Bennet,' I'll say, 'I've come to tell you that I love you,' and then the smile will go all the way across his face, he'll sweep me into his arms and kiss me.

'It's been so long,' he'll say, nuzzling his face into my hair, but my fantasy stops there because even I know that this is an unlikely scenario. There's bound to be some kind of awkwardness. Nicky's not expecting me. He might be thinking about me but he's certainly not expecting me. Is he?

I drive through a fly-speck town, just a street lined with a few houses, a ramshackle diner-cum-general store and a brand new post office. Down a side road I can see a shack that's obviously the town beer joint, covered with those signs that light up, advertising brands of beer. I wonder how anyone could live here, why anyone would choose to live here. It's the kind of town in which, if this were a film, I'd be arrested and thrown in jail on a trumped-up charge. I drive past a decrepit trailer right next to the road, with old car seats and a fridge outside on a makeshift porch. I drive through what seem like endless miles of scrubby grassland. I keep rigidly to the speed limit, terrified of being pulled over by some redneck cop and charged with stealing the car or driving without insurance – oh shit, am I properly insured? Should I have bought the extra insurance cover the hire-car man tried to sell me at the airport?

I have a dull ache in the muscles and tendons at the back of my right ankle. I have another dull ache across the small of my back, and a sharp pain between my shoulders. My head aches and my eyes are watering from squinting at the bright sky. My fingers are fizzing with pins and needles and my ears are ringing from the hum of the engine. And all the while I can hear Clio's little-girl voice talking to me.

'That's the thing with Nicky, isn't it? He gets under your skin. I almost think he lays eggs under it or something. Sometimes I want to tear off the top layer of my skin just to see what he's put under there, 'cause there's something, I'm sure about that. He looks at you like he can see inside you and then you're in his power.'

In my head it's last night again, and I'm sitting beside that swimming pool in the muggy evening listening to Clio speak, her words spinning off into the heavy night air. I think about Nicky laying eggs under my skin. I think about something growing there, something lumpy and painful and not quite human, under my ribs or in my armpits or my breasts, like a kind of cancer. And then I'm thinking about Anna, and she's telling me about the baby, and I can actually feel it inside me: Anna's baby. Except that there's something badly wrong with it and no one will tell me what. I can see the photo of Alex Esterhazy's baby in the incubator, dying before it should have been born, and then I think about what it must be like to have something growing inside you, something that's going to die. And then, suppose you're pregnant and you get to eight or nine months and you decide you don't want the baby. You tell the doctors to leave it inside you and it carries on growing and turns into something monstrous that eventually bursts out of you. And in my mind somehow it's Nicky Bennet that's inside me, growing into something monstrous and parasitic. And then I'm inside a dark place, a dark mountain, and I'm being winched steadily upwards towards something very scary, something I don't want to happen, maybe giving birth; and I guess it's a memory of a ride that Gavin forced me to go on when we went to Disneyland Paris, but I am scared stiff and I know I'm on a roller coaster and I have to ride it to the end and I don't know what the end will be.

And the next thing I know, there's a sharp pain in my forehead, which is leaning against the steering wheel, and there's a trickle of blood making its way down my face and the car has come to a standstill on the sandy, grassy edge of the road. The sunset that's reflected in my rear-view mirror is so gaudy it's as if the sky has cracked open and is bleeding all over the desert.

There's a low, flat white building spread out under the Technicolor sky. In the half-darkness there's an eerie light over the building, and eventually I can see that it comes from the sign. It's a green and pink neon sign, with the motel's name – the Sunset Motel – and the words *No Vacancies*, outlined in neon and surrounded by white light bulbs. The sign hangs lopsidedly from the top of a pole, and it's creaking backwards and forwards in the warm desert wind. This must once have been a highway, or at least a major road. Once upon a time people must have travelled along this route, before a newer, faster road was built. Because, as I drive closer, the low, flat white building resolves itself into a proper, old-fashioned motel from the 1940s or 1950s, the kind you'd hole up in if you were on the run from the police, a suitcase crammed with hundreds of thousands of dollars from a bank raid in the back of your car.

Dust and sand has blown up against the pink and green doors of the motel cabins, and collected in the bottom of the dried-out kidney-shaped swimming pool. There's a diving board poised over the deep end of the pool and, like the motel sign, it's creaking in the wind. Scattered around the edge of the pool I can make out something white: sun loungers, tables and chairs. At the front of the motel there's a small building, somewhere between a shack and a bungalow, with a sign over the door that says *Office*. There is nothing else, no light on inside the motel, no other buildings, no other cars, for miles around. There's a sound in the distance, at once familiar but unidentifiable. It's the cry of a wild animal or bird. It could be a coyote or a wolf. It could be a lonesome whippoorwill, whatever that might be. I have never been anywhere so desolate.

I stand stock-still with the car keys in my hand. I could leave now. I could simply get back in the car, turn around and head back to Los Angeles. I could get a flight home. I could go back into work and no one would ever know that I lost my nerve at the final stage, within seconds of seeing Nicky Bennet. And I've almost made up my mind to do exactly that, when I look across at the motel building and see that the door to the office is slightly ajar. I walk towards it, knowing that very soon I shall find out the truth about Nicky Bennet's disappearance.

45

There's tatty lino on the floor, and the walls of the office are covered with dark wood-effect panels. There are a few wooden chairs with faded cushions, and a wire rack attached to the wall that looks like it once held leaflets full of information about tourist attractions. Dividing the room in half is a reception desk, also covered in the same wood-effect panels. I run my finger across it; it's thick with dust. Part of the desk is hinged upwards to create an opening. Behind the desk there's a kind of living area, with an old armchair, a coffee table and a huge old fridge-freezer. Next to it, balanced on top of a bookcase, are a microwave oven and a radio-cassette player, the only modern things in the room.

Nervously I open the fridge and look inside. The freezer section's stacked with boxes of TV dinners and microwave meals, enough to last for weeks. The fridge is full of beer. I take out a bottle, flip the top off using a bottle opener that's lying on the coffee table and take a long drink to settle my nerves.

There's a door at the back of the office. I walk through it and out into the motel courtyard, holding the beer bottle in my hand. The cabins are built in an L-shape, facing in a kind of south-west direction, presumably to take advantage of the sunset views. I try the door handle of the first cabin I come to, and it opens. I walk into a room that's flooded with deep red light from the dying minutes of the sunset.

This is where he's sleeping. It must be. The bed is made up with sheets and pillows and a kind of striped Navajo blanket. There's a small bathroom at the back of the room, with a toothbrush and toothpaste by the basin where I rinse my hands and face. I pick up the tooth-brush and feel the bristles with my thumb. Then I turn back towards the big window at the front of the cabin. There's a table – a desk – by the window. There's a laptop on the desk and a printer, and on the printer is a pile of paper. Hanging on the back of the chair by the desk is

Nicky Bennet's Nudie jacket. I hold it up to my face and smell him on it. With my lips I trace the outline of the embroidered leaves and dice. I slip my arms into the sleeves of the jacket. It fits me perfectly, like a second skin. I always knew it would.

'I'm sorry it has to be this way out. Love breeds hurt and I can't stand the pain.'

The sheet of crisp white paper is lying face down on the printer, the uppermost sheet of a stack an inch or more thick. I pick it up gingerly, not sure if I should, but I'm desperately hunting for clues.

'Love breeds hurt and I can't stand the pain.' I can't describe the feeling that comes over me. People talk about someone walking over their grave. I never knew what that meant but perhaps this is it. Every hair on my body stands up on end. It feels as if I've been plunged into ice. My face, the backs of my hands, my stomach: I am cold and shuddery all over. Forget the note that Nicky left on the mirror in his trailer. That was just an echo. This is the real thing.

I am holding my sister's suicide note in my

hand, virtually word for word, stolen by Nicky Bennet.

'Oh, he's just gone to work on this project he's doing. It's "really important" to him,' Clio had said, making inverted commas with her fingers. 'It's about you, the project, sort of.'

And then her note: 'I know you want to see him again and I think it would be a really good idea for you to find out about the project he's working on. I think it will be a real surprise for Nicky also.'

Oh, my God. This is what the project is, and this is what Clio sent me here to find. I turn over the stack of paper so that it sits in front of me, printed side up, and I start to read.

INT. A TRAILER ON A FILM SET. DAY
JOHNNY FISHER sits at a mirror, staring moodily at a note that he holds in his hand. He's in his early thirties, tall and lean and tautly muscled. Handsome, but not obviously so, he has a charisma that is more challenging than bland good looks.

We HEAR a knock on the trailer door and CURT RYAN puts his head around the door. Also in his thirties, he is JOHNNY's childhood friend and personal assistant, the only person he trusts. CURT sees the note in JOHNNY's hand.

                    CURT
You've had another one, then?
JOHNNY shrugs.
                    CURT
What's it say?
                    JOHNNY
The usual. I'll always love you. One day we'll be together. We belong together for eternity. It's just . . .
              CURT (sharply)
What?
JOHNNY fixes CURT with a long stare.
                    JOHNNY
This one was hand-delivered.

I don't know much about screenplays. I tried to read a book about them once, a book of theory all about how to construct stories. I gave up when the author started to cover his pages with diagrams involving circles, arrows and wriggly lines and words like 'inciting incident' and 'inner conflicts'. Nicky's writing seems a bit clunky. You can almost hear the doomy chords underscoring those last few words. But I read on. I need to know how it involves me.

EXT. COLLEGE GREEN. NIGHT.
JOHNNY runs across the Green, chased by LIZZIE. They're both obviously drunk. JOHNNY trips and falls and lies flat on his back. LIZZIE catches him, straddles him and starts to undo his shirt.
C/U on JOHNNY. His face says resistance is futile.
C/U on LIZZIE. She's hungry for this, and shows it.
They roll over so that JOHNNY is on top, and have loud, uninhibited sex.

INT. JOHNNY'S ROOM. NIGHT.
JOHNNY is at the hand basin, wiping mud from his shirt. LIZZIE lies in bed, naked but wrapped in a sheet.

JOHNNY
So you're cool with this, yeah? I think it could be fun.

C/U on LIZZIE. She says nothing, but smiles a secret smile.

Now I am sitting on the floor, my back leaning against the bed. My feet are tucked under me and they're slowly going numb but it doesn't matter. I am reading avidly. Forget the clunky writing. I am searching each page for the name Lizzie, the character introduced on the second page as 'a slim blonde in a thrift-store dress, with a classy British accent and hungry, dangerous eyes.'

EXT. THE RAILROAD STATION. NIGHT.
JOHNNY and LIZZIE stand on the platform, inches apart. JOHNNY looks at his watch. He seems anxious to get away. LIZZIE reaches up and touches his cheek.

      LIZZIE (lovingly)
I'll see you in New York.
      JOHNNY (uneasily)
Yeah, that'll be cool.
LIZZIE puckers up her lips and makes as if to kiss JOHNNY. He moves away so that

her lips don't make contact. He pats her on the head.

> JOHNNY

Look after yourself.

JOHNNY saunters away.

C/U on LIZZIE.

> LIZZIE (under her breath)

I love you, Johnny Fisher.

INT. A NEW YORK APARTMENT. DAY

JOHNNY and CARRIE are in bed, making love. Around them the apartment is untidy, as if they've been in bed for days. Empty pizza boxes and beer bottles surround the bed.

We HEAR the DOOR BUZZER. JOHNNY ignores it.

> CARRIE

Aren't you going to get that?

> JOHNNY

What? I didn't hear anything.

The DOOR BUZZER sounds again.

JOHNNY

Shit.

CARRIE

Who do you think it is?

JOHNNY, in nothing but his boxer shorts, goes over to the window and looks out.

EXT. OUTSIDE THE APARTMENT. DAY.

JOHNNY's POV. LIZZIE is standing there, carrying a backpack and a bunch of flowers. She has an expectant smile on her face.

INT. THE APARTMENT. DAY.

C/U on JOHNNY. He beats his head against the window.

JOHNNY (under his breath)

Fuck.

CARRIE

Who is it, Johnny?

JOHNNY

No one.

He climbs back into bed with CARRIE.

DISSOLVE TO:
INT. THE APARTMENT. DAY.
It is later the same day. We know that several hours have passed by the angle of the sunlight through the windows. It's now early evening. JOHNNY is getting dressed.

CARRIE (off screen)
Hey Johnny, let's go out tonight to that little Italian place around the corner.

JOHNNY doesn't answer. He looks out of the window.

EXT. OUTSIDE THE APARTMENT. DAY.
JOHNNY'S POV
LIZZIE is still there. She's now sitting on the steps of the apartment building. The flowers are wilting. On her face is a look of grim determination.

INT. THE APARTMENT. DAY.
JOHNNY moves away from the window and walks towards the bathroom.

JOHNNY
Why don't we order in?

Funny what just a few casual words can do. 'Why don't we order in?' I can hear a callous laugh, the closing of a window, the closing of a heart. A pair of lovers inside and me – Lizzie – sitting outside, heartbroken, ridiculed, a figure of fun.

I stand up, unsteadily on my numb feet. Wincing from the pain of pins and needles, I walk back into the office. I open the fridge and take out another bottle of beer. Then I slam the fridge door shut with as much force as I can muster, open it, and slam it shut again. 'Fuck you, Nicky Bennet. Fuck you,' I mutter under my breath.

Why? Why has he written it like this? That wasn't how it happened. It was Labor Day. He was stuck in gridlock on his way to New York from Trenton. Pittsburgh. Cleveland. Whatever godforsaken steel town he came from. He was on the New Jersey Turnpike, for God's sake. The next day he tried to find me. He knew I'd be at an art gallery. He went to the Guggenheim and waited for me all morning, only I was at the Museum of Modern Art. Oh fuck, I think as I grab the rest of the screenplay and sit at his desk to read it, he's going to make me – Lizzie – the stalker. I know how it's going to end. She's going to kill herself, and leave a note just like my sister's.

INT. THE COLLEGE POSTROOM. DAY.
JOHNNY takes a letter from his post box and opens it.
C/U on JOHNNY's face as he reads the letter. His face shows confusion and concern in quick succession as

LIZZIE (V/O)
We should have been together in New York. You know you should be with me, and one day we will be together. I promise you. We'll be together for ever. You can't escape my love.

I guess I'm immersed in the screenplay. I don't hear the noise of a car. I don't hear footsteps coming towards the room. The first thing I'm aware of is a shadow passing the window, throwing darkness onto the page I'm reading. I feel a chill on the back of my neck and my first instinct is to cover the pages I'm reading with my arm, as if I've been caught out cheating. Instead, I turn my head slowly towards the doorway. Standing there, the pale streakiness of his hair highlighted by the flickering green and pink motel sign, is Nicky Bennet. He looks at me with his strange green eyes, looks deep into my soul. It's as if time has stopped. Nicky continues to stare at me. I look back at him, examining the planes of his face that I know almost as well as my own. And then, oh so slowly, he starts to smile. The smile begins on one side of his face, the twisted, lopsided smile I know so well. And then it spreads. It turns into a laugh. 'Well, well, well,' he says. 'Justine Fraser. I see you've found my screenplay.'

46

I have dreamed so many times about seeing Nicky Bennet again. Sometimes in my dreams the electricity between us crackles and fizzes and we're pulled together like magnets. Sometimes we're sitting on a bench near the beach in my home town and he's explaining why he walked out on me, and his explanation is so convincing that I end up in his arms, kissing him all over his beautiful face. Sometimes we argue fiercely and it ends in passion, mouths and bodies locked together. I have lived the moment over and over in my imagination. But of all the things I ever dreamed of doing to Nicky Bennet when I saw him again, this is not one of them: I grab my beer bottle by the neck and I hurl it at him, a sharp, wristy throw, and the bottle hits him right on the temple, just above his left eye, leaving him bleeding from a cut above the eyebrow, a cut that matches the one I have from the rental car's steering wheel. He stares at me as if I'm mad. 'What the fuck was that for?' he says, pressing his fingers to his head to stop the bleeding.

'For being such a bastard. You prick. God, you . . .' and I'm running out of words to use. I'm screwing up my hands into fists; I can feel my fingernails in the palms of my hands. I am trying desperately to be calmly, articulately angry. 'You arsehole, you fucking arsehole. I thought you were dead. You made me think you were dead. And instead you just took me, and used me, and it's just . . .'

I'm choking on the words. They catch painfully in the back of my throat. 'It's just . . . all wrong. Everything. It wasn't . . .' And as I'm speaking, right in the middle of my rant, Nicky turns his back on me and saunters away. I'm left sitting there, open-mouthed.

'Go on,' he calls from the bathroom at the back of the motel room. 'Carry on. I can still hear you. It wasn't what?' He's standing in front of the mirrored bathroom cabinet, dabbing at the cut above his eye with a piece of cotton wool, wincing slightly. I can smell antiseptic. He glances at me as I come and stand in the doorway, then turns to look intently at his reflection in the mirror, probing and examining the cut. The tip of his nose moves up and down as he grimaces. 'Anyway,' he says, 'what the fuck are you doing here? How did you get here? I guess the charmingly unbalanced Clio Callahan sent you? Bitch. She always did have a peculiar sense of humour. Her little act of revenge on me, I guess.'

I take a deep breath. 'Nicky, listen to me.' That's good; my voice sounds calmer. 'I don't know what you're trying to do with this screen-play. I mean, I guess that's why you disappeared, to write this, and it's a good story. But . . .'

He holds up his hand to stop me, mid-sentence. 'Disappeared? Have I disappeared?' He's smiling; he obviously thinks the idea is funny.

'That's what the papers are saying. Nicky Bennet Disappears. They all think you've killed yourself.'

'I haven't read any papers in weeks. No papers, no Internet, no TV.' He pauses. I can tell he likes the idea: 'I've killed myself, have I? That's so funny. God, I never meant anyone to think that.' He shakes his head and then does a kind of swaggering gesture with his shoulders, as if he's very pleased with himself.

I take a deep breath and get back to the subject in hand. 'Here's the thing, Nicky. Your script. Like I said, it's a good story and all that, but it's not very fair on me, is it? You make me look like some kind of mad bunny boiler.'

'Bunny boiler?' He spreads his hands out and shrugs his shoulders. 'What do you mean, bunny boiler?'

I can't believe he doesn't know the expression. I look at him closely, trying to decide if he's joking. 'You know, bunny boiler. Like Glenn Close. *Fatal Attraction.*'

He twists up the corner of his mouth. 'Hey, great expression. Bunny boiler. I like it. I might use it. So, anyway, I make you look like a bunny boiler. Says the woman who's followed me all the way out here to my desert hideout. Jesus, I thought at least I'd be safe here.'

I ignore this. 'There must be some kind of law about it,' I continue. 'You can't just take a real person and turn them into something they're not, can you?'

He's finished with the cut on his face. He takes one last look in the mirror, tosses the cotton wool into the toilet, then saunters back into the bedroom; saying over his shoulder, 'Carry on. I'm still listening. Tell me more.'

He's picking up the bits of broken bottle from the carpet. I walk across to the desk and lean against it, grateful for some solid support. 'It was good, Nicky, you and me. What we had . . .'

Oh God, a TV-movie cliché. I take a deep breath and start again. 'I loved you.' There: I've said it; it's out. I look quickly at Nicky. It's had no effect on him. I say it again. 'I loved you. I thought you loved me. How can you write a script like that? It turns me into a stalker.'

He stops picking up the broken glass, sits down on the bed and looks sadly across at me. 'Justine, how long did we know each other for?'

I start to answer but he gets there first. 'A few weeks, maybe? Okay, spread over a couple of years, but all the same, no more than a few weeks. Count it up. Count the number of days. Count the number of times we slept together, if you want to do it that way. Barely into double figures, hon. Then count the number of letters you've sent me. Count in the Christmas cards, postcards, the "congratulations on your new movie" cards. Oh, and you can add in all the stuff you put on the message boards as well – Jesus, I was wondering when you'd get on-line, it added a whole new dimension to your stalking. Anyway, Justine, you do the math. Every time I get one of your mad letters . . .'

I open my mouth to protest. He holds up his hand to stop me. 'Every time I get one of your mad letters – and let's face it, you're pretty good at finding addresses for me; Jesus, you even knew I'd changed agents – I think, what the fuck did I do to deserve this? I mean, how much clearer could I have made it?'

This is Nicky Bennet talking to me. Nicky Bennet, the love of my life, the man who once asked me to marry him. I'm tired, disorientated and a tiny bit drunk and I'm trying to patch together his words to work out what he means.

'Do you remember the phrase I used to use? What I used to call you at Lowell?' He's talking patiently now, as if trying to coax the right answer from a small child.

'The ginger in your lemonade. The vinegar in your glass of water.'

'Thank you.' He does a gesture of praise with his hands, raises his gaze to Heaven as if he's about to shout 'Hallelujah.' 'And what do you think I meant by that?'

I shake my head. All I want to do is curl up and die.

'Jesus, Justine. You weren't even my girlfriend. You were just a little spice on the side. I had a girlfriend. God, what was her name? The kid with the cool car.'

'Martha.'

He does a double take, surprised at me having the name on the tip of my tongue. 'Yeah, Martha. That was her name. Anyway, you seemed to know the score. I thought you were cool with your little couldn't-give-a-shit voice telling me all that stuff about your sister like you didn't give a damn. And then you changed. Fuck, I couldn't go anywhere without seeing you. And you were all, "Nicky, Nicky, can I see you this summer? Nicky, Nicky, I love you."'

His English accent, done in a high-pitched voice that's obviously supposed to be mine, is poor to the point of embarrassment. I squirm. I never said 'I love you'.

'Jesus, I had to promise to meet you in New York just to shut you up.'

'Did you go to the Guggenheim?' My voice comes out all girly, sounding very much like the impersonation he's just done – except, of course, my accent is better.

'The Guggenheim?' He's staring at me as if I have totally taken leave of my senses. 'The Guggenheim? What the fuck are you on about?'

And that's when I can feel something inside me start to die. It's as if a little flame that I've been carrying inside myself all these years starts to flicker and splutter. I take a deep breath. 'Nicky, if I wasn't your girlfriend, why did you come to find me on Live Aid Day?'

'That was the next summer, yeah? I was in Europe with Martha. In Paris. London. Wherever, I don't know, doesn't matter.' He closes one eye and screws up his forehead, as if he's trying hard to remember. 'Paris, I think. Anyway, we had a fight. I couldn't afford a hotel room.' He laughs to himself; I guess he's amused that he was ever that poor. 'I tried to think who I knew in Europe. I was kinda proud of myself for tracking you down. To be honest, I'd been under the impression that you lived much closer to London, from what you'd said. But never mind. It was a cool town. Good beach. It was fun.'

'But you proposed to me. You knelt on the beach at my feet and asked me to marry you.'

Nicky takes a long look at me and I can't work out what it is I see in his eyes. He is so close that I could reach out and touch his face, feel that familiar cool, dry skin under my fingertips. I half stretch out my hand. He proposed to me on the beach. I said yes and kissed him on his cool, dry forehead. I have just driven miles across the desert to tell this man that I love him. I look closely at his face. There are new lines there, lines I've never noticed on screen. I study them closely: a deep vertical score between the eyebrows, new crow's-feet at the corners of his eyes. He looks older than he does in his films, more used up. And then I look into his eyes again and realise the reason I can't read them is that they're totally blank.

'What the fuck are you talking about?' he says eventually, very slowly.

'That moment on the beach.' And saying it like that, I realise how much it sounds like a scene from a film. Burt Lancaster and Deborah Kerr, maybe, or Nicky Bennet saying a fond goodbye to the feisty surfer chick in *Summer's Lease*. Bette Davis in black and white, or maybe Celia Johnson, stiffening her upper lip and saying to a married lover, 'We'll always have that moment on the beach.' That moment on the beach, the moment I've told all my friends about, the moment when Nicky Bennet asked me to marry him.

'What moment on the beach?' He looks genuinely baffled, and the flame inside me does another flicker and splutter.

'When you asked me to marry you. You knelt at my feet and proposed to me. On the beach.' Nicky still looks baffled. 'In my home town. The day you came to find me.' He shakes his head and does a clueless gesture with his hands. My voice is going all high-pitched and pleading. 'You knelt at my feet. On the shingle beach. You must remember. It must have hurt.'

And that's when something lights up in his eyes. They open wide and stare at me, and I can see a smile starting to form. It starts in one corner of his mouth and darts quickly across to the other. I feel myself start to smile, too: it's going to be all right. Nicky's smile turns into a laugh, and then into something that you could almost call a guffaw. Then he claps his hands together and he's laughing so much he's almost crying. 'Oh Jesus, Justine, you kill me. So that's what it's all been about. Christ, I've got to use this. This is just awesome. All this time, you actually think I meant I wanted to marry you. That's why you wrote all those letters. You thought I asked you to marry me.'

'You did.' I can barely get the words out, I'm shaking so much.

'I remember now. We were walking on the beach. Wasn't it Live Aid Day? Everyone had their radios on, listening to it. And you were talking away in that little monotone voice of yours, and then I tripped over, fell onto my knees. You're right about one thing, it really hurt. So I'm pulling myself up and I'm kind of kneeling in front of you, and I remember thinking it looked kind of stupid. So I said something like, "It looks like I'm asking you to marry me," because it did. Yeah, I was on one knee in front of you, but only because I'd fallen. It was a joke, babe, a joke.'

He is laughing so much that I'm sure he can't see me properly. I am sitting on the corner of his desk, sitting on my hands, and he seems very far away from me. The little candle in my heart has gone out.

'I've got to get a beer,' he says, and saunters out of the motel room towards the office, still laughing. I follow him out of the room. I stand outside the office door, wondering if I should go in, if there's anything else I can say to him to save the situation. I hear him open and close the fridge door, and a click of the cassette player as he puts a tape on. 'Christ, if you thought we were engaged, you must have thought I was a real bastard for walking out on you like that when you were in the hospital,' he shouts. I can hear another laugh. Maybe it's more of a chuckle. 'It's just that my visa had expired and I thought they were about to call the police in to interview me about the incident. Figured I'd better leave before I got deported. Hey, Justine,' he calls out to me. 'You've got to let me use that whole beach thing in the screenplay. It'll be a brilliant moment.'

I lean against the doorway, breathing deeply. Nicky walks back towards me. He pokes his head around the door. 'By the way,' he says. 'I meant to say. You look good in my jacket. Kind of suits that whole thrift-store-chic thing you've got going on.' Then he walks outside into the desert night, standing on the edge of the empty swimming pool, and I can hear him humming to himself.

47

I'm not far off forty. I am halfway through my life. And for half of the life I've lived so far I have been in love with this man. He's the only man I've ever loved. I stand by Nicky's desk, holding the screenplay in my hands. Maybe I should read on to the end. Maybe it will all turn out all right. Except I can't see to read because my eyes are full of tears. When my sister Marie killed herself I didn't cry. Why does this feel like something bigger?

I sit down on Nicky's bed. I remember how I felt when Nicky left me. I'm thinking about those nights alone in my bedsit, those black nights when no one knew he had left me. Those nights when I thought my ripped-apart heart would never heal. The jerky, involuntary shudders. The stifled sobs. The teeth-grindingly black, lonely pointless pain of it all. I can't go through all that again.

When I was a teenager sometimes I'd scare myself by saying 'This is all there is. There is no God. There is no heaven. This is all there is.' And then I'd try to work out how I felt. It was like pulling the carpet out from under my own feet. That's how I feel now. Everything I ever believed is wrong.

We all need something to build on, don't we, some kind of tale that explains us to other people, something that makes us what we are, the story of our lives. For me that's always been Nicky Bennet. That's who I am, the not-very-interesting person who somehow managed once to be engaged to the world's seventh sexiest film star. I've told the story so often that it's me, it defines me: the woman who was in love with Nicky Bennet. That's how everyone thinks of me. Even my closest friends. Even Anna and Gavin. I'm the one who used to go out with Nicky Bennet. How many times have I told the story about Nicky proposing to me on the beach? God, I told Alex the story. He believed it. Martha, too. It was the one thing I had over her. Nicky Bennet knelt at my feet and proposed to me.

I imagine going home now, meeting up with Anna again. 'Did you find Nicky Bennet?' she'd say, interested and concerned about my long absence.

'Yeah,' I'd say, offhand, hoping that she doesn't ask me any more.

'And is there still a spark?'

I'd say something like, 'Oh, we've grown apart. It's never going to work.'

And then, a year or two later, the film would come out and we'd have to go and see it, like we see all Nicky Bennet's films, and then she'd know. Then everyone would know. The whole thing, the whole big, dramatic story of my life, was just a stupid misunderstanding. How could I have been so embarrassingly, shamefacedly stupid?

The tears are streaming down my face now. I put my hands to my cheeks to wipe them away and I feel the dull ache that I get in my wrist from time to time. I'm so stupid. How could I even have thought that it was love? I remember what Martha said: 'Nicky Bennet broke your arm and you still believe it was some kind of symbol of love?'

I think about Clio. She thought Nicky loved her, too. And then I start thinking about Marie, and the pain it caused my parents and my brother when she killed herself. *Love breeds hurt and I can't stand the pain*. I know exactly what she meant.

And that's when the little flickering flame inside me comes back to life, except that now it's a tiny dot of white-hot heat, like when you hold a magnifying glass up to the sun and burn a hole in a piece of wood. There's a cliché, isn't there, about love and hate being two sides of the same coin? I'm beginning to realise how true it is. I look out of the window at Nicky Bennet strolling aimlessly around the courtyard of the motel, drinking from his bottle of beer. How could I have loved him so much? I feel the love drain away; it's almost a physical sensation. And, as if to replace the love, I can feel hatred flooding in, making my cheeks flush and my heart beat so hard that it hurts.

Somehow, I don't know how, I make my way into the office. I take another bottle of beer from the fridge, feeling the heft of the bottle in my hand. I recognise the music that's playing on the cassette machine. Gram Parsons. The tape that Nicky used to play to me. It's dark outside now, the sky full of stars. By the light of the motel sign I can see Nicky. He's standing by the swimming pool. I can see his shoulders moving. He's still laughing to himself, laughing at me.

I could say I see red, except I don't. I see white, white like the tiny dot of heat in – not my heart, my heart's gone, it's dead, it's been ripped out, I don't need it any more. The white dot of heat that's getting bigger by the second, that's burning fiercely inside my chest cavity, the cavity left empty by the absence of my heart. Burning fiercely, but under control. This isn't love, it's hate, it's anger, righteous anger, anger I know how to work with. If you could see Nicky Bennet again, what would you do? I'd smash his face in with my fist.

'Hey, hon,' says Nicky as he turns towards me. And then his eyes light up because he can see what I have in my hand: the beer bottle, which I'm holding like a weapon. I move towards him, brandishing the bottle, and he laughs. Laughs. 'C'mon, babe,' he says, that delighted, challenging look flashing in his eyes. 'Hurt me. You know you want to. You know you like it.'

Just as he did on the day when he broke my wrist, he grabs hold of my hand. All the time he's laughing at me. I hold the bottle up by the neck and pull my arm back, and he's still laughing as I bring it down with all the strength and hatred I possess, smashing it into his face. It's only as the bottle makes contact with his face and Nicky flinches and loses his footing that his expression changes. His mouth forms a perfect round 'O' of surprise as he falls into the swimming pool, his arms flailing in the air. There's a loud crack as his skull makes contact with the base of the dry pool and a halo of blood forms around his head.

48

The beer bottle drops from my hand and it smashes as it hits the ground. My hands fly up to my face. Some kind of involuntary noise comes out of my mouth, something between a gasp and a shriek. I go ice-cold all over and then hot, and my whole body shakes. My legs won't hold me up any more. Clumsily I half-sit, half-fall, grazing the palm of my right hand as I put it down to break my fall. I look down at the bottom of the pool, thinking that maybe it's a mistake, a joke; maybe Nicky will sit up and laugh at me. Maybe the dark stain isn't blood but muddy water. But Nicky doesn't move. His eyes are open and his face is set in an expression of surprise, almost indignation. His nose is smashed, pushed to one side. I did that with the beer bottle. I broke his nose. There's blood trickling from his nostrils. The halo around his head has grown and changed shape, as the blood moves slowly down towards the deep end and mingles with the sand that's drifted into the corner of the pool.

I climb down into the pool, kneeling on the hard concrete. I feel Nicky's neck, where the pulse should be, and I put my hand up under his T-shirt and place the palm of my hand flat on his hairless chest where his heart should be beating. I know he's dead. His skin feels cool but his blood on my fingers is warm and sticky. I put my fingers to my mouth and his blood tastes sweet on my lips. I sit back on my heels and look at him. I have the weirdest sense-memory: a memory of the way we lay together on the Green at Lowell that first night, sticky from sex and mud, his penis still inside me, my diamanté clip in his hair glinting in the floodlights. That sense of completion, perfection, pain and exhaustion: that's what I feel like now. I've always loved the afterwards of things. I look up at the huge night sky that's full of stars. I hear a strange sound. It's me, laughing. I've just killed Nicky Bennet.

I start noticing other noises. The wild-animal sound: the cry of a coyote or a lonesome whippoorwill. And then, very faintly, the cassette that Nicky was playing in the kitchen. A man's voice, soft and plaintive and broken. A woman's voice, strong and perfect like an angel's. Gram Parsons and Emmylou Harris singing. Their voices entwined with each other, the harmonies going where you least expect them to. 'Return of the Grievous Angel'.

I've always thought of Nicky when I hear this song. Nicky Bennet, his eyes closed as he listens to the music, that look of sad rapture on his face. Nicky Bennet, my grievous angel. But it's as I hear Emmylou Harris's angel voice soar on the chorus, that's when I realise I had it all wrong. It's that word 'grievous'. It's a strange word, isn't it, not one you'd use in everyday conversation. I guess I always thought it meant sad; the look I saw on Nicky's face when he listened to the song. But it doesn't mean that, does it? It means hurtful, harmful, someone who causes pain to another person. Grievous bodily harm. Grievous angel. That's who Nicky Bennet was: my very own grievous angel. He caused me nothing but pain.

W hat do you do when you've just killed someone? I take a deep breath, stand up, and brush sand and gravel from my knees and the palms of my hands. I climb out of the swimming pool, take another look behind me at Nicky's body, and then run back into the bathroom of the motel room to be sick. I take my clothes off and stand under the shower, making the water as hot as I can stand it. A weird sobbing noise emerges from my body. I lean my forehead against the tiles. I want to run away. I want to turn back the clock; turn it right back to 1984, before I ever met Nicky. I want to be in Anna's warm kitchen on a Friday evening, drinking red wine and joking about Nicky Bennet's disappearance. I want to be sitting in the pub down by the docks with Gavin. I want to be walking on the beach with Alexander Esterhazy. I want to be anywhere but here and now.

As I get dressed I find myself laughing again. It's funny, really: the world thinks Nicky Bennet is dead and now he is. I wonder when they'll find him. *They*. Who do I mean by 'they'? Is anyone actually looking for Nicky, apart from me? I wonder who will find him. Maybe someone will just stumble upon his body. Some young couple will be driving through the desert and stop at the motel, hoping to stay the night. They'll wander around the building, shouting 'Anyone home?'

Then the guy will see the body in the swimming pool and say 'My God' and try to shield his girlfriend's eyes. What will they think happened? Will they know it's Nicky Bennet? What kind of state will the body be in? Will they know it was an accident?

Was it an accident? That thought makes me shiver. Did I *mean* to kill Nicky Bennet? I hated him. I wanted to punish him. I wanted to smash his face in. I wanted him out of my life, and now he is. Okay, so will anyone guess I killed him? Why should they? Who knows I was here? Only Clio, and why would she say anything? She would have killed Nicky herself if she'd had the courage or the opportunity, I'm sure. Maybe she knew what I was going to do. Maybe it was all her idea. She sent me here. She's just as much to blame.

I've got to leave. I've got to get out of here — get back to Los Angeles and then fly home before anyone finds out what happened. But I'm moving in slow motion, as if I'm underwater. Think, Justine, think. What do you need to do? Laptop. Must take the laptop and the printed screenplay. If I leave the script, someone will read it; or they'll investigate the computer files looking for clues, and then they'll work out what happened and the search will be on for a blonde English woman fitting the description in the screenplay. I pick up the computer from the desk by the window, yanking the power cable from the wall. I pick up the pile of printed paper and balance it on top of the laptop. I stagger out to my rental car and dump them in the boot.

And that's when I have an idea that's so intoxicating that I nearly smile. I'm remembering a conversation with Nicky. We sat on the deck down by the river at Lowell. I told him about my sister, about her death. I told him about the note she left. He told me about Gram Parsons's mysterious death in a motel in the Californian desert, about how his friends stole his body and cremated it. 'I hope someone does that for me if I die in dramatic and tragic circumstances,' he had said. I remember the spare can of fuel in the boot of my car, and this time I do smile. I bet he never thought anyone would actually do it.

I take the fuel can in my hand and return to the swimming pool. Nicky Bennet's still lying there. He hasn't moved. Of course he hasn't. It's real: I killed him. The blood around his head has congealed into a dark shape like a roughly drawn map. I sit down on the edge of the swimming pool and have to swallow back the bile that rises in my throat when I look at him. I take the cap from the can and smell the fumes. I could douse Nicky Bennet's body and set fire to it. He would go up in flames and it would all be over. He would have got what he wanted. And that's what stops me. I'm so close to pouring the fuel all over his body when I think, 'Fuck it. Why should I? Why should I give him the ending he wanted?'

And so I sit there, the can in my hand, my legs dangling over the edge of the pool, looking at the dead body of the only man I've ever loved. He's gone. It's over. Stone-dead. He can never hurt me again. He can never make me love him again. I will get in the car and drive away, drive back to Los Angeles. I will fly back home, back to my mother and Anna and Anna's baby. At some point in the future, maybe soon, maybe weeks ahead, someone will find the motel, find Nicky and try to work out what's happened. They will never know I was here. I will be long gone. It's over, me and Nicky, as if nothing had ever happened.

Any minute now I'll drive away. But somehow I'm still there hours later, chilled to the bone, with the sky lightening and Nicky Bennet's body no more than a stiffened bloody bundle in the bottom of a dry swimming pool. I wonder why it is that I haven't moved, and then it occurs to me that I'm waiting for the credits to roll.

ALSO AVAILABLE BY JANE HILL

The Murder Ballad

Stumbling headlong into a passionate fling and impromptu marriage to music star Trey, Maeve's life is about to change beyond recognition. Trey wants to whisk her off to his country house in North Carolina and Maeve follows her him without a backward glance.

But when she first lays eyes on her new home – a dilapidated old cabin in the middle of nowhere – she begins to feel uneasy. Nothing quite matches up to what she's been led to expect and, below the surface, a dark secret lies buried, a passionate and deadly love affair and an age-old murder that has never been resolved. Too late, Maeve realizes that she is all alone in a strange country, sharing a life with a man she hardly knows . . .

'A new voice in psychological suspense'
Daily Mail

'A sensational new addition to the psychological thriller shelves'
Daily Record